The Case

Roger Ashton-Griffiths

First published in 2023 by Sharpe Books.

for Sharmini, my wife

THE CASE OF CAT ADAM

1

William 'Cat' Adam was my great-great-uncle. He disappeared nearly a century ago in India, vanishing into family history at the age of twenty-five.

We have pics, so we know he was a short man, very fat and bespectacled, not at all cat-like, who closely resembled his younger brother, my great-grandfather. We don't know what happened to him, not fully, even now that I have done the research. That he vanished in 1924 there is no doubt, since we still have his letters, an example of which is the last his mother received from him in December of that year, after she had sent him a memento of the Empire Exhibition at Wembley:

August 19th, 1924
2nd Bungalow,
Palace Compound,
Dhoosar Mathavaasee
Dearest Mater,

Thanks for the pressie, which I received today. I will treasure it. But I must say that whatever you've seen in Wembley, it's not all like that over here in DM, and wouldn't have been when you were nursing in Darjeeling either. In fact, why are they even trying to build a bit of India in Wembley?

I am very busy at present, preparing for my first recital.
Your very loving son,
Cat
Master Of The Rajah's Music

Because of the letters, we do know what he was doing in Dusa Mathavasi (DM). He had been invited by the Rajah, with whom he'd been at school in Kent, to be the director of music at the royal court, and in late 1923 had travelled all the way across the subcontinent from Darjeeling, where he had been working on a tea estate. This was an enormous journey at that time, most of which he would have completed by steam train on the long passage from Kolkota to Karachi, but the overland legs at each end were major undertakings, especially the final stage to DM, which was notoriously difficult to get to.

He can only have been in Darjeeling for about a year before he travelled westwards, but we don't know why he went to India initially. Other than the occasional reference in the letters to his mother having been in India as a girl, as above for example, there appears to have been no connection between our family and the colonial project in any of its manifestations. Cat had studied at the Royal Academy of Music after school, specialising in double bass and qualifying with an LRAM – the certificate remains in the family archive. Alas, so does the correspondence relating to the loss of the double bass which he had with him when he disappeared. It appears that when Cat went to the RAM he won a scholarship, which led in turn to the loan of a valuable instrument, and his parents had to raise a sizeable mortgage on the family house in order to pay off the debt when he disappeared with it, materially affecting the family's financial status.

(There is a double bass in the museum of the Basilica of St. Mark, in Venice, which was the personal instrument of the great C19th virtuoso, Domenico Dragonetti. The double bass which went missing with Cat is believed to be the identical twin of this instrument. If it could be found, it would today be one of the most valuable double basses in the world.)

The actions of ancestors have all sorts of ramifications for later generations, as they trickle down through time. It wasn't just the family's economic position which was affected by Cat's disappearance, which resulted in the end of the line for my family's history of educating its boys privately. Cat's actions have also had a direct affect on me and my career, as I hope to make clear in the pages which follow. But before I go into the detail of my recent research into Cat's life, it would help to contextualise both my own involvement in it, the extraordinary geopolitics of a forgotten state, and how I became, by dint of being the only academic writing about it, a de facto world authority on that state.

I had grown up knowing about strange Uncle Cat, and that he'd disappeared whilst working for an Indian prince, but without knowing anything about DM. It was entirely coincidental that I arrived at Wedgwood College, Oxford, in a cohort which included the Yuvraj Samaba – Sammy – Shiv Jam Saheb, heir to the throne of DM, who was also studying history. One day, when we were all relaxing over drink or two in The Kiln, he casually told the story of a fat, white sadhu who used to wander naked through northern India carrying a double bass. He'd always assumed it was just a myth, but it seemed to me that if there was any element of truth in it, there must be the makings of an explanation as to the fate of Cat. Naturally, Sam and I became good friends, and I became hooked on DM, his homeland, and began to specialise in its history.

When we graduated (he narrowly missed his 1st, alas), he went home to take up his job as a member of the royal family, and I stayed up to do my DPhil, specialising further in the history of DM, with a thesis entitled *The Unfelt Tremor: Liminality and Survival in the Independent State of Dusa Mathavasi*. Obviously, given the nature of my research, I took advantage of my friendship with the heir to the throne, who was always happy for me to contact his advisors for information about the period around 1947, and so managed to avoid having to make a difficult and expensive journey.

It is remarkable how little is known about the tiny state of DM, even by those who purport to be authorities on the history of the subcontinent and its transition to independence. Received history states that in 1947, when Britain sailed away from India after a presence of over three hundred years, the princely states were successfully enjoined to become part of the newly-created republics of either India or Pakistan. Some of them were more reluctant than others, and the powerful Nizam of Hyderabad even considered fighting a costly war in what would have been a doomed attempt to keep his principality. But it is generally agreed that all of them acceded in due course.

It is hardly surprising, given the political upheaval and human tragedy which independence generated, so shortly after the end of a world war, that mistakes were made on many levels, in many ways, in many places, by many people. It can be argued that the very line of partition drawn up by Cyril Radcliffe was one such mistake. But Radcliffe and his committees made another mistake, an act of omission, by not reading correctly the maps created by Andrew Scott Waugh (successor to the more famous George Everest) when he was the director of the Trigonometric Survey of India. These maps are generally clear, and certainly authoritative (and available to consult at the British Library), but they stray into the limits of credibility – as opposed to legibility – when they come to describe the furthest reaches of the Indian subcontinent in the west. On the border with what was then Persia, at the furthest extent of a long, arid stretch of desert, there is a small thin line drawn between the deltas of the Kaur Dasht and Khowr-e Bahu, more or less parallel to the coastline, and about a mile-and-a-half inland. This tiny, fertile chersonese was named correctly on the map as Dhoosar Mathavassee (using the old style of transliteration), but in such a way as to make the existence of the state, given its improbable location, become invisible to later readers of the map. Because the area of land described by the line is so small, its name is written over the Jiwani Bay beside it, and this writing was soon taken to describe a feature of the seabed. Naturally, Radcliffe was interested in dry land, and only dry land, so he ignored the very existence of DM and drew a line straight through it, which he thought separated Iran from the Pakistan of his creation.

This extraordinary oversight alone wouldn't have resulted in DM becoming a forgotten state, since all the princely states had Political Agents attached to them at the time. They were central to the negotiations which led each independent ruler, regardless of rank, to surrender his land to the new republics. All of them, that is, except DM. I'm now in a position to describe at last what happened to the final Political Agent in DM, and speculatively to suggest why his disappearance – also in 1924 – from a state which the Indian Civil Service (ICS) was already beginning to have forgotten about, was overlooked, so that he was never replaced.

The outcome of the oversights of Radcliffe and, earlier, the ICS, was that DM became forgotten, too far away from the centres of administration to be noticed, and subsequently dropped from the maps. To this day, if you go to Stamfords, that estimable shop in Covent Garden where maps of every land can be had in any scale, and ask them for a map of DM, even they will almost certainly scratch their heads.

So, in short, every one of the princely states of the Indian subcontinent slipped, albeit haltingly in some cases, into the newly-wrought nations created by the British, except DM. It has continued to this day as an independent princely state, with a rajah at its head, who is, nominally, still entitled to a nine-gun salute from the British.

***

In the mid 20th century, DM was a very undeveloped place, not unlike the Arab states on the other side of the Gulf. But like them and its neighbour Iran, it was found to have oil reserves, and its modernisation began. It is still not nearly as developed as, for example, Dubai or Oman, but at the time of my recent visit, the construction of the new airport was nearing completion, replacing the derelict airstrip which had been created in the fifties. Interestingly, because of the proximity of DM to the Gulf States, and the majority Sunni population, whenever DM is referenced (usually only by oil economists, these days), it is described as an emirate, and the rajah as an emir. The paradox of the ruling family being Hindu seems to go unnoticed in what little is written about the place, although it is a matter of great importance within the country, as I shall describe.

This, then, is the land about which I wrote my doctorate, the hardest part of which process was finding an external examiner who knew enough about the place to be able to come to a measured conclusion about my work. As it was, my internal examiner, who knew of my area because she was a close colleague of my first supervisor, who had discussed it with her, laughingly commented during my viva that I could have made it all up and she would have been none the wiser. Irritating to break important new ground, only to have your labours trivialised.

Unsurprisingly, DM isn't on the syllabuses of UK universities, and since leaving Oxford to take up my first established post-post-doc job, as a lecturer in history at the University of Altrincham (one of the very new 'pop-up' universities), my teaching commitments have led me away from my research, just as surely as my new home in the north of England has led me away from both the Bodleian and British Libraries. Manchester Central Library is a fine institution, no doubt, but its circular building serves as an apt metaphor for what happens if you attempt to find references to DM on any of its shelves. I was browsing there in vain one day when an unexpected email from DM, from Sammy himself, appeared on my phone.

It began, 'Hi, Phil, thought you'd like to know that we've turned up your great uncle's lost...' and I expected the next line to begin 'diaries', or similar. It's surprisingly easy to see only what you expect to scc (just as Radcliffe and his men simply couldn't see what was in front of their eyes), and as a professional historian, I know that this is the worst of all sins. The solipsistic abandonment of objectivity leads to plain bad history!

Only when I realised that the email was making no sense at all did I re-read the sentence, which actually read, 'Hi, Phil, thought you'd like to know that we've turned up your great uncle's lost house'. House! Apparently, it had become completely engulfed by the forest at the back of the royal palace. I had no idea you could lose a house. Actually, more to the point, who knew a house had been lost, regardless of whether or not it was the house in which Cat lived? I was more than a little intrigued (although on refection, I would have been more delighted had the email continued with '… found your highly-valuable great-great-uncle's double bass').

Until I received the email, thoughts of my missing relative had receded from my attention, just like all the research projects I had had in mind when I left Oxford. Now, however, images of my uncle wandering around the countryside of India with a priceless double bass over his naked shoulder nagged me into taking action. The email had contained very little by way of detail, so I replied enthusiastically and with the suggestion that it might be a good idea for me to come, at last, to DM in person, to which I received a positive response.

The long vac was looming, I had nothing better planned, so the timing was perfect, and I went online to book a return trip to DM. It was hopeless, of course, and the best I could do, after consultation with Sam's officials, was book a return flight to

Karachi, with the promise that I would be collected from there and driven the 700 km along the N10 to DM. I was coming to the end of my second year at Altrincham, and it's just as well I'd had that regular income, as the flights cost an absolute fortune. I suppose that's the consequence of booking a *real* trip so shortly before you travel, but my great excitement was compensation enough, and two days later I was at the airport.

2

Cat Adam was in bed when the dak wallah arrived, shortly after lunch on August 24th, 1923. Being a Friday, he should have been in the estate office, at his desk, preparing the payroll, but it was still early in the afternoon, and there would be plenty of time to deal with all that stuff if he managed promptly to complete the task in hand. But the sound of mail slapping onto the Linoleum in Cat's hallway had become one which sent the wrong sort of frisson through his wobbly body, and he found himself distracted.

He had received a calamitous letter three weeks earlier, to which he knew very well there would be follow-ups. It had contained two related items of bad news, and he had been prepared for neither, even if for one he should have been. This was his benefactors' irritated demand that he return forthwith the double bass loaned to him as a scholarship student, on the grounds that he had broken the condition that it be used professionally after college, as an early-career fillip. But the agreement was that he could have the instrument until he was thirty, and he had had no expectation that anyone would check up on him during the next seven years.

The trigger for this unwelcome intrusion into what he considered his private affairs was detailed in the second piece of bad news. In prose which seemed paradoxically speechless, the outcome of some recent research into the history of his instrument was revealed, the gist of it being that the double bass which presently stood in the corner of his spartan, monsoon-damp room, leaning precariously into the angle between two walls, was not the good copy which it had been believed to be, but was actually the original, made in the late sixteenth century by the great Brescia luthier, Gasparo Bertolotti, known as *da Salò*. It had been disposed of by Dragonetti in London in 1842. Soon thereafter its real identity had been lost, when it had been deliberately mis-described in order to avoid death duties, and later sold as a copy in 1867 to the charitable trust which had since loaned the instrument to promising students on that basis. It was the research of an ambitious young academic Dragonettologist, apparently, which had revealed the whereabouts of the 'lost' instrument, and which had prompted the Trust to seek its most urgent return.

Cat could have been no more prepared as the recipient of this information than, plainly, had been the sender. In parallel voices, he exclaimed in rapt awe and lip-curling disdain simultaneously, that Parvati was not just a real *da Salò*, but a *Dragonetti da Salò*, and that the researcher was a cunt.

In the same delivery as that awful letter from the Trustees had been another, a rather formal communication from Cat's father, posted at about the same time. It detailed how furious he was with Cat, since he had not fully apprehended the fact that the double bass was loaned on condition that it be used professionally. It was bad enough, he supposed, that the instrument was doing no greater service than being plucked at the back of a dance orchestra in the planters' club at Ghoom (which it was not, as a matter of fact). Worse, now that its full value had been exposed, he would have to meet the doubtless exorbitant expense of having the instrument shipped back to England. Moreover, it was he who had given to Cat's benefactors his address in Darjeeling, in response to their urgent enquiry as to his whereabouts, since their earlier letters had been returned *not at this address*. And Cat only had himself to blame.

'Oh, pater, pater, what have you done!', Cat had sighed.

Naturally, Cat had known that the loan of his bass had conditions attached to it. He knew that it was for professional use, otherwise it had to be returned for the benefit of the next budding virtuoso. If he'd given the matter any thought (which he had not) he would have realised that the fact of his instrument being subject to recall on one ground suggested that there might be other grounds on which its return might also be demanded. He cast his head backwards and gazed longingly at the instrument in the corner.

His bibi, who up to this point had been rocking back and forth, sending slow, rolling waves up and down the mound of his naked, white torso, became still and demanded, 'अरे, के तपाईं हेर्दै हुनुहुन्छ, ठूलो केटा?'

'Huh? What?' his Nepali was still rudimentary.

'You look me!'

Cat had fallen in love with his double bass. He couldn't explain the attraction it held for him, just that it had become his favourite thing in the whole world. It was dark brown, voluptuous, gorgeous to touch, with curves to caress, it made tones which sent resonant shivers from one end of his body to the other, it caused his scrotum to contract. The idea of losing it appalled him.

Karmpal, herself substantially larger than most of the workers on the estate, now upped the frequency of her gyrations, hoping to maintain Cat's attention. His mind wandered just briefly to thoughts of using his third finger in the higher positions, before he succumbed to the inevitability of orgasming *a due* with his accompanist. 'Yaroo!' he ejaculated, in his customary fashion, as the mountainous couple shuddered together on the squealing, metal-framed cot, which sagged dangerously beneath their combined weight.

The task in hand now complete, he took his glasses from the bentwood chair beside his bed, and lay back on the lumpy, flock mattress, as he watched Karmpal wipe herself and dress. She smiled and called him *thulo keta* – big boy – once again before she left the room, briefly returning seconds later to place on his belly the letter which had arrived. He was fond of her, no doubt, and she was highly agreeable company three or four lunchtimes a week, but he had never been entirely sure that the attraction of her boss's bed wasn't merely greater than the draw of the tea tips. He might have been more fulsome in his farewell had he known that he would never see her again.

The letter, balanced on the summit of his rounded form, bobbed up and down resonantly to the beat of his heart, which was working hard in anticipation of what it might contain. He had assumed that it would have come from England, as they all did. That's where his family and friends remained, and in the nine months he'd been in Darjeeling he hadn't once travelled far from Ghoom, so had acquired no-one on the subcontinent with whom he could exchange letters. His first thought, on catching a surprising, twitching glimpse of an Indian stamp, was that the

Trustees must have instructed local agents to pursue the return of his double bass with greater aggression.

But no!

There was one person in India from whom he might possibly – just possibly – have expected a letter. She was called Mariah, she lived in Delhi, and she had broken his heart. As students together at the Academy, they had been very close, a couple, and he had adored her. She was a marvellous pianist, sent to London to study by her liberal parents (father was a Gray's Inn barrister, mother a notable poet), and together they had lovingly supported each other through the highs and lows of their studies. She had accompanied him in his recitals, he was always in the front row for hers. She had composed music for him, which he played for his finals. It was she who had named him Cat. And he called her Kitten.

In the final reckoning, when her parents had come to London for her graduation and met Cat, they turned out to be not as liberal as the couple had hoped. She came from a Christian family, so they'd anticipated no problem on religious grounds, but her parents wanted their daughter back in India, because a *suitable match* was waiting for her. And she had returned with them, dutifully, sadly, but willingly, placing her father's wishes over Cat's. It was this that felt to him like a betrayal, this which hurt the most.

Mariah wasn't the reason why Cat had come to the subcontinent. She had abandoned the promise of a good career to become the wife of her father's pupil, he had learned, very soon after she had disembarked at the Gateway of India, so he knew there was no point in following her, attempting to win her back. She was, however, the reason why he had stopped looking for professional engagements, since he found that the heart of his music-making seemed to have steamed out of Southampton with her. India had been his bolt-hole of choice because of his mother's contacts here in Darjeeling, where she had spent some time in her youth as a nurse. And the beauty of Darjeeling, for him, lay not in the hills, the greenery, the climate, rather it was that it was so far from Delhi that it hardly mattered that he and Mariah were on the same landmass.

Could she possibly be writing to him? Why would she write? Had her fucking husband arrived at his premature end? He grasped the envelope and peered at it, nervously, hoping for what might have been the best possible news, rather than the worst. But it was postmarked in some place he'd never heard of. This was a letter about neither a woman nor a double bass, and Cat was curious.

The Office of the Divan
The Royal Palace
Dhoosar Mathavassee
2/8/23

Dear Adam,

Remember me? How have you been, old bean?

We're in a bit of a pickle, here in Dhoosar Mathavassee, hoping you can help us out!

I don't know if you recall that a few of us went to Oxford together, after we left school, including Sooty. Unfortunately, whilst we were still up, his father died, and he succeeded to the title. He felt he needed a bit of help once he got back, so I've been out here working for him – I suppose I'm his prime minister, or something like that.

The thing is, we're doing some modernising around here, including finishing the church. We're also going to improve the palace, bring it up to Western standards, don't y'know. However, we've realised that none of us knows anything about culture, and all that stuff. We've got a new organ arriving any day now, for installation in the church, and it'll need someone to oversee it, plus we want to whiz up the palace with a few paintings, and we need advice.

We thought of you, naturally, you being the musician amongst us. And we think your years in artistic London must have taught you a thing or two. (Rumour has it that you developed a taste for the exotic whilst you were at the Academy as well!) And then, when Bastock Minor asked your brother where we could get in touch with you, we discovered that you're already in India!

So, the long and the short of it is this, old chum: do you want a job as the official cultural panjandrum to the Rajah here in DM?

You could start whenever it suits you, and we'll pay a proper rate for the job, I assure you.

In anticipation of your reply, I send you my very best wishes,

P. Barton

Cat was briefly amused that he found himself lying on a bed in order to read a letter which had come from the office of a divan. He took a moment or two to tune into the letter, unable initially even to think who P. Barton was. Then he remembered. He was the oh-so-goody-good captain of the year below him, everybody's favourite, whose only vice was taking delight in tormenting the fat boys, and in particular Cat and his brother. What a cunt! How fucking dare he get all pally now! Cat screwed up the letter and threw it at the waste bin beside Parvati. But he missed, and the crumpled ball of paper hit her strings and bounced back at him, with such precision that he was able to catch it.

Cat and his bass had had a two-way relationship from the first moment they met. It was an understanding. But it had always taken the form of her singing to him, whilst he bowed or plucked her. This somewhat more direct approach from Parvati took him by surprise, and he blinked blankly at the letter, returned in what felt like a reproving manner, as the perfect harshness of the open A and D strings admonished him from the corner. The pause was just long enough, and Cat realised what he was being instructed to do.

The Trustees wanted Parvati back for two reasons: firstly, she wasn't being used professionally; secondly, it had emerged that she wasn't the instrument they had thought she was. Cat decided that the first objection could be met if he could demonstrate that he was actually engaged as a professional musician, and that this was the part of the contract which was down to him. As to the second issue, it could hardly be seen as his fault if they'd given him the wrong instrument, and so he could argue that her return could happen only at a time which suited him. So, the curious job offer he'd just received amounted to an invitation to become a court musician, according to Parvati, and he concluded it could hardly be expected that he should set aside his important duties to make the trip back from India in order to hand her over.

There, that should do it! Court musician, Kapellmeister, a post enjoyed by Haydn, no less, and Hummel, not to mention Dittersdorf, the great composer for the double bass. Cat would write to his father with his new title and address (but with instructions not to tell the Trustees the new address – they would then have to deal with the old boy, which would slow things down still further), explain his change of circumstances and hope that that would put the matter to rest. At least for now.

He rolled off the bed and onto his feet, always more nimble than his bulk suggested he should be. A round smile spread across his face when he realised that, in an instant, he and Parvati had solved not just the problem of her return, but also the loss of his musical libido; he was suddenly very excited by the idea of being a court musician. He wondered how big his orchestra would be, and concluded that, realistically, it wouldn't be much more than a chamber ensemble. But what fun, and how unusual to direct from the double bass!

'The bloody payroll!' he tweaked Parvati's G string, 'Aha, but I won't be long. We've got plans to make.'

3

The smell as you pass through the open door of the plane, I have been told by others, is the same across the entire subcontinent, always a smokey, perfumed, warm haze. I find this assertion difficult to accept in its entirety; I can't believe that the air in Delhi, for example, with its infamous pollution, is the same as the air in, say, Shimla. And it can't just be to do with the amount of cow dung being burnt nearby, as I've also heard claimed. You surely couldn't cover the entirety of a vast landmass merely with the smoke of burning dung? But I found the smell to be so distinct that it overwhelmed me, at the very moment when I should have been taking my first look out at this new land.

And then the burning dryness of the air took over, and I gasped, as my mouth and nose took the hit. We have good summer days in England, so recognising a hot day when you come across one is easy, it's a familiar experience. But the degree of hotness, that's the difference. My grandmother used to insist that a Christmas cake was best cooked in an Aga, because although the heat was low, it was unstoppable. Here the heat was high but just as unstoppable. Could Nan have cooked a cake, I wondered, just by standing the foil-covered tin on the tarmac for six hours?

The experience was in very stark contrast to the preceding cramped and air-conditioned eight-hours, my first ever long haul flight, which had taken the chronic, ignorable fact of my corporeality and rendered it acute and pressing.

There was a bus at the foot of the stairs, a modern one with air conditioning, which came as a welcome surprise and looked very appealing indeed. But as I staggered off the bottom of the steps, and turned towards the bus, I was greeted by a polite fellow in a dark suit – a dark suit, I ask you! – who called me by my name and took my carry-on luggage from me. I admit to being disconcerted, wondering why the Pakistani authorities had singled me out, and for what special treatment, because I was peremptorily led towards not the bus, but a four-by-four security vehicle.

It's probable that I appeared rude, I now reflect, when another smartly-dressed, very fat bloke in the back of the car, whom I was seated next to, greeted me with an outstretched hand and a warm smile. I shook his hand reflexly, but was taciturn, fearing that something terrible was going to happen to me, during my interrogation by the local police. I knew I'd done nothing wrong, but this just added to my fears, because I had no information for them, and thus no means of stopping their brutal grilling; I certainly didn't want to be bent over and caned, like a latter-day Hari Kumar.

The dialogue between us went roughly as follows.

Mr Bunta: (formally) Dr. Adam, allow me to welcome you to Dusa Mathavasi...

Me: But this is still Karachi. Isn't it?

Mr Bunta: We are on Pakistani soil, it is true, but you are under my diplomatic protection so, effectively, you are already in DM.

Me: I am?

The car then set off, heading away from the main terminal, doubtless, I assumed, to some secret, dark building, and I was scared and confused.

Mr Bunta: Indeed, sir. Allow me to introduce myself...

Me: Please!

Mr Bunta: I am William Bunta, DM's Consul in Karachi.

Me: Oh.

Mr Bunta: (casually) I have been instructed to welcome you, and see you safely onto the helicopter for the final leg of your journey.

Me: Oh, I see.

Mr Bunta: The journey from here...

Me: Helicopter? Did you say helicopter?

Mr Bunta: Oh, yes, you wouldn't want to drive.

As Mr. Bunta explained what was happening, I became aware of a number of thoughts jostling for primacy. I was relieved to discover that I wasn't about to be disappeared by persons unknown, in a foreign land; I was astounded that the road journey to DM from Karachi was still a challenge; I was amazed that DM had a helicopter; I was impressed by the standard of Mr. Bunta's English; I was delighted by the cool air in the car; I was gleefully beside myself that I had been greeted in this definingly VIP manner; I felt sorry for my fellow passengers, who were still waiting for the bus to move, as we receded from their view; I was immensely flattered that my visit to DM was considered this important. But most of all, I felt myself resisting even the possibility of taking to the air in a helicopter, since I was sure they were intrinsically dangerous. I just couldn't think of a way out if it, however, and terror had paralysed me by the time we arrived at the side of that infernal machine. I had to be helped out of the car – pulled out, more truthfully – and frog-marched up to it.

The pilot was waiting for me, casually dressed, about my age, wearing shades of the sort pilots always seem to wear. He had a large pair of headphones round his neck, and handed me a pair of my own, inviting me to sit beside him in the front seat, in manner which I thought too relaxed, even jaunty. I said that I thought the co-pilot should sit there, which made him laugh cruelly; he was the one and only pilot. I declined his offer, and clambered into the back seat. The headphones gripped onto my head really tightly.

The blades started turning, casting a rotating shadow as they cut through the sun overhead, as if trying to slice the top off a boiled egg. Mr. Bunta may have said goodbye, or he may not, I couldn't tell because of the sound of blood rushing in my ears. He did wave, smiling broadly as the door was closed behind me; it's easy to smile broadly when you're staying on the ground. There wasn't a lot of room in the helicopter, just the bench seat I was on, and I had to sit sideways to get my legs in.

The noise! OMG, the noise! It was just unreal. As the speed of the blades picked up, reaching the point quite quickly when they couldn't be seen individually any more, the roar they made seemed to reach an absolute limit, beyond which it couldn't possibly become any louder. Then it did become louder, and I could no longer hear my blood pounding. We began to pitch a little, as if the helicopter was shuffling its feet, and then shot into the air, turning simultaneously through 270°. I tried to see if I could identify the bus I should have been on, but the airport was suddenly distant.

We set off in a straight line, heading west I assumed, and the helicopter had taken what felt like a nose-down attitude, as if it were in a constant state of falling. However, we appeared to be staying at the same height, and I was able to relax somewhat. It took me a little while to compose myself, during which time I could hear the tinny voice of the pilot over the headphones, although I thought he was talking with someone about the flight.

Ali: Are you OK back there? You're very quiet.

Me: What? Huh? Oh, sorry, didn't realise you were talking to me.

Ali: There's no-one else here.

Me: I assumed you were talking to the tower, or whatever.

Ali: Oh, they're long gone! Are you OK?

Me: I suppose. I've not been in a helicopter before. I don't really like it.

Ali: It's the only way to travel!

At this point, we crossed the beach below and started flying over the sea.

Me: What happens if the engine stops? What stops us falling like a brick?

Ali: You mean like this?

Unbelievably, the pilot then turned off the engine and, guess what, we started to fall like a brick. I might have screamed. But he did something to the angle of the helicopter, so that we were leaning back as we fell and we were suddenly plummeting to earth less quickly. Nevertheless, we were still plummeting, and I'm pretty sure that, as the sea appeared to rush up to receive us, I would have soiled myself were it not for the super-clenching of every muscle in my body.

At the point when it looked like it was all over, the pilot pulled us back further, started the engine and took off again, as if nothing had happened. I was sure we were so close to the waves that the runners dipped into them, and my jaw hurt from gritting my teeth. As we climbed, he began to talk again.

Ali: See, you don't drop out of the sky, you glide down. Perfectly safe! I could easily have landed us safely then.

Me: There was no land to land on. How could you have landed!

Ali: I was just demonstrating what's called autorotation, which is how you get down safely if the engine fails. We practise it all the time.

Me: BUT WE WEREN'T OVER LAND!

Ali: (cockily) Well, there is that, it's true. Just as well the engine started again, then!

Me: How dare you put the life of one of your passengers at risk. I will be talking to your superiors about this as soon as we arrive.

He laughed so loudly that the sound distorted in my headphones.

Ali: I'm afraid I don't have any superiors.

Me: You must have, if you're flying the State Helicopter.

More laughter.

Ali: This isn't the state helicopter. There isn't a state helicopter.

Me: Well, who's helicopter is this?

Ali: It's mine, obviously!

Me: But Mr. Bunta said that the State Helicopter had been sent for me.

Ali: I shouldn't think he did. This is my R66, and I was just in Karachi having its annual done. Sammy asked if I'd help him out by collecting you.

Me: Well, who are you?

Ali: I told you when we were taking off.

Me: Sorry, I didn't hear.

Ali: I'm Ali, Ali Qifar. I'm a friend of Sammy's.

Me: Do all his friends have helicopters?

Ali: (smugly) No, only me. I'm the rich one!

Judging him on the basis of the evidence I had before me, I decided Ali was a competent pilot, despite his undoubted recklessness, and chose to trust him. All that remained was my dread of mechanical failure. We flew over water for a while, but then hugged the coastline, and he was keen to point out to me various features of the landscape beneath, none of which I could see. All that there was, it seemed to me, was a hilly desert with a road running through it.

We chatted a lot, given that the sound in the headsets was so ropey. He told me that his grandfather had been in Dubai since before the war, running a small construction company, which had become a very large construction company as the development of the Emirates accelerated. I got the impression that most of the contracts for most of the big buildings you see on telly were given to the family firm, these days run by Ali's father and older brother. He lived mainly in Dubai, but kept the family house in DM (presumably that's why he needed the helicopter). Oh, and his university was Bristol, where he'd read Business Management. Asked about his interest in the family firm, he told me that he left it to his brother and father, and that his role was to engage in the leisure activities that they denied themselves. I realised at that point that Ali was actually a playboy, a real, genuine playboy, the first I'd ever met.

In time, I could look along the coast line beneath us and see an area of difference in the distance, quite distinct from its barren surroundings; Dusa Mathavasi. This was my first glimpse of the place which had occupied my attention for years, and I was excited. It was still too distant to make out any detail, as it appeared to be no more than a tiny speck of greenness in the otherwise buff-coloured desert surrounding it, squeezing it to the very water's edge; it looked like the first sign of mould on a slice of wholemeal bread.

Until now, I'd only had the sea or desert to look down on, neither of which had supplied much by way of reference points, and I had been aware only of a slightly-vague, relative sense of movement. But looking straight ahead, as DM loomed larger and larger, I could see the outline of the chersonese quite clearly, shaped roughly like a foot, pinched at the borders with Pakistan and Iran by closed inlets of the two river deltas.

We travelled at a tremendous lick, and astonishingly soon we slowed down and were passing over streets and houses, where I could see cars and people moving. Ali announced that he would take me for a tour round the state before we landed. Idiotically, I assumed this would be a bit like those terrifying moments when you're coming in to land at Heathrow, when they fly really low up the Thames, impossibly slowly, before turning left over Kew

Gardens at just the moment when you think you're about to reach the airport safely, only to go back and do it all again. I hate the feeling that the plane can't possibly stay in the air at that speed, and dreaded what I thought would follow now, especially since as far as I was concerned, we had indeed all-but safely arrived.

Alas, it's not like that in a helicopter.

I don't know how low we were flying when Ali put on the brakes. It wasn't the same as his earlier dangerous stunt to demonstrate how safe we were – we didn't fall from the sky – instead we just stopped moving, lingering in thin air. Absurdly, I was reminded of a line in the poem by Dante Gabriel Rossetti, 'Silent Noon', when he writes that the dragon fly 'hangs like a blue thread loosened from the sky', except that there was nothing pastoral about this experience, with the blades overhead thrashing not the ripened wheat, but the air relentlessly into submission, and the sensation it produced in me was far more colic than bucolic. I actually vomited into my mouth a little, and had to swallow it. The thing is, we weren't so high that the distance to earth had become abstract, like in a big plane, and nor were we so low that the distance became irrelevant (and by irrelevantly low, I mean sitting safely on the tarmac). We were at just the right height for it to look like a very long, but very real way down, and we weren't making progress in any direction, which is much, much worse than merely flying too slowly. Obviously, I knew helicopters can hover, but I'd simply not expected to find myself sitting in one whilst it did.

Quivering, I peered trough the window, down on the roof of a enormous modern structure, which Ali informed me was the palace. To the rear, it was embraced by a thick crescent of trees, and in front, heading directly to the sea, ran a straight road lined with buildings. One of them had the unmistakable minaret of a mosque, which looked like it was reaching up to scratch the helicopter's belly. The bulk of the town straddled this central avenue, and Ali pointed out various buildings, but they all seemed so small, compared to the palace, more or less undistinguishable from the houses and shops around them.

We edged forward, keeping the Gulf to the south, on our left, towards the toes of the foot, where it was plain that all the oil development had taken place, with an array of large round tanks lining what looked like a sizeable dock complex. The new airport was also at this western end of the chersonese, its outline and form visible, but clearly still under construction.

(I must admit that from up there, the *foot* looked more like a common-or-garden spit of land, rather than the somewhat grander-sounding chersonese it's been known as historically, but for the sake of consistency I will stick with the Classical term.)

To my abject horror, I could see that the new runway had been constructed across the remains of a star-shaped bastion. Two of the five points still described the side along the water's edge, but most of the four land-bound sides, and the defensive ditches running in front of them, had already been covered with tarmac. It was unmistakable (I thought), the remains of an Early Modern European fort, presumably either Portuguese or Dutch. Now, given that I am the only academic authority on DM that I'm aware of, it struck me as extraordinary that I hadn't known of the existence of this fort. You might suppose that I felt shamed, but far from it; since I was completely sure I'd read everything ever written about DM, and had found no reference to this fort whatsoever, I was also completely sure that nothing had ever been written about it. I sensed an academic coup in the making. Describing a find such as this, the sort of thing usually uncovered after years of research and fieldwork, is what gets a chap a chair at a proper university. Praise be for helicopters!

Somewhat to his surprise, I asked Ali to go into a hover again, so that I could take a better look, but he cheerily noted that we were running out of fuel. We turned left, briefly flew over the sea, turned left again and were flying back towards the heel, along the coast, and to our final landing in Ali's back garden. When I say garden, I should be clear that I mean a walled lawned area about the size of a football stadium, with a massive house in the middle – I think it would be fair to describe it as lip-curling, post-modern bling! – which, he informed me, because of matters of protocol, was actually smaller than the royal palace, if not by very much.

The length of the chersonese is only about nine kilometres, and its width fewer than three, so our tour of the state had been mercifully brief, and I was delighted finally to be on the ground. I found myself to be stiff as I climbed down from the helicopter, but at last I had my feet on the soil of Dusa Mathavasi; I was exhausted, overheated and elated.

And at that point, a camel bounded over and knocked me to the ground.

4

Cat stood on the quayside in Dhoosar Mathavassee, gazing in awe at the beautiful uru which lay at berth before him. He had made the journey from Darjeeling by sea, travelling down the tributaries of the Brahmaputra to Chittagong with a cargo of tea, before hitching rides on a variety of vessels. He had changed ships at Calcutta, Madras, Colombo, Mangalore and, finally, at Bombay, where he had found the Sea Nymph tied up, loading rice for a coastal voyage northward, calling in at Karachi and then DM. Of all the ships he'd been on, small and large, during his month-long journey, it was this one which had given him the most pleasure.

None of the crew had spoken English well enough for him to have had a proper conversation, but the time he'd spent aboard had been full of friendship and sharing, as the hand-crafted wooden vessel made progress under canvas, through the slow, rolling waves of the Arabian Sea. Communication with hilariously exaggerated gestures had supplemented Cat's still-modest ability in Hindustani, but he had been able to amuse the crew during periods of rest with his ventriloquial skills, the fun of which didn't depend on clarity of meaning. And he and they had made music together, plaintive folk songs and jaunty shanties alike, when Cat had become the percussionist, drumming on upturned pans from the galley which, not long before, he had helped empty. He had particularly enjoyed the food on board which, simple in nature but plentiful in supply, was freely available; he had enjoyed a rare week of true satiety.

Parvati had spent the voyage below, strapped carefully into her enormous plywood case. It was in this case that she had arrived when Cat first acquired her, and he had considered at the time that it was massively too strong, because it was massively too heavy. For the most part, whilst a student in London, he had transported her in a soft, canvas bag which he had found unused in the college storeroom, conveniently. The hard case was the reason why he had decided to make the journey to DM by sea rather than by rail, because he'd had that experience travelling to

Ghoom on his journey eastward, and didn't care to repeat it; a double bass in a canvas bag on the London Tube was bad enough, but in a monumental sarcophagus on an Indian train it was all-but impossible. And now that case was being winched from the hold, in full view of the crowd gathered on the quay.

Knowing Parvati's true identity, Cat was happy that she was hidden from the prying eyes of the onlookers, who were seeing dangling from the crane a very large, scruffily hand-painted black box, nothing more than an over-large travelling trunk, the property of this over-large European tripper. Until, that is, the lid of the case became unfastened, swinging open on its hinges, just as the crane arced round to transfer the precious cargo from ship to land. There, in her nakedness, hung Parvati, as wooden and curvaceous as the uru from which she'd been lifted, strapped into the green baize interior of the case, for all the world to gaze upon as if she was showing her pantaloons.

Cat caught his breath. His primary concern wasn't the embarrassment of seeing his double bass so immodestly exposed, it was the fact that now only a single leather strap prevented her from tumbling out of the case, into the water or to smash on the concrete of the pier, or both. He ran forward, despite his undulating sea-legs, with arms outstretched, as if to catch her should she fall, a gesture which would undoubtedly have been as suicidal as it was impetuous if it had been translated into action. He cried out, 'don't let go, my love, hang on tight!', grateful, reflectively, that he was in a place where he supposed no-one understood him, as he watched the crane gently lower her to the ground. Other hands came forward to help steady the box and ease its gentle touch-down, and it was clear that many people were commenting on its unusual contents, even as Cat slammed shut the lid.

It was damnably hot, and Cat was already thermally challenged, without the additional excitement of this brief but urgent crisis. Having sailed northwards up the coast, he knew that the monsoon had broken the summer heat lower down the subcontinent, but DM was too far north to benefit from the cooling effect of the rains. It was still high summer up here, with the hot loo wind only slightly calmed, and this provided another reason to regret Parvati's brief exposure, since she needed to adjust to a new climate slowly. Throughout the last part of the journey, as temperatures had begun to rise, Cat had kept her canvas cover dampened lightly, and folded into the bottom of the case to maintain a uniformity of humidity. A shock such as she'd just suffered could have serious consequences – cracking like a glass filled with boiling water – and, in this place, no luthier was likely to be on hand. Mind, anyone who could build an uru, Cat speculated, could almost certainly maintain a *da Salò*, even if the scale was so different.

As for himself, Cat's arms and legs were always fully covered, partly to save him from the sunburn to which he knew he was easily prone, but mainly out of respect for the mores of a people for whom the sight of a mountainous white body, clad only in, say, shorts and a sports shirt might cause offence. Unlike others whom Cat knew, he felt he had an entirely realistic sense of his own body, of the hugeness which had caused him to be dogged throughout his life, and especially at school, the fat boy – the fat owl indeed, because of the little round spectacles he wore then – teased by all and any who felt they had a right to comment on his appearance. The train ride to Ghoom had been appalling not just because of having to transport Parvati in her case, but for the number of times that strangers had made comments about him needing two tickets, because he was taking two seats. He hated being the size he was, being aware of how much easier so many things would be otherwise, and now, having sprung to Parvati's defence, was a good example, as he found himself decidedly short of breath, sweat oozing from his forehead.

'I say, old bean...'

The clipped English accent had come from behind Cat, so he swung round to see who could possibly be addressing him thus, and was surprised that all he could see were brown faces.

'...you don't look like one who's arrival here has been altogether copacetic.'

'I beg your pardon?'

A small man, whose white, three-piece suit contrasted markedly with his chestnut skin and black goatee, stepped forward and extended a hand in greeting.

'You look out of sorts, Mr Adam.'

'Do I?' Cat was confused.

'You do.'

'Well, I just had a bit of an emergency...' Cat nodded his head to suggest the relationship of the crane to Parvati's case, and that things could have gone better.

'I know. I witnessed the event.'

Cat was annoyed that an English speaker had in fact been on hand to hear him cry out to his double bass in intimate terms. 'Yes, well, these things, as they say. And you are?' He took the outstretched hand into his own and shook it.

'I'm the British Political Agent here in Dhoosar Mathavassee, and my name is Enoch da Costa.' He doffed his sola topee. 'How do you do, Mr. Adam.'

'How do you know my name?'

'Well, there are a brace of observations I must make on this matter, the first of which is that it is my job to know what His Highness the Rajah is doing, and to advise him according to my belief and expectation with regard to the will of His Majesty's government.'

'Right.'

'The second is that, knowing that His Highness was expecting a corpulent former school friend by the name of Adam to arrive, with a double bass, on a dhow from Bombay – you see your telegram was received – I was inclined to the view that I could reasonably make the assumption that you are he. Am I correct?'

'Er, yes, you are, quite correct.'

'Splendid! Then, shall we organise some coolies to take your luggage to the palace compound, whilst you and I ride in the tonga I have waiting?'

At this, Enoch da Costa, gestured with his hand and the crowd parted, to reveal behind them a dusty plaza, which served both as quay yard and civic square, at once bustling and torpid. Bony porters pushed roughly-fashioned hand carts, shifting sacks and produce to and from the small line of ships tied up, shouting and laughing in their pale cotton dhotis and sodden khaki pugrees. At the same time, groups of men sat inactively here and there, on a wall or on barrels, some playing games on packing-case tables, some taking instruction from a white-clad imam, some smoking and glancing aimlessly out to sea as they mended nets. The smell of freshly-landed fish was strong, the sound of the flies they attracted pervasive, and the sun all-dominant. Amongst the uniform dullness of the clothing there was no brightness, no-one more flamboyantly attired than the political agent, and although there were boys going about their business like men, there were no women. Cat sniffed; he liked women.

Taking in his surroundings, he rather casually told Enoch that the skipper of the uru was waiting for payment.

'But, I don't understand," Enoch halted mid-step, 'how did you secure passage without any money?'

'Oh, I had some, gave it him in Bombay, but he seems to insist that he needs more, reckons that the food wasn't included, or some such. Anyway, I'm not made of oof, and the other boats cost money as well, don't you know.'

This was true, and the payroll money, which Cat had borrowed from the plantation in Ghoom to finance his journey, had run out. At some point, he reminded himself, he must make sure that the royal treasury here returned the money to his former employer, it being only correct that it paid for its Master of Music to travel to his new post. But it wasn't urgent, he felt, since no-one back there knew where he'd gone.

'Just settle the bill, there's a good chap!' Cat sensed the possibility of resistance, and stepped out to cross to the shade of the waiting tonga, leaving Enoch, startled, to do as bidden. The plaza was merely a widening of the coast road, which went on its way both left and right, not much more than a well-used dirt track. There were no cars, which anyway would have struggled on the pitted surface, but many bicycles and carts drawn by animals. One of these, a substantial vehicle with four wheels, was waiting to receive Cat's luggage, its driver looking on in dismay as the vast black box was carefully manoeuvred towards him horizontally by a team of four porters, with the respect and care which Cat's gimlet look had demanded. Thinking that any great exertion in this heat would have been just as injurious to his health as rocking motionless in the sun's biting glare, Cat opted to move at a tortoise pace, shielding his head with his hands, regretting the loss of his old straw boater overboard quite early on his journey. Enoch, better protected, soon caught up with him, and gave him a look which Cat thought ungenerous.

Both the cart and Enoch's tonga were waiting on the far side of the plaza, beside the opening to the palace avenue, which led northwards, and at the distant end of which could be seen what must have been the royal residence. Even from here, at the bottom of the avenue, Cat could see that the palace had been built on elevated ground, not high but higher than all the surrounding structures. Had he been looking in the other direction, he might have seen instead the looks exchanged by the two drivers, as they realised between them that the payload of a double bass in a sturdy, camel-drawn carriage was as nothing compared to the burden of Cat Adam in a lightweight, two-seat tonga. Enoch did, however, catch the exchange, and understood immediately the unspoken point, whereupon he summoned a second tonga with an imperious but discreet gesture.

Seeing Enoch mount the second tonga, Cat understood what was going on as he took his seat. Having heaved himself into the carriage, whilst the driver hung on to his mule lest it should take fright, he glanced at the space beside him and tacitly acknowledged that there wouldn't realistically have been room for both of them. Resignation had long been a feature of his oversized existence, so he glanced longingly back at the uru for the last time, where he had been comfortable, before jolting forward at the head of the small convoy.

With comfort now in mind, Cat realised that he hadn't given much thought to the matter of his accommodation in DM, presuming simply that it would come with the job, as at Ghoom. But now he was on a road which led directly to a royal palace, it occurred to him that he was expecting to be able to enjoy a far more luxurious standard here than back there. He supposed he would be given a suite of rooms in the palace, now that he thought about it, in a manner fitting for someone of his rank within the court. And glancing up the sloping avenue towards the palace, he was pleased with what he saw in the distance.

The avenue was lined with modest buildings, carelessly stocked shops with open fronts, and offices with louvred windows. There was a couple of havelis, but not the grand type he'd seen in Cal, rather they were plain and, like every other building, succumbing to the black mould which usurps old paint in such a climate. There were no pavements, nothing to distinguish one from another the dusty spaces used by carriages, bicycles and pedestrians, and the milling of people threatened at every point to spill over into the path of the tonga. Here there were women, the majority with heads covered with the tails of their sarees, who seemed to be about the business of shopping; but still no colour beyond the palest of blues and faded rust.

As Cat made his progress, barely-clad urchins darted out from their places of invisibility, to run alongside his tonga begging for alms, causing the driver to shout 'tok tok' repeatedly. He had no intention of parting with any paise, but was unsure as to the correct attitude to assume in this new place, and turned as best he could in the confined space to see how the Political Agent dealt with the swarm of interest. He saw that the children ran up to Enoch's tonga as keenly as to his own, but upon spotting who the occupant was, pulled disappointed faces and let him pass by. Enoch, in turn, disdainfully refused to see them, gazing purposefully straight ahead. Cat thought it made him look foolish and cruel, especially since he wasn't even a proper Englishman himself, so waved and smiled at the children, who laughed and waved back even without the encouragement of his small change.

The heart of the city was poor and undeveloped, Cat could see, in stark contrast to the glory which he anticipated as they rolled ever nearer the palace. With his younger brother in training to be an architect, he had acquired a vicarious interest in buildings, and described to himself in technical terms the large and, within its context, grand flight of stairs which were becoming visible in the distance, leading up from the carriage yard beyond the iron gates, not unlike a miniature Sans Souci, where Cat had toured with his college orchestra. The steps ascended from a green terrace to the first floor of a low, wide building, more decorated than the ground floor beneath, with four arched windows either side of the triple-arched portico and raised hexagonal towers terminating each end of the range. Above stood a handsome central cupola which reminded Cat of the dome of the National Gallery in

Trafalgar Square, and the whole was decorated with neo-classical-Saracenic devices – pilasters, an arcaded entablature where once might have been crenulations, Corinthian columns supporting the portico – and was finished in white stucco. Cat was delighted.

On the right, about two-thirds of the way up the clamouring thoroughfare, the line of buildings was broken to reveal the church, set back in its own grounds, which Barton had mentioned in his letter to Cat. As he had suggested, it was nearing completion, the nave and chancel in white stucco, which gleamed as brightly as the Political Agent's impeccable suit, under a roof of plain clay tiles. It was surprisingly large given its setting, with a spire beginning to rise within a tangle of wooden scaffolding above the west door. The grounds, Cat had to suppose, were intended over time to become a graveyard, although he wondered where the Christians might be who could one day occupy this dusty corner. Still, so long as it had its organ and he had his orchestra, he wouldn't concern himself with matters of that kind.

As the church passed out of view, the avenue briefly rose more steeply before it opened into another square, similar in size to the quay yard at the other end. Fronted by the palace railings, the area was covered in golden sand, and it was clear from the freshness of the cart tracks that some effort was made to keep the surface smooth and level. Indeed, Cat's attention was drawn from the details of the palace, which had become now more sharply visible, by the sudden scurrying of four elderly, stooped ladies with brooms, who appeared one from each corner of the square, and whose task, plainly, was to smooth out the sand ahead of approaching palace traffic. They were as nimble and efficient as they were pathetic, he thought.

It was becoming clear that the grandeur of the palace was somewhat illusory, now that sections of missing stucco had become visible, and Cat could gauge the extent to which the whiteness was patinated by the ubiquitous black mould. Incredibly, Cat thought, half the glass from the windows in the cupola was broken, and several pieces from the cresting on top of the entablature were missing, as if someone had knocked the building's teeth out.

Barely in time, two of the sweepers withdrew from the path of Cat's tonga as it approached the central gate, standing with their skinny legs more or less to attention as the gates swung open. Cat might even have thought about throwing down a tip had there been time, but his carriage jolted through the gates without halting, as the two guards who held them open saluted carelessly. They carried on their shoulders rifles and were dressed in livery, although it wasn't clear from this whether they were policemen, guards or just servants. Cat assumed they were all three in one, and nodded at each them as he passed by, assuming the superior air of the Master of Music.

There was a tight turning circle in front of the palace, also covered in sand, allowing the tongas to draw up alongside the flight of steps, which now looked worryingly steep from where Cat was sitting. He heaved himself out of the carriage, taking great care as he lowered himself to the ground, because his ankles had become unreliable lately. The driver once again considered that the welfare of his animal was of greater importance than that of his passenger, to whom he offered no assistance whatsoever. Enoch, behind, was dainty in his dismount, gratefully accepting the obsequious hand offered by his driver, and dusting down his white suit as he stood upright. The cart with Cat's luggage disappeared to the left, on a track which led off the circle and passed behind the palace; doubtless the servants at the back door were on hand to deal with his things, to convey them to his suite of rooms, but would they treat Parvati with sufficient respect?

'Welcome to the Durja Bangala, Mr. Adam!' Enoch gestured in a manner too grand for the broken-down building which he addressed. Cat thought he detected another ungenerous look, in fact a barely disguised sneer, on the face of the PA. It was rather as if this fellow, who, given his youth and ancestry, was in a position rather more senior within the ICS than was typical, felt it was all a bit beneath him. 'I apologise for the tatterdemalions who bothered you as we made our progress up the royal avenue, and I regret that I am...' Enoch looked up at the palace, rising above him in near dereliction, and was unable to finish his speech. Cat, astonished by the PA's posturing, was unwilling to ease the awkward moment. Imagining that Enoch da Costa was the type to be lost for words only very rarely, he decided to let him flounder in his embarrassment. '...yes, well, we have arrived...' Enoch's shoulders fell.

'Right, shall we?' Cat took a deep breath, and prepared to mount the crumbling staircase, choosing the right-hand side because a large section from the middle of the handrail on the other side was missing. It was going to be a stiff, unsteady climb, at least twenty steps, he estimated, and handrails mattered under such circumstances.

Enoch quickly overtook Cat, his pace being somewhat less measured, and waited for him on the top step. Before Cat could join him, one of the pair of doors within the shadow of the portico creaked open, pulled by an unseen hand, and an elderly servant in a white angarkha and dhoti stepped out to greet the PA. Cat had paused for a moment at the halfway point, when both men turned away from him to speak to each other without being overheard, which occasioned controlled shaking of the head by the servant and a shrug of frustration from Enoch.

'This is Ajaz, Mr. Adam,' Enoch made the introduction when Cat finally stepped onto the terrace, 'he's the family's factotum of very long standing, and he will be able to answer any queries you might have about the running of the house.'

'Salaam alaikum,' Cat held out his hand, panting.

'Wa 'alaikum al-salaam, Sahib' replied Ajaz, exchanging a glance of approval with Enoch as he bowed his head, 'Please follow.'

'How long have you been here, Ajaz?' Cat had learned that treating servants well was the route to attentive service, and polite small talk was always a very good way to start.

'Oh, long time, Sahib. I started as houseboy in the day of Rajah's grandfather. They were glorious times!'

'More glorious than now?'

Ajaz considered before answering drily, 'I'm sure I cannot say, Sahib. I have been instructed to take you through to Rajah's drawing room when you arrive, so if you would step this way.'

They passed through the doorway, into the shade of an inner hall, and then into the light central atrium, which was open to the damaged cupola above. Cat reflected that it must once have been a grand reception hall, the durbar, and, on the other side of the black and white chequered marble floor, the royal throne was indeed still in place, directly ahead of the entrance. Its covering of red and gold damask was very faded, very stained. There was a heavy wooden door with once-gilded carvings to the right-hand side of the throne, leading to the private rooms beyond, and Ajaz led Cat and Enoch through it, before they turned right into the plain, dark corridor which ran through the centre of the palace, lit only by small, distant windows above the doors at each end.

'Alas, no enfilade!' observed Cat, attempting to make conversation.

Enoch scoffed and muttered, as if pained, 'In this palace?'

Cat could hear the sound of hilarious laughter coming from ahead, which seemed incongruous in this dingy space. They passed a door on the right which was ajar, providing a little extra light, then stopped at the door on the left, about halfway down the passage, on which Ajaz knocked before they entered. The laughter immediately ceased, as Enoch led Cat through into the drawing room.

'Your Highness, may I present Mr. Adam...', Enoch allowed his head to dip briefly, as if that was as much of a bow he could bring himself to perform.

Cat smiled and nodded at Ajaz, who held the door open, and passed beyond Enoch into the room. There he discovered at one end the Rajah, waving aloft a cricket bat whilst sitting on the shoulders of a blind-folded European, and at the other Barton frozen in the act of googlying a turban for the Rajah to strike.

'Barton – still the keen cricketer, I see,' Cat knitted his eyebrows, 'and Sooty, as ever, the batsman.'

His Highness Hurree Jam Saheb gasped, and Barton took a sharp intake of breath.

'What did you call me?' demanded the Rajah

'You do realise that disrespecting His Highness is a capital offence round here!' gasped Barton.

The blind-folded man tutted.

Cat was astonished, didn't know what to say in the face of this icy reception from his old class fellows. There was a long silent pause, during which Enoch made as if to intervene, before thinking better of it, when suddenly the three sportsmen burst into laughter so spontaneous it seemed as if it must have been rehearsed. Hurree fell spectacularly from his mount. 'Adam, you sap!' he laughed, bouncing to his feet, 'you should have seen your face!'

Barton stepped over and placed a hand on Cat's shoulders. 'Honestly, old man, you didn't think we were being serious, did you?'

He stank of gin.

'You rotters! I've only just stepped off the boat and already I feel like I'm back in the dorm, putting up with everyone being beastly again.'

'Sorry, old man,' smiled Hurree, 'just a bit of fun. Anyway, welcome welcome welcome!'

'Yes, just a laugh, that's all,' tittered Barton, 'but we don't call him Sooty any more, seriously. It's not appropriate, is it!' He threw the turban to the Rajah, who straightened it out as best he could before jamming it onto his head.

The third individual removed his bind-fold and blinked at Cat. 'Hello, Adam, remember me?'

Cat didn't remember him at all, but was wary of saying so, not yet having got the full measure of what was going on.

'You'll remember Mr. Wigly, I'm quite sure, Mr. Adam, from your glorious school days?' Enoch came to the rescue.

Cat hesitated for a moment, allowing his thoughts to clear. Yes, he did remember a Wigly from school, although he wouldn't have recognised this moustachioed fellow as him had he not been told. He recalled that Hurree had stayed with Wigly one Easter vac, and they had become notably friendly with each other; there had been talk that their closeness was of that special variety which arose from time to time in an all-boys public school, but which generally amounted to nothing. Cat wondered what Wigly was doing here, until he saw him take Hurree by the hand and lead him towards the drinks table.

'Another peg, Your Highness?' he giggled, 'And what about you, dear old Adam, what will you have to drink? I like your square specs, by the way.'

'Hallo, Wigly, thanks. It's a little early for me, I'm sorry, especially since I feel like I'm still at sea! I was wondering about a bite to eat, though, if you chaps...'

All three roared with laughter, preventing Cat from finishing his sentence. He turned to look at Enoch, hoping for some assistance, but he was impassive, observing his drunken inferiors at play as if they were zoological specimens. Ajaz, however, caught Cat's eye, and nodded almost imperceptibly, indicating that he would make provision for his needs. But then he stiffened suddenly, as another young man entered the room.

'So, your new friend has arrived. Such pains you've taken to make him feel welcome, I see!'

'Mr. Adam,' Enoch assumed a more attentive attitude, 'may I introduce Prince Shankarrao, His Highness's younger brother.'

'How do you do, sir,' Cat offered his hand, but it was not taken.

'My little brother's just back from university, Adam, and he's very serious about life, aren't you, Shanky. I think it must be because he went to the London School of Economics, wouldn't you agree, Pip?'

Barton smirked.

'The thing is, Mr. Adam, that I find myself incapable of living life without reflecting on the advantages to which I have been born, and the responsibilities which I must therefore accept. It is not for a royal prince to live his life in a state of drunken debauchery, when instead the call of duty should be his master, and sobriety the means by which he answers it.' The fresh-faced youthfulness of Shankarrao couldn't disguise the burning sense of purpose which lit his eyes, with which he swept the room before turning on his heels and exiting.

There was silence, then hyena-like guffawing from the drunkards, Wigly dabbing his eyes with what had been his blindfold.

'If you come with me, Sahib,' Ajaz stepped forward to address Cat discreetly, I will show you to quarters.'

'Thank you, Ajaz,' Cat let out a sigh of relief that he was being taken in hand by the only sensible person in the room. 'I think I need to find my bearings. And perhaps that bite to eat…?'

'Come back soon and have a drink with us, Adam!' instructed the Rajah.

'Yes, sooooooon!' echoed Wigly and Barton in unison.

5

I hadn't known that camels were capable of playfulness, presuming them to be either domesticated beasts of burden, or else in their feral state, chilling in the desert, trying as a herd to avoid capture. But there was no question, even for this novice in camel ways, that the animal leering down at me from a height was happy. If it had been a dog, then it is clear that its tail would have been wagging.

Curiously, as I lay there beneath the sun, partially dazzled, my first thoughts were for the camel's welfare, since it had knocked me over very close to the helicopter, and the blades were still slowing. I decided that its designer would had done due diligence in the matter of not decapitating pilots and their passengers, but still I had myself been mindful of what still seemed a possibility as I'd climbed out, and had made sure to keep my head down. It occurred to me, though, that it was extremely unlikely that anyone would have taken into account the possibility of a lofty ungulate sticking its head into the path of the rotors, which would surely have been chopped off instantly.

Ali stepped in to help me, tugging at the animal's halter. My previous contacts with camels had been limited to zoo visits when I was a child and, later, as a member of the crowd of well-wishers in Oxford, gathered to send off whichever cleric had drawn that year's short straw, thereby earning the dubious honour of walking one of these famously recalcitrant beasts all the way to Cambridge. I recall that there they were always scruffy, with bits of fur hanging off and a leery look about them. This one, which was now drumming rhythmically with its front feet, was exceptionally tidy, as if groomed for a royal county show.

Ali: Sorry, this is my pet camel.

Me: Yes, I can see it's a camel.

Ali: She was just pleased to see me. She gets over-excited when she hears the chopper coming in to land.

Me: It wasn't what I expected, I must say!

Ali: No, of course not, I'm very sorry. I'll speak to her trainer about her behaviour in the morning. You're ok, are you?

Me: You have a camel trainer?

There was a pause, as if this was a stupid question. He whispered into the camel's ear, whereupon she immediately stopped her purposeful drumming and stood politely by, thus illustrating the necessity for a camel, if it is to be trained, to be well trained.

Me: I was worried she might have cut her head off in the helicopter blades.

Ali: (laughing) No, no chance of that. She's trained to keep her head down.

Me: Silly me, of course she is.

Ali: Anyway, we don't cut heads off round here. We hang people.

There was a peculiarly sombre edge to Ali's voice as he made that, I thought, strange remark.

Ali: And this is Billi Boy.

A cat had slunk over and was winding itself around my legs.

Me: Oh, hello, Billy.

Ali: (amused) No no, *billi* is the Urdu word for cat. This is Boy, Billi Boy.

A white-clad servant had by now arrived, bowing to me and then to Ali in turn, although it did look a little like he was bowing to the camel as well, since she was standing directly beside her master. Ali passed the camel's halter to the servant, giving directions in, I guessed, Urdu, about, I guessed, my luggage. Together we walked towards the terrace in front of the enormous house, avoiding the brace of deer which emerged from who-knows-where to gambol in front of us, the warthog snuffling amongst a small group of trees in the distance, and the parakeets which flew overhead. It felt like I had arrived in a Disney cartoon.

I understand, reflecting now on those first few minutes on the ground in DM, that subliminally I had expected the place still to resemble something like Mirat in *The Raj Quartet*, even though I knew objectively that it had been greatly modernised in the decades since the war. Such is the power and attraction of the heterotopic space in fiction, I suppose, when it generates an immutable memory and ontological status, therefore, which bears no relation to reality. Mind you, this place was definitely posh.

When you first arrive somewhere new, especially after a long, time-shifting journey, it's difficult to take in more than just your first impressions, and they had been so extreme that I must have entered a state of overload, so that I don't recall much of the Qifar house, beyond its vastness and having a cup of tea brought to us on the terrace, as we reclined in white, rattan furniture and watched the automatic sprinklers pop up mesmerisingly one by one over the entire garden. That was taken as an indicator of the onset of nightfall, and a sign that it was time to take me to the palace, where I was expected.

Ali sent his servant a text message from his mobile, giving instructions to prepare a car for the final leg of my journey. I wouldn't have been surprised if I'd been whisked away in an open-top Rolls-Royce, complete with gold-plated everything, but it was a rather more modest four-by-four which turned up to collect us, in a dark colour and with darkened glass. And it was bullet-proof, I learned, when I remarked on the weight of the door as we climbed in; I tapped the window with my knuckle on the inside, which responded with a dull thud, as if it was a section of granite kitchen top. Was it necessary, I asked, beginning to wonder if I'd come unwittingly to a dangerous place. But Ali assured me everything was fine, as we set off through giant metal gates which the armed guards opened only as we drew up to them, and closed the moment we had passed through into the outside world.

The journey by car took longer than it had in reverse by helicopter, unsurprisingly, but it was still relatively short; DM isn't a big place. We turned onto the coast road and drove west for two or three kilometres before we arrived at a roundabout, in the middle of which was an enormous piece of public sculpture, which Ali called *The Aerial*. It was becoming dark, so I wouldn't have been able to get a good look at it anyway, but regardless I was thoroughly distracted when the driver turned right at the roundabout by turning right at the roundabout. I would have expected, of course, to turn left and go all the way round, through

270°, but it appears to be the custom there to circumnavigate a roundabout in either direction, depending, I presume, on which way round takes you more quickly to your desired exit. I expressed surprise – it might have been a squeak of distress, frankly – before Ali assured me the driver was behaving in a manner which was normal for DM. Everything I had encountered since we landed was probably normal for DM, and I wondered if it was just my jet-lag which made everything seem strange, but looking backwards at the sculpture when its lights flickered on, as we left the roundabout, I noticed for the first time that we were in fact travelling with an armed escort bringing up the rear, in the form of an open-top jeep with four uniformed men with large moustaches, brandishing machine guns. Normal for DM was likely to become a matter of concern, I feared.

I recognised enough of the road we turned down to know that it was the straight road over which we had hovered, which led to the palace, about a kilometre ahead of us on top of a rise, brightly lit and decidedly brash. The roads were excellent, with good surfaces, and this one had a central divide, in the manner of a boulevard. There was plenty of traffic, although everything was moving along nicely, with many people out and about, walking casually under the street-lighting and peering into the windows of the shops along the way. There wasn't a branch of M&S, let's be clear, but if there had been it wouldn't have looked out of place.

And suddenly, as we approached the palace, there on the right was the mosque with the tall minaret, set back within its own grounds. It was shining and fresh, very Arabic in style, and seemed much larger on the ground than it had from above. Like the palace, it too was flood-lit, from its first course of tiles to the very tip of the minaret, where an enormous silver crescent moon reflected the light back down to earth. It wasn't a lovely building, cold at first sight, more about the statement it might make to those passing by than to those who would enter to pray. The grounds were paved in marble, and crowds sat around on benches and steps, young and old, enjoying the evening warmth after the scorching heat of the day.

Ali explained that the mosque was only recently finished, and that his family was very proud, from which I took it that his family had paid for it. I had been about to make some remark about its size being disproportionate to its setting, but managed to stop myself just in time, so that I made a sound which I hoped expressed instead something of a sense of wonder and admiration. I think I got away with it.

We approached the roundabout at the head of the boulevard, with the palace lying directly ahead of us, and I was fascinated to see which way round the driver would go, since there was no clear advantage in either direction. There was another sculpture in the middle, this time a rather bold, partially-abstracted statue of a person, but I couldn't make out who or what, and didn't feel up to tackling the subject with Ali, so passed by in ignorance; to the left, as it happens.

The sculpture looked old-fashioned compared to the palace, which we now approached up a central driveway. Remembering the mantra of one of my tutors at Oxford, that modernism is new things from old materials and postmodernism new things from new materials, the sculpture was merely an abstraction in plain old stone, whereas the palace was a monstrous thing in white, blue and pink stucco, such as could be the home of an eastern out-shot of MI6. It was symmetrical, absolutely huge, the ground floor an uninterrupted colonnade of many tall, white columns, looking like a parodic take on an antebellum southern mansion. The outer quarter of the facade on each side extended upwards in brilliant blue stucco to a second floor, with tall, rectangular windows aligned to the columns beneath, whilst there was a twenty-metre break in the central section, filled by the eruption of a central drum-like structure in pink, perfectly round and rising four levels above the colonnade, pierced around its circumference at every level by smaller round windows. The drum was then topped with a flat square roof, on legs, which looked for all the world like the helipad you see on hospitals, even though I knew already that the only helicopter in DM customarily lands in its owner's back garden.

The palace was set on a rise, surrounded by swathes of fine, green lawn through which cut the central driveway, leading up to a hard terrace across the full width of the building. There were no railings that I could see, or any other visible obstacles to members of the general public who might have wanted to wander up to the front door, but then I saw that the tiny figures dotted along the vast length of the building were all armed guards. The effect was a heady, confusing mixture of come-and-get-it openness, combined with the cold dominance of Edward I's Welsh castles. Albert Speer would have loved it; I hated it.

We stopped by the front door, where the doors of the car were opened for us by uniformed guards, saluting, whilst our own armed escort hovered behind, at the point where the driveway met the terrace, clearly intending to prevent the non-existent terrorists who hadn't followed us from mounting the attack which was obviously not imminent. Given how calm everyone was, frankly, I was at a loss to understand what all this security meant; I supposed that the palace authorities were just operating on a better-safe-than-sorry basis, absurdly over the top even though it seemed.

I wondered what had happened to my luggage, as I'd not had sight of since it was loaded into the helicopter's boot at Karachi, but there was no opportunity to ask. Ali and I were surrounded by a very brisk and hard-looking contingent of soldier-policemen with badges saying 'commando' on the shoulders of their green uniforms, marching us in a phalanx through the central archway, into the marble reception hall and across to a lift, which was open and waiting for us. The sound of boots echoed off the marble all round. Ali gestured that I should enter first, then he followed, together with a liveried servant who had been waiting to one side, who pressed one of the buttons and stood looking discreetly up at the ceiling as the doors closed and we began to ascend. Ali suddenly guffawed.

Ali: Nothing like making an entrance, eh!

Me: What the hell's going on?

Ali: Oh, don't worry, everything's fine! It's just that we had a bit of bother recently, so we're putting on a show of strength for anyone who's looking. It's hilarious!

I was unconvinced that it was all that funny. And who was the 'we' to whom he was referring?

Me: What sort of bother?

Ali: Don't worry, nothing which concerns you. And we've got it all in hand anyway.

This was quite the smoothest, poshest lift I'd ever been in, and it hardly felt like we'd moved when the doors opened to reveal the Yuvraj waiting for us, smiling broadly, with arms outstretched.

Sammy: Philip! At last, you've made it! Come in come in come in.

He wrapped me in a hug as I stepped out of the lift, and I was genuinely touched by the warmth of his greeting. He was bare-footed, in jeans and a tee-shirt, and he looked very well indeed, suggesting that life was treating him generously. And then I saw beside him Arabella Jade-Reece, the icy, pale blonde who had been his girlfriend at Wedgwood and who, I had to assume, still was. I was wrong, they were now married.

Me: Sammy, what a pleasure to be here. Arabella, what a surprise. How nice to see you.

I pecked her on both cheeks, and judged from her impassive response that she was as delighted to see me as I was her.

Arabella: (icily) Yes, fancy!

Tense as she was, she still sounded like the posh girl from Huddersfield she had always been, the girl for whom coal came in sex, as my Nan would say. I tried to remember why I didn't like her, and thought it was probably because she'd never liked me, the boy from the comprehensive school. This would add spice to an already fascinating trip!

Sammy: Come through, dear old friend, come and make yourself comfortable.

He led us all through the lobby, itself large but already far more human in scale than the public floor we'd left below, and into what could only be described as a domestic lounge. It was carpeted, had soft furnishings arranged around three sides of a square, all in tasteful, pastel colours, and was delightfully cool, thanks to the air conditioning which hummed gently in the background. Mercifully free of the bling I had expected, judging by the exterior, the ceiling was at a sensible height, and the walls painted in a soft brick red. I noticed that the outer wall curved gently, and concluded we were up in the central drum area.

Sammy gestured that I should take a seat on the sofa, behind which a chubby little elephant-headed god sat on a table, surrounded by burning joss sticks, which made the whole experience strangely reminiscent of our undergraduate days. Google would later tell me this was Sri Ganesh, the Hindu god of prosperity, amongst other things, and the quiet comfort of my surroundings suggested that he was fully in command of his brief. Everything seemed very pleasant indeed, and I wondered, as I sank into the glorious sofa to which he gestured, whether Sammy had continued burning joss sticks ever since we'd left Oxford.

A servant was on hand to takes our drinks orders. I was really, really tired by now, but bearing in mind the stories of offence given by refusing a sheep's eyeball in the Bedouin tent, I asked for a gin and Slimline. Ali wanted a vodka and tonic, whereas Arabella wasn't thirsty, and I saw her give Sammy a look when he asked for a brandy.

Me: When was this place built, Sammy?

Sammy: Oh, we've only been in for a year or so. It's all part of the redevelopment package for DM.

That's the problem with being a historian, I decided, that you keep an eye out for things once they've already happened. I knew about the oil and the potential changes it might have been bringing, but not the actual changes which it had already brought.

Me: Oh, right, so where were you living before?

Sammy: The dower house is on the outskirts of the city; it's been the de facto palace for decades.

Me: And the public function of the palace – all the marble stuff downstairs?

Sammy: Yes, you're quite right, that was the problem, the real reason for building the new palace. It's the administrative everything now, nearly. Before, offices and departments were lodged in whatever space we could find in the city, all over the place. It was very inefficient!

Me: And, er…

I wanted to ask where the money had come from, but realised that if Sammy wanted to talk about that at all, historian to historian, he'd probably want to do it in private.

Me: ...who was the architect?

Arabella: (butting in) Oh, we were very lucky indeed. We got Petros Anastapopolous.

I hadn't a clue.

Arabella: (proudly) Petros Anastapopolous!

Repetition changed nothing. And I resisted the urge to suggest that, since it was built on elevated ground, the palace might be thought of as Anastapopolousacropolis.

Sammy: He's a friend of Arabella's father.

Arabella: Well, be that as it may, he's also one of Michael Graves's top students, Sammy. Don't sell him short.

I hadn't heard of Arabella's dad's buddy, but wondered by what mysterious process he'd come by the commission for this enormous pile in this faraway place. My gin arrived.

Arabella: We were delighted when the Sammy's father approved Pet's design.

I was stuck for something to say, so said the obvious, annoyingly.

Me: It's very postmodern.

Arabella: (smugly) He prefers the term New Urban, actually.

Me: Who does? The Rajah or the architect?

Ali: (knocking back his vodka) Yes, well, on that note, I'll be going.

Sammy raised his eyebrows and made a micro-gesture in my direction.

Ali: Oh, yes, of course – I'll come and pick you up in the morning, Philip, show you round a bit. Ten o'clock?

Me: Great, thanks. Land or air?

Ali: Sea? We've got a lot of it!

Me: Oh, er…

Ali: Actually, by land. So you can sleep easily.

I admit that I was pleased to hear this.

We all said our goodnights, and I took my leave, ushered by my personal servant (if you please), to a splendid bedroom suite on the floor above, where all my luggage was already unpacked and hanging up or folded in drawers. The enormous bed was turned down, with the single remote control for all of the lighting, air conditioning and media resting on the table beside it. Lakshmi was extremely polite, showing me how everything worked, and left me with the information that the wi-fi password was Panini4000, a curiously Italianate reference, I thought, in this place so far removed from the heart of classical Europe.

With thoughts of toasted sandwiches now invoked, I realised I hadn't eaten for ages, but was just too exhausted to do anything about it.

6

Cat was directed by Ajaz back along the dingy corridor, with Enoch following close behind. They reached the point where they'd entered from the durbar hall, and Cat turned left into it, assuming there would be a grand staircase leading up to the bedrooms, but he found himself alone as he rolled into the middle of the empty space.

'This way, please, Sahib,' directed Ajaz from the doorway.

Cat shrugged and turned on his heels, back into the corridor where a turn was taken into a dark rear hall, out through a back door and down some stairs into a service yard at the back of the palace. There was a bustle of activity, as maids in uniform-grey shalwar kameez, and men in soggy livery went about their business, moving between the palace and the range of outbuildings which defined the yard. It was evident, from the splendid smell of cooking which caught Cat's attention, that here, external to the palace, was where the kitchen was situated.

'Yes, Mr. Adam,' Enoch read Cat's mind, 'this is the servants' entrance.'

'I don't understand...' Cat had been expecting something more befitting of his position at court.

'All will become clear momentarily,' Enoch walked on.

Ajaz led them through a narrow passage between two of the rough brick outbuildings, where the space opened up into landscape, revealing a lake, about the size of a cricket ground, surrounded by a green, wooded area. Amongst the trees, on the shore nearest the house, a hundred yards away, stood a pair of small bungalows, not ten feet apart, timber built and roughly whitewashed, with corrugated tin roofs and each with a veranda in front, facing the water. They reminded Cat of his accommodation in Ghoom, and he realised with dismay that one of these was going to be his new home. He had been expecting a sumptuous room in the palace, perhaps with running water, maybe electricity, but he knew already that it was back to oil lamps and a thunderbox. There was nothing resembling a garden around the bungalows, rather they had been built directly onto the bare, woodland floor, and of course there was standing water, lots of it, which probably meant a proportionate number of mosquitoes. But at least there was plenty of shade.

'We are to be neighbours, Mr. Adam,' noted Enoch, striding purposefully forward, a man who had accepted his lot bitterly.

'I see. In that case, Mr. da Costa, I think we should be on more relaxed terms. Please call me Cat.'

'That I will, gladly. I sense in you, Cat, the possibility of conversation, and I'm pleased you're here. I'd be delighted if you would call me Enoch. Anything you wish to ask, Enoch will be just next door. I'm generally in. There isn't a lot to do in these parts, and my work isn't onerous.'

Enoch stood like a guard by the step up to Cat's new house, and shook his hand, a gesture of friendship.

'Thanks. It'll take me a while to gather myself. I need to have a sit down – and maybe that bite to eat?'

Ajaz nodded and bowed slightly, 'I will send someone, Sahib, right away.'

Cat stepped up onto his veranda, ready to take leave of his new friend without being at all sure that he liked him. Enoch, however, plainly felt the moment was right to speak candidly. 'Professional men, let us say clerics and doctors, in the rural eighteenth century would have been obliged to be friends for lack of any alternative amongst the peasants they served. The irony here and now is that the peasants are the occupants of the royal court.' With which he nodded politely and left.

The interior of 2nd Bungalow was as plain as Cat had feared it would be. He entered directly into the living room through the front door, realising that it was in fact the only door, and found it sparingly furnished with a bamboo two-seater sofa and arm chair, with ajrakh cushions, and a low table with a woven rattan top, all of which clearly formed a suite provided specifically for this room. Far from new, it was roughly made (locally and in a vernacular style, Cat presumed), and delicate in scale, with the sofa looking just about the right size for a single chap to get comfortable in. The chair could serve as a footstool, perhaps, or for Enoch when he visited; Enoch was both thin and, quite probably, the only visitor Cat could expect.

In the opposite right-hand corner of the room he could see that Parvati's case had been brought in and, thank heavens, was standing the right way up. And in the left-hand corner opened the rough wooden door which, plainly, led into the adjacent bedroom. Between Parvati's case and the bedroom door was a space too narrow to accommodate Parvati when she was naked, so it became immediately clear that the case would have to go elsewhere, so that she could have the corner to herself.

Cat edged through the gap between the chair on the left and the table, to get to the bedroom door which, when opened, revealed the unappetising vista of the thunderbox directly ahead, scantly separated from the rest of the room by a flat screen. Otherwise, there was an iron-framed double bed draped in an off-white mosquito net, which stood with its head against the dividing wall, and on which his personal effects were neatly laid out. There was a tiny dressing table at its foot, which doubled as a wash stand, and a diminutive wardrobe beside that.

Everything was made in the same bent bamboo, except the thunderbox, which was well finished in a dark wood and looked rather venerable as a result. Nevertheless, a thunderbox in a small bedroom was a bad thing at the best of times, especially when the bedroom in question was as tiny as this one, with only a pair of small casements by way of ventilation – and Cat had long acknowledged that the need for ventilation arising in his wake was generally greater than for the average man. The bungalow throughout was diminutive by any standards, particularly for a larger-than-average occupant, so some creative thinking was required, and Cat quickly arrived at a plan for what he thought might be just the first of a series of home improvements.

Parvati's case was fitted with castors on both the body and door, so that it could be opened without falling over, when it created two sides of a substantial upright cube. If the thunderbox could be removed to one end of the veranda, then the existing screen could be placed to obscure the view at the open side, and Parvati's case could be positioned so that it might be opened to provide privacy on the other two sides. This seemed to Cat like an ideal solution to two problems, and he determined to ask the staff responsible for emptying the thunderbox to reposition it accordingly.

But would there be staff to empty his thunderbox, he wondered, in this down-at-heel rajahate? Could Ajaz be the lone servant? Surely not, since his luggage had been brought in and, he noted as he opened the rickety wardrobe, his clothes hung up.

As if to cue, there was a knock at the door.

'Sahib, I bring for you food,' a tiny, high-pitched voice filtered through from the veranda.

Cat was struck by the loveliness of the girl who stood at his threshold, despite the greyness of her uniform. She was tiny, with delicate, fair skin, raven hair tied back, and sweet brown eyes which glistened at him.

'Milkar burri kushi hui', beamed Cat.

'Namaste - it is Indira, Sahib,' she smiled back, bobbing a delicate little curtsy.

'Well, hello, Indira.' Cat was delighted.

It was evident from the fact that Indira's hands were pressed together, making a namaskar, that she was not so much bearing food as intending to, suggesting to him that her English didn't stretch to the refined use of tenses. Since Cat was always eager to improve his Hindustani, he wondered whether there might be the possibility of mutual benefit with the exchange of lessons, but he stopped before he developed the idea too far. She was too young – perhaps fifteen, certainly not more – too pretty, too delicate to be interested in a fat man like him, and it would be deeply, deeply wrong to even think about taking advantage of such a lovely creature. Oh, so lovely.

'What food Sahib like?'

'Oh, Indira, thank you for asking so nicely. I like any food,' Cat became self-conscious in the presence of one so perfect, and made an apologetic sweeping gesture, 'as you can see, I like any food at all. I get hungry.'

It wasn't clear that Indira had understood Cat's point, and she looked blankly at him.

'I eat all food - sahre bhojan...'

'Tik, Sahib,' she grinned, adding as she turned to leave, 'you big man!'

'Cow!', thought Cat, irritated. She had showed him less respect than a man of his position, let alone forbearance, deserved. If she was going to be that cheeky, he might as well have not suppressed his initial inclination, tried to have developed a relationship of mutual benefit! But no, he knew, inside, that he was reacting in this steamy climate according to his natural but exhausting proclivities. He'd done it many times in the past. He'd always had an eye for the prettiest of girls, but they had never had an eye for him, and he had learned long ago that his greatest successes in love had been achieved amongst ladies with more ample, womanly forms.

Plenty of time for all that later, as for now he realised that the main lady in his life had received very little attention recently.

He had to shift the sofa away, nudging it with his shins, in order to create enough room to swing open Parvati's case. And there she was, as voluptuous as ever but somewhat bad tempered, Cat perceived, having been ignored for so long both aboard the uru and since, with her only breath of fresh air a narrow escape from death in the burning heat of the day. Here, at least, in the shade of the trees and beside the water, the air was cooler and more humid, much more suitable for an ancient double bass to begin to acclimatise to her new surroundings.

Cat gently, almost nervously, began to unbuckle the cracked leather strap around her fingerboard, knowing that this was all that had saved her at the quayside. To his great relief, she didn't complain, and Cat's trembling fingers relaxed, in the hope that she wanted the same as him. Carefully, he lifted her so that her endpin was clear of the socket in the bottom of the case, pulled her towards him and pressed her to his chest. His hand stroked the ridges in her scroll, whilst he pressed his cheek hard against her strings, listening to the resonance of her body as it vibrated up her neck. He leant back to test her tuning, and found that only the E string was flat, so he gently tightened the key, whispering as the nut creaked under the movement, 'there we are, my love, just a bit tighter', until she was ready for him.

He reached for his bow, but realised that there was no room to move. He and Parvati were sandwiched between the sofa and her case, with nowhere to go. Gently, he leant her back into the case, whilst he turned the sofa and table on their ends, and carried the chair outside. He shut the bedroom door, making that corner available for Parvati to lean into, and struggled with the case, rolling it towards the door, over the threshold and onto the veranda, where he paused for breath; there was shade here, but it was still too hot for serious physical exertion. Recovering, he returned the chair to the room, placed the sofa and table on their legs, but moved all three nearer the door and window, so that there was enough room for he and Parvati to move freely as they made music together.

And then he took up his bow, wiped it with rosin, took Parvati into his embrace, and played a G in twelfth position. Always a spectacle to hit a high note like that, cleanly at first touch, his finger position was perfect, needing no fine adjustment to the intonation. He eased his whole left hand into a slow vibrato, and Parvati wailed ecstatically as he pressed into a down-bow with his right arm, filling all of the space he'd created. Tears came to his eye, as Parvati sang a scale downwards, chromatically, through two octaves, and then through a further third, until the open E string boomed like mahogany. She led him up again, back to the high G, in a plaintive natural minor key, the B flat and D natural confounding his own easy expectations, and beyond into the range of harmonics, available only to the very best, where she allowed him a sharpened seventh, and they lingered together on a G so high it belonged to the violin. He had to force himself to breathe, wishing she would sing ceaselessly to his touch for ever more.

After the longest, slowest up-bow, they rested, leaning on each other, not drained but recoiling, ready to start again. Cat panted slightly, his moist cheek held against Parvati's neck, his hand softly damping the vibrations of her strings. There was a knock at the door.

'May I enter?' Enoch asked from outside.

Cat, startled, barely able to speak, grunted his assent, rotating Parvati away from the door, to protect her modesty.

'H'm, quite good,' commented Enoch, as he strutted in, his head on one side.

Most players of quality would have been offended by Enoch's apparently off-hand comment, but Cat was a player of very exceptional quality and, as such, was able to remain aloof from the criticism of lesser men. He knew he was the best because he'd been told so, by any number of people of greater musical standing than the political agent of a backwater state on the edge of India, and so he simply would not rise to the challenge. Indeed, the very fact that he held in his arms Dragonetti's *da Salò* was an indicator of his exceptional virtuosity, even if the conditions of the loan had become a little confused. Remarks such as Enoch's were the sort of observation made by pretentious oafs who were completely devoid of either musical ability or experience, he felt.

'Thanks,' he responded drily.

'The sound travels easily between our abodes. Do you know the Dittersdorf...'

Cat turned his head towards Enoch, not a little surprised to hear that name in this place.

'...the D major?'

Cat replied calmly, sneering inside, 'I think you must mean the E major.'

'Oh, yes, sorry, I was assuming that you, as the soloist, would generally use the scordatura tuning, a major second higher, and that consequently you'd know the piece in D major. Of course, the orchestral part, and therefore the piece itself, correctly, is in E major, I agree.'

Cat could see no trace of an edge in Enoch's remark, no hint of sarcasm, not even an obvious air of know-it-all-ness.

'Of course,' he continued with his facts, 'using the Viennese tuning – D, A, D, F sharp, A – of the old five-string instruments, the scordatura tuning was generally just a minor second up, so the concerto is sometimes described as being in E flat, but that's increasingly rare these days.'

Cat didn't know this. In fact, he had never heard of the old five-string double bass with its Viennese tuning, but he chose not to admit it.

'As it happens, I carry the score with me wherever I go!' sniffed Cat.

'Oh, excellent! I'm very fond of it. Perhaps we can play it together sometime?

'What do you mean?'

'I'll play the piano part.'

'Oh, I'm sorry,' Cat had him now, 'I've only got the orchestral score with me, not the reduction.'

'Oh, not to worry, I'm sure I'll manage from that. I read quite well.'

Was he serious? Could Enoch really read at sight an orchestral score, even one as straightforward as the Dittersdorf, and render it on the piano? That would be an exceptional feat of musicianship.

'I was intending to play the piece with my orchestra.'

'Your orchestra?'

'Yes, that's right. For our first concert together.'

'What orchestra?'

'My orchestra! I'm here as the Master of the Rajah's music, you know!'

'I think, perhaps, there's been a little confusion, my dear Cat.'

'Oh?' Cat could tell already this wasn't going to end as he wished.

'There isn't an orchestra, and it would probably be incorrect to describe you as the Master of the Rajah's music. Strictly speaking.'

'Then why am I here?'

'You're here because your school friends thought you were the man to bring them to up to speed in European cultural ways, to go with their new European church. You'll realise that, in my present role as political agent, I am prohibited from the subjective use of adjectives in my everyday attempts to describe things as they are, or rather, as I see they are, but if you'll allow me on this one occasion to break my own rule, I would say, confidentially, strictly between ourselves, that you have been brought here in the pursuit of a member of the family *Anatidae*, and that that pursuit will be – which forbidden fruit shall I choose? yes – *fruitless*.' Enoch was pleased with his little wordplay.

'But the organ? I'm here to oversee the installation of the new organ!'

'Ha,' Enoch sneered, 'if you thought you were going to get command of something like a new Rieger or Frobenius, then I regret you have been sorely misled. The *organ* is already in place, having been delivered last month on a ship which came alongside to winch it off as a unit, more or less wrapped in brown paper and string. It is a *harmonium*, not an organ, and it was manufactured by Hilton & Sons in Forfar. I have played it several times now and, in and of itself, it is a perfectly serviceable instrument, but hardly what one would call an *organ.*'

Cat stared blankly at Enoch, understanding fully what was being said, but quite unable to make sense of his relationship to this place and what he thought his job was going to be.

'But I received a letter from the Rajah, or rather from Barton, asking me to come to be Master of the Rajah's music,' Cat blinked through his square spectacles, 'look I've still got the letter. Wait here.'

He leant Parvati back into the corner, placing himself between her and Enoch so that he could first pat her belly unseen, and went to retrieve the letter from his writing case on the bed. 'See for yourself,' he insisted, waving the envelope triumphantly.

Enoch took the letter, and read it with a solemn air. 'Yes, you see, it doesn't quite say *Master of the Rajah's music* does it. Not really. It actually says *cultural panjandrum*, although I must say, I myself would have preferred the term *cultural philosopher*, I think, because of the relative contrast it creates with the notional suggestion that the palace occupants, by writing this letter, are casting themselves in a philomathical mould.'

'For god's sake, Enoch, what are you talking about?'

'The important thing is to understand that this letter was probably written by the Divan when he was drunk, under the direction of the Rajah, who was almost certainly also drunk. Look, may we sit down?'

Cat quickly sat on the sofa, waving a magnanimous invitation to Enoch to take the chair. There was a knock on the door, and

Indira entered without pausing, carrying with her a tray loaded with an ample range of tasty-looking dishes of food.

'Sahib,' she curtsied to Cat, casting what he took to be an impudent smile in Enoch's direction, as she placed the tray on the table. Worse, Enoch winked back at her, although it plainly wasn't meant to be a gesture for Cat's eyes, as he attempted to do it whilst Indira came between them; her slightness and sprightly habit rendered her effectively transparent.

Cat was pleased with the food laid before him, as he had become exceedingly hungry. He contemplated offering some to Enoch, as the correct thing to do, but decided against it as he had less need of currying favour than of filling his belly. Indira left, once again making eye contact with Enoch as she pulled the door shut behind her.

'Who is that girl?' asked Cat, irritated again.

'Oh, she's no-one, just our personal maid. She looks after the bungalows and their occupants. She's our servant.'

'Well, she's bloody impudent!'

Enoch nodded his agreement thoughtfully, as if drawing on some particular experience with her about which he was unprepared to speak.

'Now, listen, Enoch,' Cat assumed a commanding air, 'it is very important to me that my position in court is given as Master of the Rajah's Music. It doesn't matter why, but it relates to a problem back home, which has no bearing whatsoever on my work here.'

'Well, I suppose, given that you are the only musician here, other than myself, but since I have a full-time job which demands by definition that I be described as an amateur, thus making you not just the only musician but the only professional musician...'

'Enoch, just stop will you! All I'm asking is whether you'll back me up should anyone ever enquire. Just be ready to agree that I am indeed the Master of the Rajah's bloody Music, please.'

'I imagine that that will be in order. Certainly, there is no-one else competing with you for that role.'

'So that's a yes, then?'

Enoch turned his eyes to the ceiling, preparing his thoughts before pronouncing on the matter.

'Is it? Yes or no, Enoch? Just yes or no.'

'H'm,' Enoch was pained, 'I… I...'

'Enoch!'

'Oh, yes, then, very well. Although I should say...'

'Thank you, Enoch, that will do.' Cat addressed the tray before him, his juices running freely. 'Tell me about the church – why they are building it?'

Enoch fell for Cat's diversionary tactic, and launched into a lengthy account of the construction of the church, at no time taking any more than the barest effort to disguise his contempt for the project. Cat was able, meanwhile, to enjoy his food unhindered as the history unfolded.

The response of the sitting Rajah, following the uprising of 1857, had been to attempt to appease the British, lest their vengeful remedies should be directed towards either the royal family or any of the nobles who served DM. The state itself hadn't risen against the EIC, since the relationship between the Hindu rajah and the British was solid in one direction, and between him and the Muslim population good in the other. However, the blood-lust amongst the colonisers was very great indeed, and it wasn't certain that it could be prevented from overspilling into this state, so a policy of overt westernisation was adopted. This pre-emptive measure extended as far as the commissioning of designs for a neo-Gothic church, to encourage the immigration of trading Europeans into a state which would then seem like a home from home.

However, the end of the East India Company's monopoly, which was the direct result of the uprising, meant a fundamental change of policy in trading, which was the beginning of DM's decline. The British Raj, when it took over, wasn't sufficiently interested in the state's pomegranate plantations or fishing output, and the decline which had become so evident now, in less than the lifetime of a man, was set in motion. DM became a fringe state in which the government lost interest, and the money ran out just at the point when the church foundations had been completed.

'So why's it been finished now then?' asked Cat, mopping up the gravy from a plate of nihari with some paratha.

'One of the ways in which the royal purse has been depleted over the years has been to continue to send the males of the line overseas for their education, to your old public school indeed, and then Oxford, so the essentially western outlook of the royal family has never diminished. If you combine that fact with the inexperience and - what shall we say? - sybaritic approach to policy making employed by the present Rajah and his English Divan, it may throw some light on the decision to improve the fortunes of the state by readopting the policies of the post-mutiny period, and to westernise. It is clear that British rule of India can't continue in perpetuity, and there may be some merit in the idea of opening up to the west in preparation, but not by finishing a church when the infrastructure otherwise is so poor, and when the population have lives of such low quality. The coffers, my dear Cat, are now empty, and it will be the consequence only of decisive action which will save this state from bankruptcy.'

'Oh,' Cat looked startled as he sucked a bone from the dish of paya which he had on his knee, 'does that mean I'm not going to be paid? They said they'd pay me the going rate.'

'I think the notion of you receiving a regular sum from the palace is something you should put out of your mind.'

Cat sucked too hard, and the marrow he'd been attempting to draw from the bone shot into his mouth, followed by the bone itself, which dug painfully into the back of his throat, threatening to travel further down whichever pipe it met first. Aided by the natural gagging reflex, Cat was able to save himself, but not without experiencing an alarming sense that his life had been endangered.

'Fear not, my new friend, I am empowered in my capacity as a plenipotentiary to draw on the resources of my government to provide support for certain elements of the business of state, and so I will be able to make provision for you, to *see you right* as some would say.'

'Fuck me!' choked Cat, recovering less quickly than he would have liked, 'what have I come here for!'

'Are you okay?' Enoch asked, an eyebrow raised as if this was merely a matter of academic interest, 'shall I call for the doctor?'

'There are doctors here?' Cat spluttered.

'No. There is a doctor. One, a single doctor. And strictly speaking she is a servant of the zenana, here to care for women in purdah. She has been prevailed upon in the past to help others in need, however. There is no hospital, and the sole remedy for the seriously ill is a voyage to Karachi, which is available only to those who can both afford it and who are likely to live long enough to benefit.'

'Best not get ill, then...' Cat pulled himself together, and placed the empty bowl back on the table.

'Ah, the cry of the short-lived colonist since the malarial days of early Bombay – *best not get ill, then*!' Enoch could demonstrate a wistful air when he chose.

Without either an orchestra to direct or an organ to install, and with no expectation of the vast purchasing power with which he had hoped to buy modern art for the palace, Cat was at a loss as to what he would do with himself, other than hide behind his job title. Returning to his earlier reflections about rural isolation, perhaps he should take up Enoch's offer to play music together. 'Piano, you said – where is it, is it playable?'

'Ah, I think that was probably a careless thought, now that I give the matter my attention. There is no piano.'

Cat's despondency bottomed.

'But there's the harmonium! No-one else has any use for the church, so we may as well make the best of the resource, eh, even if it does amount to bull-fiddling whilst Rome burns.'

Cat, his throat recovered and his belly full, decided he was tired after what had been long day, spent in transition between the sea and land, voyaging and arriving. He had had ambitions for his new post which, clearly, were a long way from being achievable, but he nevertheless had a title which would keep at bay the Trust, at least for a while, and so keep him and Parvati together. And that would do for now.

'I think I must sort myself out and have a good sleep, Enoch, if you'll excuse me. We can talk about playing tomorrow, if you have time.'

'Hah, if I have time? My job is to represent His Majesty's Government and its interests in Dhoosar Mathavassee, wherein His Majesty's Government has no interest whatsoever. I have very little to do as a consequence, and I can barely wait for the home leave I'll be due in six months.'

Leave wasn't something Cat had contemplated, having put out of his head even the possibility of returning to England, lest Parvati be seized from him. But now, with Enoch's remark, it crossed his mind that he didn't know when he would see his family again. It was clear that he wasn't going to make his fortune in DM, so there would be no triumphal homecoming as a wealthy nabob. And, worse, he'd arrived at a place where good health couldn't be guaranteed. He knew then that the only way in which this could be a place where he lingered long would be if he were to become the unfortunate whose distinction was to be the first occupant of the new church yard.

7

Wow! What a bed!!

I slept amazingly well, cocooned in a controlled environment and floating on the most comfortable mattress I'd ever lain on. When people exoticise the orient, I think they not only objectify the region conceptually, in the Saidian sense, but also implicitly acknowledge that the occident, guilt-riddled Christendom, simply won't allow itself the enjoyment of luxuries of this order. Myself, I don't doubt I could make a six-pack of this particular cultural soft under-belly with ease.

I suppose you get used to having servants too, but I was not yet. I didn't feel fully at liberty to get up in the manner of my own choosing, since I could hear Lakshmi knocking about somewhere in the suite of rooms, and it seemed that I needed instructions, or permission, rather as if I was in hospital awaiting orders from sister. So I lay and waited until he discreetly entered, and stretched as if I'd just awoken, and was now ready to be assisted.

Lakshmi: (bowing) Good morning, Sahib.

Me: (feigning a yawn) Aa-aa-ah, good morning, Lakshmi.

Lakshmi: Sahib sleep well?

Me: Yep, not bad.

Lakshmi: You want shower or bath?

Me: (wrong-footed) Ooh, er, well, a bath, why not.

Lakshmi: I run.

He walked, to one of the wardrobes, from which he produced a bathrobe, lay it on the bed, bowed again in the most courteous way and disappeared into the bathroom. I seized the moment to leap out of bed and pull on the robe, for the sake of my modesty, and went to the window to see what I could see.

Once I'd worked out how to operate the electrically-controlled blinds (they were mounted vertically between sheets of glass, gliding sideways into a hole in the wall), I found myself looking over the land at the back of the palace. Beyond the flat roofs of the lower sections, which projected rearwards, I could plainly see the crescent of woodland which I'd seen from above the day before, in the middle of which was the reservoir. I knew already that this was a creation of the British in the nineteenth century, during the period when they retained some interest in DM, achieved by digging an enormous hole and filling it with water from channels connecting with the Kaur Dasht and Khowr-e Bahu. By creating a reservoir, they hoped to provide the means of irrigation for both crops and people, encouraging the development of what they considered to be virtually an island state, cut off on all sides by sea and desert, and potentially a useful bit of real estate on the western edge of the subcontinent. We know now, of course, that that's not how things turned out.

The greenness of the wooded area was quite astonishing when seen from this reduced distance, undoubtedly a result of the standing water, thick and lush by any standards but certainly compared to the dusty brown of all that lay around otherwise. Seeing a place is an essential aid to understanding its history, and I wished then that I'd been more energetic and visited during my doctoral studies, when it would have become plain just how arid and inhospitable DM must have been before it was irrigated. What lay before me was an unequivocal lesson in the importance of water, whether it be artificially channelled or otherwise, and a clear illustration of how far DM had come in terms of its development; cue my bath, which was deep, at a perfect temperature and bubbly.

As I emerged, I found my breakfast set up on a table by the window. I thought it a little odd that I was isolated like this, having expected to join the family round a table. I raised the matter with Lakshmi.

Me: Is it usual to have breakfast alone in your room?

Lakshmi: Yes, Sahib, everyone busy during day. No time chit-chat.

Me: Oh, I see. What time is the Yuvraj generally free?

Lakshmi: Today His Highness out on business.

I was slightly surprised that no-one had mentioned that I would be, effectively, alone this morning, until Ali turned up in a couple of hours, for the tour he'd promised me. It's possible the Rajah and Rani were somewhere nearby, but I'd not yet met them, so couldn't possibly have wandered off to say hello; in a place this big, they might not even know I was their guest. So I ate my breakfast quietly, dressed myself in my own clothes which, extraordinarily, felt like someone else's since they'd all been pressed (including my boxers!), and went walkabout, restricting myself to those areas which were clearly domestic but not private.

I presumed that a level down would be a good place to start, having been the floor to which I was first taken yesterday, and I knew there were stairs to it, because I'd come up them the night before, but I couldn't find them anywhere. Fortunately, I found the posh lift, so used that instead, and enjoyed again the feeling of being teleported without any discernible movement, although this time there was no-one on duty to press the buttons for me.

I recognised the landing, but was much better able now to take in the surroundings, having apparently breezed through it yesterday without seeing anything of the objects around me. And what objects they were! In any other setting, you might describe them as being fit to adorn a royal palace, and that that's literally what they were doing didn't detract from the insistence of the cliché.

Where, for example, there might be a console table in a smaller hallway, here was a three-piece suite made of gilded and carved wood in what could so easily have been a parody of the Empire style, were it not for what I thought was its defiant modernity, its bold, square shapes, with deeply undercut figuring. In the centre of the group was a low, plate-glass table, standing on shiny cast metal legs, on which sat a glass sculpture by Dale Chihuly (I recognised it because I don't like his work), and in the corner beyond there was a standing pot by Grayson Perry (same story). I mean, none of it was to my taste, but there was no arguing with the quality, or cost. And on the parquet floor where, in your imagination, you might not be surprised to find a sculpture of, say, an elephant carved from local wood and inlayed with ivory, there was instead a thirty-centimetre-high hippo made thus. A Clydesdale wouldn't have been more out of place, and would have raised just as many questions about post-colonial expectations, but it was a pleasing object, nonetheless.

The walls were covered in paintings, and by no means the sort of humdrum domestic portraiture I probably expected. There were certainly pictures of members of the family on display, but they used a range of media, oil to collage, metal scales to embroidery. The earlier portraits, it is true, were more conventional than the more recent work, going back into the nineteenth century. There was a line-up of all the Rajahs, and I had my first glimpse of the face of the present Rajah, who looked rather stern, I thought.

My favourite of all the objets d'art/curiosities/mementos/heirlooms was a very curious item, I thought. It was a serving dish with a cover, made in heavily engraved silver plate, a handle at each end of the platter and one centrally on top of the lid. It is possible to imagine that there are some circumstances under which there would seem to be nothing exceptional about this object, but all of them would involve being at some distance from it and, quite possibly, drunk; the unavoidably striking feature of the thing was its size. It was so large that it would have been impossible for a single man to carry, and whereas other, more modest serving cloches might have been suitable for the presentation of, say, a quail, this one would easily have accommodated a roast ostrich (to continue the trope of African species). It brought to mind the golden age of the Mughal emperors, when limitless luxuries were available to the court, but raised questions of authenticity because the history of DM does not include its full incorporation into the empire, even when its extent was at its greatest under Aurangzeb. I was curious to know how this platter had earned its place in the palace.

I continued my explorations, opening heavy mahogany doors and peering into rooms one by one, all of them very stylishly furnished. Nothing, I have to say, seemed personal, or to admit of any eccentricity or personal quirk, and I sensed a heavy hint of Department Store suffusing every room. I mean, who couldn't be happy living here – but it's not how I'd do it if it were my palace.

I wandered off to other floors, wallowing in the scale of the building (knowing that I was still in the central rotunda, the private living area), and found similar spaces with similar decorations. Some of the internal doors were locked, whereas those at the boundaries of the rotunda were all open, but were fitted with large, stout locks and sliding bolts (in highly-polished brass, of course), clearly intended to isolate the occupants from the world beyond. When I opened one I found that it was heavy in the way that the door on the car had been, and I concluded it was bullet-proof, the equivalent of the drawbridge and portcullis in mediaeval castles. It dawned on me then that the entirety of the central rotunda was a fortress, and I began to feel like Jonathan Harker exploring Castle Dracula, when he realises he is alone.

Where was everybody? I was beginning to find it all very disconcerting, so I returned to my suite of rooms and decided to read my Twitter feed, my channel back to what would have to pass for the real world. There, without any particular diligence on my part, I stumbled upon a great many tweets about the terrorist attack a couple of weeks ago at some place no-one had heard of in the Gulf, some place called Dusa Mathavasi.

I was dismayed that I'd not thought of browsing for news about DM before I'd got here. It was a bit like arriving at Paddington to find your train cancelled, when it would have been so much better to have checked online in advance. Everything was plainly laid out for me; I read about the murder of the Chinese engineer in charge of the construction of the airport by an Islamic extremist; I read that the terrorist had been captured and was currently being held in the state's gaol; I read about the enhanced security which the Rajah had ordered, which explained the show of strength which accompanied my journey from the Qifar residence to the palace; and I read that such an attack had been anticipated and was considered overdue, which, I suppose, accounted for the fortification of the palace.

I was quite disturbed to find that I was in a tiny city which had a newly-acquired problem with terrorism. Here the potential for imagining that *it might not happen to you* thanks to the laws of probability was very greatly reduced, because being in DM, with its minute population, meant being in the front line, without the shield of several millions of other people to whom it might happen first. And being a constituent member, for the time being, of the royal household added an extra layer of hazard, surely? So, if it's difficult to imagine that it might not happen to you, then it becomes easy to think that it *will* happen to you, and that's quite alarming. The fortifications in the palace might, it appeared, not be hypothetical, just for show, rather those heavy doors with the shiny bolts might one day actually be all which could come to separate a squad of armed and determined terrorists from the occupants of the royal palace. And by *occupants of the royal palace*, in truth, I meant instinctually *me*.

I was very keen to talk about the situation with someone, anyone, but I was absolutely alone, without even Lakshmi within earshot, it seemed. I needed to know more about the circumstances of the murder of the poor engineer, what the police had done in response, whether they had intelligence of further attacks being planned. But mostly I just needed reassurance, I can see now; this wasn't a situation I'd ever rehearsed, and I was close to panic.

I lay on my bed, seeking some slight consolation from the wonderful mattress, and stayed there until a WhatsApp came in from Ali, saying he was in the lift and coming to collect me. It's certainly as well I had notice of his arrival, because my imagination had run away with itself by then, and I might have feared the worst when the lift stopped at my floor; the opening of the hushed doors would have acquired a wholly menacing aesthetic.

Me: (trying to seem calm) Hey, Ali!

Ali: Mornin', Philip! Did you have a good rest?

Me: I slept very well indeed, thank you. But, uhm…

I described to him what I'd read, all of which he confirmed as being the case, but he assured me that everything which needed to be done had been done, and that they had received expert advice on matters of security from a retired Pakistani army colonel, who knew about these things. The domestic part of the palace, moreover, didn't just have steel doors dressed up as wood, he informed me that it also had a roof which was made to withstand the impact of some sort of a bomb – a mortar shell, perhaps – but the finer details were lost on me. Essentially, I was living in a royal bunker.

Repeatedly, as he spoke, he referred to 'we', and I was unsure as to who constituted what, I assume, was an inner circle, but took him to mean simply the Rajah and those close to him, as befits the court of an absolute monarch and his buddies. As I suppose I expected, he was keen to make it plain that the situation was in hand, with nothing to fear, and that we should just get on with our lives.

In answer to his question as to what I'd like to see first on our tour, I admitted that I was all but consumed by my burning curiosity; I wanted to see Uncle Cat's house.

8

Cat awoke early, to the pleasing sounds of birds singing in the trees all around his tin-roofed cabin, and of the delicious sound of Indira bringing in a breakfast tray. He thought it could only be her because of the delicate whiiish she made as she moved around, placing the tray down almost without noise, save for the faintest rattle of a cup on a saucer. He gazed up into the vault of the grubby net suspended above him, wondering how long it would be before a mosquito flew in through the hole which propagated from the failed stitching around the hanging loop.

'Good morning, Indira,' Cat addressed her through the dividing wall.

'Good morning, Sahib!' came the tiny reply.

Cat was about to thank her for bringing him a tray when he heard Parvati's indignant voice, brushed against in her corner by Indira, and he cast aside the net to leap out of bed in a defensive fury. He threw wide the door to the living room, shoulders squared, ready to thump a girl so small he could have blown her over. She gazed at his rage aghast, immediately aware that her accidental contact was not something which could be tolerated.

'Sorry sorry,' she quivered, shocked by Cat's rage, 'I did not meant touch.'

Cat breathed deeply through his nostrils. From somewhere in his belly, he recognised that his reaction was disproportionate, and that he must let his temper subside as quickly as it had risen. He realised also that, since he had slept only in his pyjama bottoms, he stood threatening this trembling butterfly before him with that same belly's enormous, rolling shape in plain view, and he was overcome by embarrassment. He saw her eyes dart downwards, involuntarily, taking in the horror of his half-naked form, his blotched, stretched skin, his recessed belly-button, and was ashamed.

'Yes, well,' he mumbled, apologetically, 'my double bass is very precious to me.'

'Sahib?'

'Precious. You know *precious* – utsaah.'

Indira couldn't help but grin, 'Sahib mean utkrsht, I think.'

My, she's cheeky, thought Cat. 'Well, whatever I mean, I mean it's precious! So never touch. Do you understand? Never touch!'

'Ha, yes, Sahib-ji, I promise.'

'Achchha,' he muttered, backing into the bedroom and closing the door behind him, relieved to be out of sight once more. Whatever Cat's failings, poor hearing was not one of them, and he heard quite plainly the sound of Indira tutting behind the partition wall, accompanied by the exhalation of a little puff of air, doubtless an act of self-reflection on her part about how rudely she felt she'd been treated. 'Oh, and Indira...'

There was a silent pause next door.

'Haa, Sahib?'

'...ah, I wasn't sure if you were still there!' Cat cried melodramatically.

'Haa, am, Sahib.'

'Good. Please ask Ajaz to come and see me.'

'You want see Ajaz?' the voice was shaken.

'Indeed I do!' Cat adopted a grand tone as he said this, and would have hooked his thumbs into his waistcoat pockets were he wearing one.

'Yes, Sahib.'

He heard his front door close gently, as if a mouse had crept out whilst no-one watched. There was no reason for the girl not to be a little afraid of him, he reasoned, given her propensity for insolence, and he hoped she was worried that he was going to squeal on her to the head servant. But that wasn't at all what he wanted him for in reality; the matter of the thunderbox had acquired some urgency in the night.

Exhausted by his travels, Cat had retired early and initially slept well, despite the anxious overview he now had of his new position. But he had been disturbed from his slumbers by something he didn't recognise and, once awake, had lain in his new bed, in his new home, fretting about what seemed like an unsure new future, whilst listening to the new sounds all around. The insects on and around the lake made a din, to be sure, but it was constant cheep and not in itself disturbing. The water lapped gently at its edges too, but that was soothing rather than a distraction. And accompanying the gentle splutter of his oil lamp, which he had turned down but kept alight in the corner of the room, was the sound of his bungalow creaking as the timber rafters and iron roof contracted at different rates in the cooler air. More disturbing than any of these, by far, was the gentle moaning he could hear from next door, from Enoch's bungalow. He thought it apparent that some effort was being made to mute the groans, either that or that Enoch was having a nightmare with his head buried conveniently in his pillow, but it was an odd and unexpected sound, eerie in the isolation of darkness.

In his bemusement, as he listened to Enoch's weird aria, Cat realised that there was a bowel movement under way to which he had need to respond, and that despite that need being urgent, he knew he had to put on his pyjama top in self-defence. He had become enough of an India-hand that he had entered his mosquito net fully clothed, and changed for bed beneath it, even though this involved much wriggling and squirming for one with a difficult body in a confined space. The point was to avoid having bits of skin exposed any more than was essential, since past experience had taught him that he was one of nature's juicy people; one of the principal advantages of having a partner at bed time, a fact taught at neither Haileybury nor SOAS, was that A could waft a towel around and keep the insects more-or-less at bay whilst B changed, ready to perform the same service in return. So, after much contorted spinning within his little tent, accompanied by some super-human clenching, Cat was in a position to cast aside the net and sit on the edge of the bed, assuring some fortitude in his sphincter before hazarding the journey of two yards to the thunderbox, which he reached without a second to spare.

As he had sat, waving a sheet of old newspaper around to keep the foe off his bare bits, pyjama bottoms lowered as little as possible, he realised that Enoch's moaning had ceased. Presumably the dream had passed, and he had entered into a more gentle sleep, but in any case there was no sound to be heard from next door. But the mosquitoes! What a menace, drawn not just by the prospect of some tasty Adam blood for their midnight feast, but also by the attraction of the still body of water upon which he was enthroned, with its added benefit of volatile stinkyness. Indeed, as he had prepared for bed earlier, Cat had spotted that there were several healthy-looking larvae actually swimming in the water in the thunderbox, which he had presumed now were metamorphosing into the virile bugs flying all around, having drunk long and deep of the enriched liquor of their juvenile existence.

Moreover, any hope Cat might have had that the increasingly-pestilential odours surrounding him, fruitily filling every corner of his bedroom, could protect him from this plague of insects was lost. This was far worse than the usual night-time call, and he had felt forlorn.

It was clear that placing the thunderbox on the veranda wasn't merely the solution he had thought it would be, because the problem was actually so very much greater than he had anticipated. And his last, lonely thought as he returned to lay his head on the pillow, hopeful of more sleep to come, was that he needed to summon Ajaz at the first opportunity to arrange the move.

With the arrival of daylight, the menace of the mosquitoes vanished, and Cat felt freer to make his morning ablutions on the thunderbox without fear of attack. But as he sat there, the extraordinary sound of Enoch's falsetto returned once more. There could be no mistaking it for what it was this time, as it wasn't muffled, and it wasn't coming from 1st Bungalow.

Having dismounted the thunderbox and washed his hands on the diminutive dresser, Cat cast open the door to his bungalow only half-prepared for the spectacle which greeted him. He'd thrown his kaftan round himself, deciding that the noise Enoch was making was actually singing. In fact, it was well done and in tune, not bad singing, just so far away from Cat's expectations that he'd not immediately recognised it for what it was, as if it was a sweet mango coloured blue. Enoch was singing 'I Know That My Redeemer Liveth' from Handel's *Messiah* outside his door, in a soprano falsetto, and, although there could be no accounting for this fact, it was plainly the case, so Cat was only half astonished when he caught sight of Enoch trilling, soap in his hair, and wearing nothing but a loincloth, dipping up and down in the lake as if he was by the ghats at Benares.

'What are you doing?' Cat asked.

'Oh, *good morning*, Cat!' Enoch's tone was one of mild rebuke, since he had received no formal greeting before being abruptly quizzed, and manners amounted to everything in these places, he felt.

'Eh, what, oh, h'm, good morning, Enoch. Might I ask what it is you're doing?'

'You might,' Enoch briefly submerged himself, 'although I should have thought it was immediately apparent.'

'Yes, it is, I suppose. I can see that you're bathing, and I can hear that you're singing.'

'Well then, surely the question you desire to ask of me is not *what* but *why*?'

Cat sighed inwardly. 'Very well, Enoch, *why* are you singing a soprano aria from an eighteenth-century oratorio whilst you bathe in a lake on the western edge of India?'

'That's better. Now, taking each point in turn, in reverse order if I may, I'm bathing in a lake on the western edge of India because this is where I live and work, I'm singing an aria by Handel because I like his music, and I'm singing in the soprano range because I trained as a male soprano.'

Whilst there was an ineffable logic to Enoch's simple explanation, it opened a chasm of incomprehension for Cat. He thought he'd try Enoch's approach in reverse. 'Why did you train as a male soprano? Why are you singing at all? Why are you bathing in the lake?'

'I trained as a male soprano because male altos are too common. I'm singing because I have sung in my bath since my mother encouraged me to do so as an infant; it lifts the spirits and kick-starts a brain like mine in the morning. I'm bathing in the lake because there's nowhere else.'

'Oh, I had assumed there was a bathhouse somewhere,' Cat muttered, defeated.

Enoch was correct, it wasn't what he was doing which had given rise to Cat's curiosity, but that he plainly didn't consider any of it unusual, and the questioning had come to its natural end because there was no sense in pursuing answers where none existed. Enoch sang soprano arias as he bathed, and that was the end of the matter.

'Will you join me?' Enoch splashed water over himself extravagantly.

This presented a challenge to Cat. He was very keen to bathe, facilities having been limited on the Uru, but he wasn't keen to strip off in front of anyone, and certainly didn't want to immerse himself in his lovely silk kaftan, the last gift Mariah had given him, brought all the way from Delhi after one of her trips home.

'Come on, old man, I won't look!' Enoch identified Cat's hesitation for what it was.

'I'm not awfully keen… that is to say… I'm, er...'

'See!' Enoch stood up in the water, arms stretched out, revealing the startling puniness of his frame, 'I'm all skin and bone. My body's a joke! Come on, there's no-one around. It'll be fine.'

Cat havered, deeply troubled. However, he couldn't help but recognise that Enoch was correct, that he was in fact all skin and bone, and that there was something laudable, enviable even, about the way he seemed to have cast off any hint of pride. Perhaps, in this new place, Cat could embolden himself?

'What if Indira comes along?'

'The hummingbird? She won't, she has other duties at this time of day. Do come and join me!'

'But there are other people too!'

'My dear Cat, don't be so dotish. This is not the place for modesty, I assure you. I mean, look at *me*, there can be no doubt that Zulfikar could engastrate your fine, manly body with my bony carcass – you are a delicious grouper compared to my shrivelled bummalo, yet both belong in the water.'

'Who the hell is Zulfikar?'

'The royal chef, obviously!'

'Yes, obviously. I'll get my things, I suppose.'

Cat retreated to his bungalow, not merely to retrieve his soap bag, but also to put on a pair of underpants. There was no question whatsoever of nakedness, especially since Enoch's eagerness to get him into the water, whilst he sang soprano arias, might have carried hints of the desire for a shared experience involving cleanliness of neither mind nor body. Cat had learned to enjoy a very liberal outlook as a music student in London, but he certainly couldn't be interested in Enoch in *that* way. And, in any case, he reasoned that bathing in yesterday's underpants would result in them being laundered at the same time so, checking that there was no visible reason not to be seen in them, he pulled them on under his kaftan and returned to the shore.

'Do come along, you shrinking violet!'

'Yes yes! You're going to tell me the water's getting cold!'

'If anything, it's getting hot. Best drop your exotic peignoir and get in here before the sun rises too far and dries us to sultanas!'

Cat cast his eyes round, to be sure that there was no-one nearby, and allowed his kaftan to drop to the ground, where too he cast his eyes, like a pubescent twelve-year-old.

'Come along, old man! In you come.'

Cat stood for a moment, feeling the breeze dance gently on his bare skin, a sensation he'd not enjoyed for as long as he remembered. And enjoy it he did. He raised his arms to allow the air to get to his armpits, felt immediately its drying effect on his perpetual sogginess. This was very pleasant indeed. He raised his eyes, smiling, but, then horrified, saw that Enoch was smirking at the sight of him.

'You rotter! You beast, Enoch! I thought better of you, laughing at me,' he folded his arms protectively across himself, and turned his back towards the lake.

'No, you misinterpret, Cat, I'm not laughing at you,' Enoch asserted with some urgency, 'I would never do that, as I have been laughed at myself. It is cruel. I am smiling because the moment of joy on your face made me happy. I promise!'

'Really?' Cat peered over his shoulder, 'You swear?'

'*Fraus hominum ad perniciem, et integritas ad salutem vocat*!' Enoch sought to soothe, adding for good measure, as he submerged himself once more, 'I never dissemble.'

Cat shook his head. There was an undeniable openness to Enoch, unfathomable even though that made him, and it seemed probable that he was being more supportive than he might, accidentally, have appeared.

'Please look away. I'm coming in.'

Enoch nodded sagely and bobbed round to face away from the shore. Cat turned hesitantly, checked the immediate area for onlookers, and advanced on the water. As he dipped his feet in, he found it was cooler than he'd anticipated, but not so cold as to be unpleasant. He stepped in further, feeling the sandy grit beneath his soles, between his toes, and a line of coolness lap up his legs. Those dreadful periods of nude swimming at school, just one of the panoply of physical and mental abuses wrought upon the boys, had succeeded in so far as that Cat knew how to swim, but only with the barest competency, and he was relieved here that the ground dropped away so gently. The water reached his testicles, normally the first point at which a change of temperature could shock, but he discovered that the coolness was a joy, as his wet underpants began to cling closely, sensuously to his skin. His belly followed, up to his diaphragm, at which point cold water could have made for a sharp intake of breath, but it was easy, it was delightful. Cat ducked himself, and felt chilled for the first time in months.

'I'm in. You can turn back.'

'Jolly good. Well done, old chap,' Enoch smiled empathetically, 'This is one of my favourite parts of the day.'

Cat bobbed about, chuckling, finding the experience a great joy, whilst endeavouring to keep as much of himself submerged as he could. He laughed as Enoch laughed, sharing the moment, and took in a mouthful of water which he ejected in a majestic plume.

'Oh, no, Cat, don't do that,' Enoch insisted, still in a cheerful manner, 'don't take the water into your mouth.'

'Oh my god, is it polluted? Is it full of shit? You're telling me now?'

'No no, not at all. As a matter of fact, the palace is above the city, so all the feculence enters the rivers downstream of here. That's the problem. Worms.'

'I don't follow...'

'There is a healthy population of aquatic life in this clean water, and consequently a healthy population of parasitic worms too. One such, *Camallanus magna*, was described in 1822 by

Francis Hamilton in *An Account of the Fishes found in the river Ganges and its branches.* It is a parasite of *Macrognathus pancalus*, a fish frequently found hereabouts.'

'Is there anything you don't know *something* about, Enoch?'

'Why, no,' chuckled Enoch, 'there isn't really! I enjoy knowing things. Anyway, the fascinating thing about *Camallanus magna*, which is a roundworm, a nematode, by the way, is that larger examples have been found to have grown beyond the limits of the gastrointestinal tract of its host, so that it can be found to be projecting out of the fish's anus. Cat – Cat – where are you going?'

'If you think I'm going to bathe in water where there's a chance of picking up an arse-worm...,' Cat's sense of modesty had vanished as he scrambled to reach dry land.

'No no no, hear me out! All I was suggesting is that you shouldn't swallow the water, that's all. The worm can't enter your bottom from below, only from above, the long way! Do come back in, Cat, and finish your bath. You'll feel much better for it.'

'You want me to wallow around in infested water? Seriously, Enoch? In a place where there's no doctor?'

'Oh, well, on that score the locals have access to a perfectly well-tried anthelmintic, so there's nothing to fear. I have taken it myself. Ah, I see the arrival of our seneschal.'

'Don't change the subject! Anyway, what's a seneschal when it's at home?'

'A seneschal is the principal steward of a great house. Everybody knows that, Cat!'

Cat had not known that, but now that he did, he spotted Ajaz walking towards them. Neither in nor out of the water, he hesitated as to what his best action was to be, and decided that the risk of being parasitised had to be lower than the certainty of being embarrassed, so clamped his mouth shut and fell back into the water, creating a rolling wave which nearly knocked Enoch over.

'You wished to see me, Sahib?' Ajaz asked Cat, giving no indication that he thought it strange to be addressing a fat, nearly-naked European rolling around in the water like a dugong.

Ajaz was a stocky individual, with a very large, once-broken nose, looking like he might formerly have been a boxer, and from his inferior position in the water, Cat found him to be much more intimidating than he had seemed the night before. 'Oh, yes, uhm, good morning, Ajaz. Salaam alaikum.'

'Wa 'alaikum al-salaam,' Ajaz responded, with a tiny bow and just the suggestion in his tone that he might have had better things to do than exchange pleasantries under these circumstances, 'what can I do for you?'

Cat had righted himself in the water, and squatted chest-deep to preserve his dignity. 'Oh, yes, uhm, I wanted to ask you for a favour...'

'What can I do, Sahib?'

'I wondered if it would be possible to move my thunderbox onto the veranda?'

Both Ajaz and Enoch looked blankly at Cat, neither able to imagine what it was that he had in mind, yet each imagining quietly the horror of being able to observe this very large man straining at stool. Whilst Enoch remained uncharacteristically speechless, Ajaz recovered the moment and with aplomb pointed out that that was a most unusual place to wish to have one's thunderbox. Enoch nodded his agreement.

'Ah, well, you see...'

Cat gave his reasoning, describing as tastefully as he was able the problem of odours in his small cabin, and detailing how he intended to use Parvati's case to create a makeshift cubicle. He added that there was a problem with mosquito larvae swimming in his thunderbox, admitting that placing it outside wouldn't prevent that, but at least the metamorphosed insects would fly off into open space, rather than hunt for their first food in his bedroom.

'Yes, I have had that problem,' acknowledged Enoch. 'I like to think of the contents of my thunderbox as their *anamniotic* fluid!' He looked between Cat and Ajaz, pleased with himself, but neither got his joke.

Ajaz pondered the suggestion for a moment, before admitting that it was a good plan, adding that he thought possibly that outside toilets were the more modern way of doing things, the way forward in matters lavatorial, which he would discuss with the Rajah when the moment was right. He dipped his head politely and left the water babies to shave.

9

The posh lift had a mysterious setting which required a key; Ali had one to hand, of course. It was for a stop on the floor below the main entrance, where I'd arrived the day before, into a private area which connected with the palace garage, judging by the petrolly smell. Here too was the back door, a detail which seemed strangely suburban given the rest of the building, as if it could have had a cat flap fitted. Having stepped out into the lobby, Ali made us wait whilst he sent a message.

In fairly short order, a squad of four commandos appeared by the back door, all berets and moustaches, looking very casual with their machine guns slung over their shoulders, whereupon Ali said it was safe to proceed. Only moments before, prior to being beamed down, he had been asserting that everything was in hand, and that we should just get on with it, which had to mean that normal life here involved close protection from a bunch of seriously hard-looking individuals, even if it was only for a stroll in the back garden.

And, in a sense, the lawn we walked over was in reality a back garden. It was certainly a private space, inaccessible to the public, and surrounded with a low wall. Whilst it wasn't in any sense secure, like the Master's Garden at Wedgwood for instance, the wall was a clear and unambiguous statement of separation, and it would have been possible to play a decent game of croquet there without fear of being interrupted by non-players on the green (it was actually a very good lawn, I noted).

Surrounding the lawn, indeed enveloping it, giving the impression that it was merely a clearing in the woods immediately behind the palace, were the trees I had seen from my window. And it was towards those that Ali led me, through a small gap in the wall and down a short flight of steps, where there was a track which appeared to circle the palace in each direction. Beyond that there was a pathway into the woods, which we entered, emerging after a hundred metres or so into a newly-cut clearing, with its floor still covered in the stuff which gets left behind when you cut down trees. To the right as we entered, some men were working on scaffolding about three metres high, building something which involved welding and producing bright blue sparks which seemed quite out of place in this verdant little glade. The smells of welding and felled trees conflicted in a most unpleasant way.

To the left, at last, was what I'd travelled all this way to see. There, towards the water's edge, were two small huts and a greatly-decayed old car, all of which had plainly been ignored for decades. The car was a sort of black/rust/once-green colour which defied description (except that it would've been impossible to get that effect from a single paint tube), and the soft parts had mainly decayed, leaving, for example, seats which were just rusty coil springs and horse hair. The hood, which had been in its lowered position when the car had been abandoned, was nothing more than a frame, looking like a skeletal, old-fashioned baby's pram. The wheels still had on them the suggestion of tyres, but two of them had collapsed inwards so that the car sat at an angle, looking as if it had accumbed to drink the water.

Me: Why are these things here, Ali?

Ali: (gesturing towards the scaffolding) A good question! We only discovered them because we made the clearing for this. We had no idea they were here.

Me: But it's part of the palace grounds. How can you not know?

Ali: Well, I s'pose the focus over the last few years has been developing the town and then building the palace, and everyone's literally been looking forwards.

Me: It's extraordinary! And no-one alive remembers these huts?

Ali: Nope, seems not. The Rajah remembers his grandfather telling him this is where the Political Agent's accommodation was, likewise your great-uncle. Otherwise, there are some stories that spectral moans were heard once upon a time, so the buildings 'must be haunted', which might account for no-one having been here. But I think really they were just ignored long enough that they disappeared into the woods.

For buildings to disappear from both view and memory seems to be unique; where else could this have happened? And the car? How did it get there? I have since found no evidence even that it was actually registered in DM, as the number plates were illegible (their painted figures having long ago flaked off), but I have to assume either that it was, or that there was no requirement for registration at the time. Google would inform me that the car, which I photographed, was probably a Morris of the early twenties, so I can only surmise that it was a reckless purchase made by a reckless Rajah – which can only mean Hari – a plaything which can hardly ever have been used, as there wouldn't have been roads on which to use it.

Rajah Hari was the older brother of Shankarrao, the present Rajah's great-grandfather. He was, by all accounts, a thoroughly bad thing, who not only dissipated what little money was in the coffers on extravagant foreign trips and such like, but also surrounded himself with cronies from his public school, with a strong suggestion that the palace became a hotbed of homosexual entanglements such as would have been utterly scandalous at the time. This is the period when Uncle Cat would have been here, although I hadn't known, up to this point, which of the two Rajah's he was here to serve.

I turned my attention to the two huts, at last, and saw how deeply entangled within the embrace of the woods they had become. I have to assume that one of these was the Second Bungalow to which Cat referred in his letters, and, by extension, the other was First Bungalow. The one to the left had a tree growing through its roof, leaving no doubt whatsoever which of man and nature was winning this tussle. There was a veranda, much decayed, which we picked our way across, to push the door open – in fact, it fell off – so as to get our first look inside. Blackness and dust, decay and damp, the interior was in a dreadful state. There were two small rooms, divided now by the trunk of the tree, but once by a partition wall, the remnants of which could still be seen. The lounge was furnished with meagre rattan furniture (the cushions, as on the car, had rotted), and the bedroom with an iron-framed bedstead and the remains of a mattress. A curiosity was the manacles – handcuffs – which hung from the head and foot of the bed, made crudely by a blacksmith, I would guess, which somewhat unambiguously situated the practises of the occupant of this hut within the class of actions which we now would describe as kinky sex. Rags of clothes lay on the collapsed floor of a wardrobe, nothing which seemed easily identifiable.

Me: (taking pics) Has anyone been in here already?

Ali: No, deffo not. We saved them for you.

Me: It would have been a time capsule maybe twenty-five years ago, but it's just gone too far over now. What a shame.

Ali: (chortling) Yes, but what about the bondage cuffs! Aren't they hilarious!

Me: Well, yes, certainly unexpected. Maybe the stories about the court at the time are true?

Ali: What a bunch of boys, eh!

We exited carefully, the structure clearly being unsafe, and turned our attention to the other hut. This one was much harder to approach, since a screen of saplings had grown up in front of it, looking to my mind rather like Robinson Crusoe's palisade. We managed to bend back a couple of them and squeeze onto the veranda where – imagine my delight – stood what looked like a giant trunk, large enough to contain a double bass. I know it was too much to hope for, that the *da Salò* could have been locked up here quietly for nearly a century, not least because it was clear from the other materials in this environment that it would have rotted away, but my excitement was very real nonetheless.

We approached the trunk, taking pictures as a record, and found that it stood beside a smaller, much-decayed wooden box, with a galvanised bucket inside – the toilet, on the veranda! – suggesting that life here was very hard back then. The trunk had once been painted, but now had the same patina as the car, minus the rust, and the corners were rotted away. It was held closed by two complicated bolt arrangements, one each at the top and bottom, which were very difficult to shift, having set in position over time; they had a similar appearance to the manacles in the other hut, so I had to conclude that they would have been locally made. With some effort, and a highly effective kick from Ali, the bolts opened and the lid of the box creaked open.

It's possible, I concede, that I might have emitted a manly shriek when a skeleton fell out onto my foot. There was a brief, terrifying moment when the bony arms seemed to wrap themselves around my leg, before they fell off the rest of the body, like a moment in a Ray Harryhausen film.

To be clear, there was no *da Salò* inside, although that was plainly what the case had been designed to contain. The general shape of a double bass was described by dividing partitions, which looked like they might have been covered in green baize once upon a time, and there was the stringy remnant of a leather strap which would have buckled round the neck of the instrument whilst in transit. At the foot of the case was a set of small drawers, two on either side of the gap which the end pin would have occupied, which had long-decayed leather tabs with which to pull them out, and which contained a set of double bass strings, a spare end pin, a couple of blocks of rosin and an empty Huntley and Palmer's tin, which was badly preserved.

The skeleton itself aroused much curiosity amongst our guards, whose attention had been drawn by the noise I'd made, I fear. As a result, they had squeezed through the palisade, and there were suddenly eight stomping boots on the veranda, which seemed like it might give way as a result. The men were persuaded that all was well, eventually, and that they should remove themselves, but not before a lot of peering had been done and commentary given. The smell from the case wasn't nearly as awful as I would have expected, knowing that a body had been decaying within for nearly a century, but there was an odour, to be sure, and it wasn't pleasant.

Ali and I squatted to examine the remains of the poor wretch who had died, and immediately spotted that there was a dot of light to be seen shining through the lid. It was apparent that a bullet had passed right through, presumably killing the entrapped person as it did so, although there was no evidence of damage to the bones. That we were looking at the remains of a man was clear, despite the slightness of the skeletal frame, because enough hair had survived to show that he had had a goatee beard. In addition to that grotesque detail, fragments of clothing were present, although it wasn't possible to determine what their nature might have been.

There were a handful of sheets of paper lying in the case, which remained just-about legible, bearing the letter head of the Political Agent, Enoch da Costa, a name I hadn't encountered during the course of my earlier research, curiously. On the back of these were drawn some lines of music, although it wasn't possible to make out what the tune was. Most importantly, there was a badly tarnished pocket watch and chain, which had fallen to the bottom of the case, on which was inscribed, *To Enoch, from your great chum, Johnny*. This was telling for a number of reasons, not least confirming, in conjunction with the letter heads, that these were the remains of the missing last Political Agent. Inescapably, the inscription also suggested that Mr da Costa was part of the homosexual ring at court, the importance of which I came to surmise only when I was back in the UK, as I tried to find out more about him.

The archived records of the Indian Civil Service are generally very clear and well-ordered, as might be expected. Having ascertained that da Costa was the missing Political Agent, I dived into the archive back home and discovered something extraordinary about him. Rather, I didn't discover something extraordinary about him. That he was employed by the ICS is clear, because there are records of him buried deeply in the payroll. But there is no mention of him in any other records, no reports about him, or from him, or concerning him, no telegrams received or sent, nothing. It's as if a significant effort had been made to wipe him from the record, to disappear him from the chronicles of the ICS. What other reason can there be for this other than to protect the zealously-guarded reputation of the Service? So it would seem that the scandal of his behaviour at the court of Rajah Hari was felt to be so serious that, essentially, his bosses back in London left him in DM to rot. That they didn't know that he had been locked in a double bass case and shot, so that he had been left to rot literally, signifies the extent to which DM had become a matter over which they wanted to wash their hands completely. A quite remarkable episode in the history of the High Born Service.

I was happy to have established the fate of the missing PA, but as I stood looking down at his wretched remains, I felt a little disappointment that there was nothing else to be gleaned about the fate of my great-great-uncle, or the *da Salò*. The contents of this hut were in an even less well-preserved state than the adjoining hut, with no papers or personal possessions surviving. Although there had never been even a whiff of a family rumour that Cat had been gay, I was drawn to the conclusion that he had become part of the scandalous homosexual ring and, as a result, disappeared at the point when Rajah Shankarrao took the throne. And it was clear now that what had been recorded as the peaceful takeover by Shankarrao was in fact a bloody and violent affair. As has often been stated, history is written by the victor, and when he wants to be seen as the good guy, he doesn't necessarily tell it like it was.

What the actual nature of Cat's disappearance was I would find out only much later, and that rather by chance. For now, on my first full day in DM, I appeared to have arrived at a full stop.

10

Cat had eaten already, on the basis of just-in-case, when Enoch knocked on his door at the appointed hour. He'd had a busy morning since bathing, during which he had played Parvati for an hour, to help her acclimatise to the new climate in DM, before laying her back in her corner to rest. And he had supervised two palace lackeys, tasked with the responsibility of carrying to the veranda not just the bucket from his thunderbox (which would have been moved daily anyway, Cat hoped), but the box itself, which was a solid bit of local cabinetry, heavy and awkward to manoeuvre in the confined space of the bungalow. It had involved choreographing a complex dance between the box and the double bass, so that one should not come into contact in any way with the other, yet without simply taking Parvati outside, out of harm's way, because the day had become too warm already.

'Come in, Enoch,' shouted Cat, in response to the knock.

'Oh,' Enoch stopped short, catching sight of Cat's empty meal tray, 'you've eaten. I thought we were going to have some lunch?'

'Oh, yes, we are, don't worry, that was just a little snack to keep me ticking over, don't y'know.'

Enoch's intention was to take Cat on a walk about the city, before the temperature peaked around two o'clock, when they would settle in the little bhojanaalay at the water's edge which was his favourite. There was often a breeze by the sea, but this place had the additional benefit of a pankah, which was unusual in these parts as it meant prices were higher.

'But not nearly so high that the British Crown can't afford them!' Enoch had laughed.

Dressed once again in his pristine white suit and sola topee, he walked Cat in the direction of the gap in the wall which led through to the rear of the palace, from which they had emerged the evening before, but turned right and followed the track round to the side, the path by which Parvati and his luggage had travelled on the camel cart. He had advised Cat that, as they would be walking through the city, rather than riding, he was to follow strictly all the instructions given, in order to avoid any *undue difficulties with the natives*. Just as soon as they were outside the palace gates, there was suddenly a crowd of interested locals paying attention to them, and Enoch became very stiff and formal.

'Don't communicate with them, don't look them in the eye,' he instructed.

It was too late already, since Cat was waving and smiling at a pair of urchins, brother and sister he presumed, who were about to fall in line and walk beside him. They were ragged in appearance and, frankly, not clean, but they had pretty, friendly faces. 'Ahpke nahm kya hoon?' he asked.

The pair giggled.

'What's wrong?' laughed Cat.

'You just said *What is your names*? - you used हूँ instead of है.' Enoch nagged like a crusty old Latin master, 'Really, if you're going to persist with your dog-Hindustani amongst these damn natives, you must at least make the effort to conjugate correctly.'

'Oh, fuck off, Enoch!' hissed Cat.

'Well, really!'

'You're a bit of a damn native yourself, might I point out!'

Enoch grew very quiet, but looked furious.

'Mera nam Cat hain,' he addressed the children once more.

They tittered again, shyly, before the girl plucked up the courage to speak. 'Salma,' she pointed at herself then her brother, 'Osman'.

The other children in the crowd began to shout out their names – Mohammeds, Zenabs, Illyasses, Mariams – as the gathering grew. Cat waved and laughed with them all. There was a festive air, bouncing and laughing children all around.

'Look what you've done! I told you, Cat!'

'I'm sorry, Enoch, I can't see what the problem is. They're just friendly nippers, they just want to get to know us.'

'They'll pick our pockets. They'll grow into a rabble. We'll lose control.'

'We're not in control, Enoch, this is their city, this is a princely state, it's not British India! They are ruled by the Rajah...'

'Yes, and that's the problem.'

'What do you mean?'

'The Rajah is incapable of ruling, in my eyes. Unless something is done about him, this state will fail. And if the state fails, then it becomes a hotbed of dissent, and a locus for trouble in the surrounding British areas. In times gone by, the British simply used force to replace a bad ruler with a better one, one who would do their bidding and not impede the interests of the Crown, but we can't do that now. Times have changed.'

'What are you suggesting?'

Enoch didn't reply. They had reached the church square, and he peeled off to the left, snapping at Cat to follow him. As they approached the door on the north side, watched by the men working in the scaffolding above, the crowd drew back.

'Come along, come and see inside,' Cat urged them, 'I've haven't been inside yet myself, come and look with me...'

Little Salma stepped forward, but was held back by her shyer brother.

'They won't come,' muttered Enoch icily, 'they hate it. All they see is an act of peculation.'

'An act of what?'

'Money wasted, wasted on a place of worship for a religion which no-one here follows. And can you blame them?'

Enoch entered the church angrily, Cat scurrying to keep up. But once inside, almost immediately, Cat saw Enoch's tense shoulders drop as he stepped out of the public eye. He seemed to breathe more easily, walk with a more relaxed gait. Despite the scorn with which he'd spoken about the harmonium, he made straight for it with a broad smile on his face, genuflecting theatrically towards the altar as he passed. Cat eyed him, realising that he'd just seen the official persona, the Political Agent with *a job to do*, the same person whom he'd glimpsed yesterday upon his arrival. Gone was the curiously-whimsical but jolly fellow he had been back at the bungalows. It was true that, being the boss of a workforce consisting only of himself, he was in a position to be on- and off-duty as and when he saw fit, but the contrast between the two Enochs was greater than Cat might have expected.

The church was deserted, and Cat's first thought was that something was wrong. He screwed his nose up, squinted through his spectacles trying to decide what was missing, and realised that it was a matter of perception, that Gothic buildings should always be old. Even Gothic revival was old-ish by now, so it felt very odd to be in a building designed in the 1850s yet only just completed; every Gothic building had been new once, undoubtedly, but he certainly didn't recall being in one as shiny and unused as this one. The bare walls, completely free of memorials to the great, good, divine or loyal, were in pristine white distemper, whilst under foot was a floor consisting entirely of polished encaustic tiles. They were as would-be-mediaeval as the tall, thin, leaded lancet windows which sparkled in the brilliance of the daylight flooding through. To the west, on Cat's right, the altar could have been made by the same hand and in the same, dark wood as his thunderbox. It was draped with a simple, white cotton cloth, and standing on it was a blackened wrought-iron cross which, because it looked to have been locally hand-made, seemed very modern in this starkly faux, imported building. The nave, to Cat's left, was filled with serried pews, which were new, cheaply made in pine, looking like the sort of mail-order furniture Gamages would sell, if their range extended to church appointments. Cat's first feelings for the church were not positive.

On the south side, straddling the divide between nave and chancel, where Cat would ordinarily have expected a step or some other marker, stood the harmonium, positioned so that the player had his back to the wall. With his topee resting on top of the instrument, Enoch was playing now and, being a small man, all that could be seen of him was the top of his head. As he pumped the pedals, his hair jiggled about in one direction, whilst his (Cat thought) excessively romantic posturing caused it to flop around in another, causing an amusingly dynamic, three-dimensional range of pileous waves. Cat was pleased not to be able to see his face, which he imagined would be contorted in the expressive manner of the enthusiastic amateur *demonstrating his musicality*. That said, the quality of the playing was very good.

'What is that piece?' asked Cat, sidling over to the altar for a closer look at the cross.

'This? Oh, it's just part of a little set I composed. It's juvenilia,' Enoch craned his neck so that he could see Cat over the harmonium, like a tortoise reaching up for food.

He was playing a contrapuntal piece of some complexity, refreshingly modern, which he seemed to manage with extraordinary facility, especially given that his feet were burdened with the task of maintaining the air pressure. Cat wasn't about to admit it, however.

Enoch continued, playing and pumping all the while, 'This came about when I had access to the organ in my prep school – I was experimenting with twelve-tone serialism, although of course that was years before Arnold Schoenberg had codified his version of the technique. It's a simple piece, but I think it suits the directness of this instrument, and I can transfer the pedal part into my left hand, which is useful since I have to...' He stopped playing abruptly and stood up, pulling out the handkerchief from his top pocket to wipe his brow. '...phew, it's hard work. Never mind, I'll get used to it as we practice.'

Cat had arrived beside the harmonium, and cast his eye over its two manuals, each with four stops. It was a modest instrument by any standards, once again too new, showing no signs of years of neglect, in the way that harmoniums in chapels always do. The case was finished in a mean, thin, dark lacquer over a low-grade oak veneer, and he thought it unlikely it would last very long in this severe climate. 'May I have a go?'

Enoch slid off the bench to allow Cat access, which involved moving it back, finding the compromise between there being enough room for Cat's belly without it folding over the lower manual, yet not so far from the pedals that his short legs wouldn't be able to operate them. Once in position, he thought for a moment about what to play which would seem fitting for a Master of the Rajah's Music in the presence of this irritatingly gifted amateur; not virtuosic, because that would look wantonly flashy, and was beyond Cat's second-study keyboard skills anyway, and not pianistic because this instrument was definitely no piano. He decided that some Mozart would hit the spot, being about musicality and taste rather than mechanical skill, and also because he could remember some. He pulled out all the stops, pumped and readied his fingers to play an E flat chord.

'Ooh!' chuckled Enoch, 'we like a big chord, do we!'

Cat raised a pained eyebrow as he played the second chord, a more-widely spread C minor, and he was about to play the third chord when Enoch laughed and hopped like a happy child who had won at snap.

'First inversion, E flat major – yes yes yes, it's the overture to *The Magic Flute*, *Die Zauberflöte*, k620, 1791, libretto by Emmanuel Schikaneder, premiered at his theatre, the Freihaus-Theater auf der Wieden in Vienna, in 1791.'

'I only played the first two chords, Enoch!'

'I know, I know. It's unmistakable! I've got the vocal score in my bungalow, as it happens – we can do some of the arias from it.'

Cat raised his second eyebrow, regretting the answer he knew would follow,' And which arias did you have in mind?'

'Why, the Queen of the Night, of course, silly! I do a particularly notable Königin.'

'I can't wait to hear it,' he grimaced, already worn out by the pumping.

'Come along, dear Cat, we'd better get a move on. I fancy you'll be ready for lunch soon, and I'm beginning to feel peckish myself. Oh, I'm so excited to be able to make music with someone.'

The strength of the sun had increased very greatly during the short time they'd spent in the church, especially since they'd become used to the coolness of the interior. The instant he stepped outside. Cat stopped, his breath momentarily taken away in the dryness of the midday heat, and sweat began to drip freely from his forehead. The children were all waiting patiently for them at the edge of the square, so he rolled towards them and, mopping his brow, addressed his followers, 'Topee ke dukahn?'

Enoch flipped back into official mode, and tutted, 'Really, Cat, if you want to go shopping please ask me.'

Salma, pushing Osman into line, stepped forward, and they each took one of Cat's hands, to lead him, he assumed, in the direction of a hat shop.

'We're back in their city again, Enoch,' Cat said over his shoulder as he was led away, 'y'coming?'

Enoch followed, grumbling to Cat and barking what he meant as instructions for the children. His command of the language was obviously very good indeed, as he spoke so quickly that Cat couldn't really tell what he was saying, but it was clear that the children could, and that they were completely intent on ignoring him. Salma, far bossier than her younger brother, tugged on Cat's hand to steer him back onto the main road, turning left in the direction of the quay.

The road was the same bustle of confusion it had been the day before, when Cat and Enoch had driven along it in the opposite direction, but now that they were on foot and even more conspicuous, everyone stopped what they were doing to stare, not just those with nothing better to do. Cat felt no sense of threat, saw nothing which amounted to animosity towards these intruders, but detected a clear sense of weariness amongst a population for whom life brought few comforts. Very soon, Salma hauled Cat's mountainous form off to the right, tugging on his hand until he yielded to her will. 'Yeh disha, Cat,' she commanded.

'You're a tough little character, aren't you!' observed Cat, and she grinned back cheekily without understanding. She couldn't have been more than seven or eight, he thought, and Osman a couple of years younger.

Leaving behind the main road, they entered a maze of narrow passages, which gave a clue as to the age of the city's origins. No planning had ever been involved in the development of these streets, or the buildings which lined them. Never higher than two stories, but towering in the context of their closely-packed surroundings, the walls were largely undecorated, bare, coarse, grey cement or dun clay, the monotony of which was punctuated by the ubiquitous patches of black mould. Water trickled along whatever slight gradient there was, generally in the direction of the sea but not always, and in places it puddled; Cat stepped over or round these. Some of the houses were closed, but some had open fronts and served as workshops, or to display wares for sale, most of which were day to day necessities. There were smells, there was noise, there was labour; nothing spoke of luxury or leisure.

They pressed on, often against a swell of people, and rounded yet another corner, one of so many that Cat had lost his sense of direction altogether. Salma and Osman both suddenly stopped dead, each pulling at Cat's hand to prevent him going further. They had seen a dog ahead, which they decided they didn't like the look of, completely missed by Cat in his attention to the details of the human activity all around. Salma pointed to the cringing animal and Cat could see plainly that it was unwell, that its mouth was dripping with foam. The children quietly held him back whilst the poor animal skulked past, growling. Cat watched the miserable creature go, noticing Enoch's look of dread as it passed him by. And suddenly, they were off again. Another few corners, always in shadow, past merchants selling who-knows-what directly from limp, half-empty sacks, mechanics repairing decades-old bicycles, children selling chai in little, unglazed cups, and they arrived in front of a shop selling hats.

'For god's sake,' Enoch caught up with Cat, 'can't you do me the favour of acceding to my adjurations when we're out together? Is it so much to ask? I simply shouldn't be seen in these quarters!'

'Why not?' Cat was bemused.

'I am not here to influence the futures of these people, I am only here to represent His Majesty. It is the interests of the Crown upon which solely I'm focussed, so as far as these people are concerned, I'm not here. I don't exist.'

'Yes, you said as much, Enoch, but yet you clearly do exist and you are definitely here. And whatever you have in mind for this place will inevitably have some bearing on the lives of these people. I think you ought to be able to look them in the eye!'

'It is complicated!' Enoch was very brittle, very far removed from any place he considered safe.

'Good, I look forward to hearing all about it over lunch. But first, a hat!'

The stragglers amongst Cat's band of followers had fallen away as they had walked deeper into the old town, presuming correctly that the quest underway had some purpose, and would thus offer neither amusement nor the opportunity for tips. In any event, Salma had effectively monopolised this new resource, not least by the forceful use of her brother strategically to take Cat's spare hand, so excluding any possibility of infiltration by another. Cat was amused that she thought she was portraying herself as adorable, when it was clear to him that he had become a business opportunity. But she was good at what she did, having led him promptly to a hat shop, keeping him safe along the way, and now, an adult in a child's body, she haggled the price of a Sindhi cap down to what she considered a reasonable level before allowing him to part with any money.

After she had returned them to the main street, she looked dolefully up at Cat as she released his hand. She made no obvious sign that she was asking for a tip, rather assumed an attitude of cuteness, like the helpless puppy she plainly was not. Cat took no offence; if her guile lacked the maturity to be invisible, she had nonetheless provided a good service, and Cat reached into his pocket, pulling out too many coins.

Her eyes glowed, and she gasped, 'Shukriya, Cat!' before she and Osman skipped away into the shadows.

'H'm,' Enoch couldn't help himself, 'what a bright little girl. Were there opportunities available in this miserable place, then I am confident that she could make something of herself.'

Cat decided that was as touching a remark as Enoch was capable of making, in his official capacity at least.

11

Ali and I spent some time in the bungalows, combing through the litter of corruption in the hope of finding further evidence. The quest was fruitless, alas, and likewise our examination of the car, which had been rather plain in its finish, judging by the surviving scraps of unremarkable oil-cloth with which the interior had been finished; there wasn't a scrap of monarchical braided silk to be seen. Ali said he would organise for the skeleton to be given a proper end, although we had to decide what that might be, since we assumed da Costa was a Christian, and there was neither the appropriate burial ground in DM, nor anyone remotely qualified to read the service, even assuming a Book of Common Prayer could be found. A Muslim burial was simply out of the question, Ali thought, which left no choice other than cremation, a process more normally preserved for the sole use of the Hindu royal family.

(I did retrieve da Costa's watch, which cleaned up rather well when I got it back to England, where the jeweller who undertook its overhaul announced that it had been a watch of the highest quality, very expensive. I have retained it as a memento of the trip.)

That evening, Ali invited me to join him and some friends on the roof of the palace for drinks. Although I was still surprised by the casual manner in which he seemed to take ownership of things which happened, I said I thought that would be fun.

Me: Will Sammy be there?

Ali: Yeah, he'll turn up at some point, I think.

Me: What about the Rajah? I've not met him yet.

Ali: (laughing) Oh, I think that's highly unlikely! It's a young scene.

Me: A scene? Drinks on the roof is 'a scene'?

Ali: Yeah, there's not a lot else going on in these parts – there's no pub, I point out!

Me: Well, there wouldn't be, it's a Muslim-majority state.

Ali: (chortling) That's no reason not to have a drink!

Me: So all of DM's young people hang out on the palace roof?

Ali: (raising an eyebrow) Well, god, no, not all of them. It's only the people who are friends. Obviously.

Me: An inner circle!

The evening weather was perfect, and I arrived on the roof (by the posh lift, of course) to find myself wrapped in gently moving warm air, more like a pleasant draft than a breeze, although the source was off-shore no doubt. The contrast with the daytime heat was very striking, and a great relief. There were both men and women sitting up there, a group of about fifteen people, very relaxed and casually dressed, all around my age, some coupled-up, others merely part of 'the scene'. The space was large and notably well-appointed, a terrace for leisure rather than a roof on which to sit, with a floor like the deck of a ship, a central circle of sofas and chairs around a series of low tables, a bar to one side and a number of servants to act as the bridge between a drinker and his desire.

The thing which struck me most forcibly upon joining the group was the volume of laughter, the abandonment, the carefree enjoyment of life for people with nothing whatsoever to grouse about. They were young, socially successful, well-off and, I assumed, healthy, the blessed of the new age in DM. As I got to know them over the following days, I learned that most of them were in this position because their fathers and grandfathers (not mothers and grandmothers) had succeeded in business as the state developed, with its oil money trickling down not very far into their pockets. They were all foreign-educated, speakers of perfect English amongst themselves, and of barked Urdu to their servants.

I couldn't work out initially why they were all on this roof together, what was the underlying motivation, why their manners suggested it was their habit to be here. They obviously all had homes to go to! As I listened to the conversation, which was largely to do with either who-had-done-what-to-whom or else family business matters (rather than their onerous days of graft in the office or painstaking deeds of charity), it became apparent that they were all cast in the same mould as Ali, as playboys and playgirls. He was clearly the head playboy, judging by the reverence with which he was treated, but the others weren't far behind. They were jolly and welcoming, tremendous boozers (Chivas Regal seemed to be the scotch of choice, or vodka for those preferring their spirits without character), and a lot of fun to be with.

And then Sammy entered, whereupon everybody jumped up and stood more-or-less to attention, silently waiting for him to be jolly and informal, when they all resumed their seats and carried on, except that now he was the centre of attention. Even those not talking to the Yuvraj directly had somehow twisted in their seats so as to deliver subliminally the message that they were hanging on his every word. And they were no longer as much fun. I realised that I was looking at a court, in the full-blown early-modern sense, filled with people who wanted to catch the monarch's eye in the hope of preferment. As courtiers must have done from the earliest of times, they had learned to entertain themselves with slight diversions whilst waiting, like coiled springs, to be attentive to a ruler who was out of reach for most of the day. Evening drinking on this roof was the equivalent of archery in the grounds, promenades along the gallery and the dancing of pavans and galliards.

I was already feeling frustrated at my lack of progress with regard to Uncle Cat's life in DM, and sitting up here amongst this group of drinkers reinforced my sense that he was still very distant from me. I could see that there must have been a social life back then, just as there was today, and this reminder that I was no closer to learning what it was like for him added to the disappointment of not having unearthed anything about him. I knew more about da Costa, it was true, but I didn't know what he looked like, it wasn't him I came to find, and it hit me suddenly that I actually cared about Cat, that he was more to me than a curiosity or a point of academic interest.

After a short while, Arabella followed her husband onto the roof, causing no sort of a stir at all. She was welcomed cheerily enough, but it was clearly the case that no-one felt she personally could do them any good. Whereas not long after, in sharp contrast, I saw Ali's eyes bulge briefly as he spotted something across the roof behind me, whereupon he jerked fully to attention and stood rigidly, joined in very short order by everyone else, including Sammy (and, reflexly, me), in order to receive the Rajah and Rani themselves. It was a stressful moment.

But it was the moment when I became one of the inner circle, because, it turned out, their Royal Highnesses had made this exceptional trip to the roof to welcome me personally to their home. They were a charming elderly couple, very gracious and warm in their greeting, and I felt rather honoured to have been received in that way, whilst throughout everyone else stood to attention in complete silence. As soon as they'd gone, everyone sat down and started to relax again, except now it was towards me that their knees pointed whilst they played at carefree chit-chat amongst themselves.

A particularly attractive female, who had been usurped from her position of privilege at the side of the Yuvraj when his wife arrived, now sidled over to sit beside me.

Me: Hello! My name's Philip?

Lulu: (purring) And mine's Lulu.

Me: Pleased to meet you, Lulu.

Lulu: (growling) You can call me Lu.

Me: Thanks very much. Please, er, call me Phil.

I had no idea where this conversation was going, at this point, and admit that I was a little tongue-tied because she had the sort of beauty which has been used as a trope of power and seduction for centuries; had I a thousand ships under my command, I would undoubtedly have launched them on her say so, in a (rampaging) heart beat.

Lulu: You're very special, you know.

Me: (stammering) I... I... am?

Lulu: (resting her hand on my knee) Yes, you are.

Me: G-gosh. W-why's that?

Lulu: Because not everybody new to the roof gets a special visit from the Rajah.

I knew then where the conversation was going, and attempted to find Lulu correspondingly less attractive. Unfortunately, her enormous eyes, spectacular frizz of curly black hair, sinuous figure and unspeakable femininity meant that I was destined to fail in my struggle, and I remained resolute in my conviction that she was utterly gorgeous.

As I watched her butter me up, really quite without shame, I became aware of her shalwar kameez, which was a spectacular printed affair on a ground of peacock-blue; I know very little about fabrics, but it seemed certain that this was exceptionally fine stuff. It had a tantalising slit at the neck, in which could be found both function and purpose; its function for her was to let her head through, whereas her purpose for it was to reveal that region where the proximal ends of her clavicles met the jugular notch (according to Google), and where the light-brown, peachy skin looked so delicate that it seemed to insist it should be tenderly cared for. By me.

Me: Uhm, ah, which was your university, Lu?

Lulu: I did criminology at the University of Blackpool.

I wouldn't have thought that that short sentence could possibly have resonated so sweetly in my imagination. But it was delivered in a breathy whisper which sounded like a bottom sliding across the antique leather of a Chesterfield,

Me: (ridiculously) Ah, so you'll know all about catching people and locking them up!

Lulu: Hardly, but since you mention it, what about your uncle's sexy bondage equipment!

News travelled fast, it was clear.

Me: Well, uhm, he was my great-great-uncle, actually, and I think… that is, we don't know... whether they were actually his or the Political Agent's.

Lulu: Who cares, they obviously had a lot of fun back in those days.

I suppose I'd either failed to deliver the signals which Lulu was looking for, or else she just got bored with me, since she saw a gap in the circle which she thought she should fill, and upped and left. I was joined very shortly by a young man called Cheekoo (he said), who also wanted to chat me up, presumably thinking that Lulu's departure signified more than it did.

Cheekoo: Hiiiii there, me Cheekoo, you Jane! I saw the vixen leave and thought, ooh, there's an opening for me.

Me: (taken aback) Hi, Cheekoo. I'm Philip.

Cheekoo: I know who you are, fella! Do tell me about the bondage bed you found today – does it run in the family?

What a bunch they were turning out to be, this inner circle. I looked over towards Sammy, and saw a man at ease, laughing with his friends, and wondered if he had actually *done* anything today. Beside him, Arabella had the strained look of one forcing herself to be jolly (which she'd always had – I never knew what Sammy saw in her), and I wondered what sort of day she must have had; I guessed not much involvement in government, so what, then?

12

As the night began to draw in, Cat sat triumphantly on his thunderbox, enjoying the freedom of the open air on his exposed skin, rather as he had that morning by the lake. It was true that there were mosquitoes in abundance on the veranda, but there were just as many within 2nd Bungalow, where the evening air was far less convivial. He had found in his baggage the large, folding fan which he'd discovered lying around somewhere in Ghoom – clearly unwanted by its former owner – with which to waft the mozzies away when they approached, and so had exposed a little more skin than he might otherwise have dared. Parvati's case, as a modesty screen, functioned extremely well, and he was very content with the outcome of his little improvement.

With the light now fading, he peered into the baize interior of his enclosure, the cloth thinning in several places, reflecting on how old and worn it was. He had no idea when the case had been made, since Parvati was already in it when she had come to him, but it was undoubtedly aged and could even have been Dragonetti's original, a thought which caused to him to bemoan the loss of status of double bass players in this modern age. No doubt old Domenico had attendants by the handful to look after the transport of his instruments, making his travels a simple matter, whereas Cat's solo journey across the subcontinent to Ghoom had taught him how difficult it could be to move a double bass on land without help. His return to the west coast by ship had been so much easier, as she had been winched aboard every vessel and off again upon arrival; and then the memory of the near disaster on the quayside here at DM returned, sending a chill shiver down his sweaty spine.

It was some sort of a wonder that nothing like that had happened before, he realised, contemplating what he could do to secure the case properly. He needed to be confident that such an incident could never occur again, for Parvati's sake as well as his own, so what was required was some sort of catch, a fail-safe, which would lock by default whenever the lid was closed.

Moreover, although he didn't anticipate moving anywhere very soon, it would be for the best if he attended to the matter promptly, since a chap never knows when he might have to pack up and leave at short notice. He'd seen a number of small workshops on the detour into the old town today, and decided he should visit one at the first opportunity to commission something which would do the job.

However, whilst Cat felt implicitly that he was exceptionally skilled in a number of ways, he certainly didn't consider himself to be any sort of an engineer, and couldn't imagine just how such a lock might work. The problem was that the lid of Parvati's case wasn't like an ordinary house door, closing into a frame, and all he could see in his mind's eye were locks for variations of that configuration. In fact, the case functioned more like a clam shell and, accordingly, was already fitted top and bottom with ordinary hooks and eyes to keep it closed, but these didn't operate automatically. He concentrated on the matter for as long as was necessary to decide that he wasn't equipped to come up with a solution; but he thought he knew someone who probably was.

Enoch had continued to present himself as a renaissance man during the day's outing, or, to one less charitably inclined perhaps, a thorough-going know-it-all. There seemed to be nothing he didn't know something about, no subject upon which he couldn't propound, no language he couldn't speak. Cat understood that a man adept at delivering bullshit can seem to be more knowledgeable than in fact he is, but Enoch had demonstrated a genuine understanding of music, both its theory and history, far beyond that which a layman would be expected to have, and it wasn't impossible to believe that his wild, divergent explications on apparently limitless subjects were similarly supported with learning. He had at one point, over lunch, moved the conversation from his thoughts on the ancient bicycles passing by the bhojanaalay, to the arrangement of main bearings favoured by Henry Royce in his latest straight-six engines, so it seemed reasonable to Cat to assume that he might have the engineering nous to think through what was likely to be a trivial problem for the right sort of brain.

Cat had decided today that he found Enoch fascinating. Not the least of the fascination was why he, an Anglo-Indian, was a member of the Indian Civil Service, one of the *heaven-born*, known in every circle as a hyper-elite group, the most intelligent and resourceful, always men and always white. There were some Indians working in the service, it was true, but always at a much lower level than Enoch who, as a Political Agent, was a senior figure with serious responsibilities. It was very surprising to Cat, who had come across any number of snooty British toff-types on his travels in India, that Enoch had been allowed into that particular club. And it wasn't just that he was Anglo-Indian, as he was by any standards an odd sort, not at all someone who had come out of the mould of the British colonial servant.

Enoch had picked up the tab for lunch earlier, which wasn't a large amount despite Cat ordering double portions to sate the hunger he had developed as they walked. The food was delicious, spicy grills of fish and lamb, with rice, sag and dahl, and Cat had eaten with his fingers in the manner of the people from further down the subcontinent, a practice he had acquired in Colombo on his journey here; it made the food taste better, he thought. Enoch had eaten prudishly, with a knife and fork, in the manner of an uncomfortable Englishman, and had momentarily given Cat *a look* as he had first dug his fingers into the rice, although he soon relaxed as he realised there was no-one in the restaurant interested in observing him behave formally. Cat had also received an envelope which contained a goodly quantity of cash to compensate for the salary which he could expect not to receive. Enoch termed it an honorarium, and Cat had expressed his genuine gratitude, saying that he thought it would *tide him over*, which in turn brought him a rebuke, and the instruction that he should try to rely less on the use of cliché.

Moments like that revealed a personality which Cat thought, at best, curious. He had no sense that there was anything malevolent about Enoch, that he was intent on causing anyone any harm, but equally there was no indication that he thought about how he might actually do any good. He seemed professionally committed to what he saw as his role within the ICS whilst on duty, but to have no interest beyond having fun when he was off duty. And that was where the curiosity lay, Cat decided, that he was a man of learning and culture, a man who craved intellectual stimulation, companionship, love maybe, yet who had accepted a job which brought him about as far as it was possible to be from all of the things he held dear .

As he had dropped his trousers prior to mounting the thunderbox, Cat had caused Enoch's envelope to fall out of his pocket, and he had leant forward fartily to pick it up. He counted the contents accurately now, as he whiled away this pleasant time, and was delighted with the amount he discovered within. He had already realised that having cash was a moot point in DM, since there was really nothing much in the shops on which to spend it, and all his daily needs – food, accommodation, a servant – were covered by the palace anyway. This cash amounted to savings, therefore, and he wondered where was the best place to keep his stash safe, away from the too-bright eyes of Indira not least, and decided that the drawers at the bottom of the case, beneath the soft cover still folded there, was unlikely to be of interest to her, given the dressing down she'd received earlier for not keeping her distance from Parvati.

Where did Enoch keep his cash? Presumably he had quite a lot of it somewhere, enough to look after the business of the ICS, since DM suffered from a paucity of banking facilities. Cat decided he must have access to the palace treasury, wherever that was, and to have stored large amounts of His Majesty's oof in there; there was unlikely to be much lying around and unwanted, he concluded with a sigh.

The absence of things on which to splash money presented a problem. He wasn't in a rush to spend a single paisa of his own resources, in reality, but not even having the theoretical opportunity to do so meant he couldn't reasonably approach Enoch for further funds on the grounds that he'd gone broke, and it was clear that the amount given was a favour to – Cat hesitated – damnit, yes, to *tide him over*. It wasn't a salary, that much was made clear, so if he wanted more, he'd have to come up with a way of justifying it. Perhaps an elaboration around the amount owed to the payroll in Ghoom, when the time came; it had seemed too early to raise that matter over lunch.

The shielding provided by Parvati's case wasn't quite complete, and through the narrow slit between it and the wall, he noticed Indira's shadow arrive silently, before she knocked on the bungalow door.

'I'm in here,' Cat hissed, causing Indira to leap backwards as if she'd stumbled across a cobra.

'Ah, Sahib,' she sighed after a moment, 'what you do behind there?'

'I'm having a poo, obviously!' Cat thought the question shouldn't have needed asking, and was correspondingly blunt.

There was a pause for reflection before she asked, 'Willie Pooh, Sahib?'

'Huh?'

'Day without friend like jar without one drop honey left in.'

'What are you talking about, girl?'

'Sometimes tiny things take up most room in heart.'

'What are you blatherin' on about, you ass?'

'Enoch Sahib teach me Willie Pooh, Sahib...'

'Willy poo? I don't know what you mean! In any case, I'm sure this is a different sort of poo.'

As if to order, what Cat felt might be the last of the evening's movements occurred, noisily, giving Indira an inescapable clue as to the alternative meaning, of the other sort of poo. She squealed uncomfortably, greatly pained.

'Oh, Sahib – oh, Sahib...' she struggled to recover, 'I... I bring water for bungalow.'

'Jolly good, perfect timing, Indira.' Cat was beginning to appreciate the merits of having a servant, 'just leave it on the wash stand, would you.'

'Yes, Sahib. Does Sahib want food?' her voice revealed inescapably her disgust as she placed Cat's eating and defecating within the same context.

Cat wondered whether this was a moment of insolence, but decided to give her the benefit of the doubt. He also wondered what the answer should be, since he had been invited to the palace for dinner this evening, but thought a little snack in advance might not be a bad thing; it might stop him eating so much that others around the table would notice and, worse, comment.

'I don't have very long, Indira – I'm due at the palace tonight,' he couldn't help but puff himself up by the use of that phrase, 'but if you could get me a couple of samosas or something quick, that would be cracking.'

Indira didn't reply. She entered the bungalow briefly, to do what she needed to do, and pulled shut the door behind her as she left. Cat, confident that his thunderbox time had come to an end, hid his cash in the compartment at his feet, dismounted, cleaned himself and went in to wash his hands and dress.

Enoch was due to knock at seven-thirty, so there wasn't very much time to get into white tie. Cat habitually kept his evening dress at the ready, as a musician must according to his tutor at the Royal Academy, but was disappointed to find that the climate had softened his starched shirt and collar. No time to deal with that now, and in fact a softer collar felt much more comfortable than he was used to, he decided. Moreover, he wondered if it was even possible to get a collar and marcella bib boiled in this place, which would mean relaxing his standards for concerts and public appearances, so…

…no, he had forgotten momentarily the underlying untruth of his position here as Master of the Rajah's Music. Nonetheless, when the PA arrived, they would walk together to the royal palace to meet some of the best of DM society, at what was described as a formal meal to recognise Cat's arrival. So it was clear to Cat that he did have some sort of status in this place; he'd certainly never attended a banquet given in his honour.

As he returned to his lounge, dressed, he discovered that Indira had been able to enter and leave a plate with two samosas on the small rattan table, without apparently having made any noise at all, and Cat was well into the task of eating them when Enoch knocked.

'Just a moment,' Cat tried to sound like wasn't eating, as he stuffed the last of his snack into his mouth, and chewed anxiously, 'won't... be... a...'

'My dear Cat, I have seen you in your underpants,' laughed Enoch on the veranda.

Cat, not immediately grasping the meaning of Enoch's remark, ceased chewing for a moment before realising that his unwillingness to be disturbed had been taken to indicate that he was incompletely dressed, rather than that he was eating again. He swallowed, hard, wiped his mouth with the napkin from the tray, and opened the door to reveal Enoch suited fully in white, top to bottom, white tail coat, white tie, white patent oxfords.

'Good heavens,' Cat's reaction was beyond his control, 'you look like G.H. Elliott!'

'Oh, I see,' Enoch's response was distinctly cool. 'You mean, presumably, that I look like The Chocolate Coloured Coon?'

Cat realised that that was exactly what he had meant, in effect, but that at the same time he hadn't wished to cause any offence to his neighbour. 'No, no, no, my dear friend, that's absolutely not at all what I meant in the slightest – I mean… I meant that you look bright enough to take centre stage at the Palace, is all.'

'Is all? And such clarity of vision without even your glasses on.'

'Yes, er, I was just looking for them when you knocked – oh, here they are!' Cat grabbed his spectacles from the table, where they lay beside the tray. Not only was it clear that Enoch had spotted the tray with its empty plate, but that he also saw Cat's still-greasy thumb leave a clear print on one the lenses, which had to be rubbed clean with a handkerchief.

'Do you find yourself now to be in a state of readiness?'

Cat nodded, too embarrassed to speak.

'You might be interested to know, since you raise the issue,' Enoch rose in superiority above the moment, 'that I have in fact already taken centre stage at the Palace.'

'You have? When?' Cat stepped onto the veranda and pulled the door shut, relieved that the conversation was moving on.

'It was in 1912, at the first Royal Command Performance, before Their Majesties.'

'Crikey! What was your act?'

'My act? My *act*? Do you think I emerged from the gutters as an entertainer in variety?'

'I… I… well, you must have done something on stage – isn't that your act?'

'I appeared under my own name, thank you very much.'

'Just as *Enoch da Costa*? What did you do?'

'Well, no, not exactly. I appeared as *Enoch da Costa: The New Mozart*, and I played a piano sonata of my own composition.'

'Sounds like an act to me!' Cat remarked as they struck out for the back door of the palace.

'Well, if you wish to be so literal...'

'How did this come about?'

'Oh, another time, old man, another time. What are your spectacles made of, incidentally?'

'Ah, well, it's some brand new stuff called Erinoid,' Cat boasted.

'Yes, I thought so. It's a casein-based plastic, derived from milk,' noted Enoch as he stepped off the veranda.

Cat sighed deeply and followed.

13

Once I'd realised that Ali was indiscreet, and so decided to guard what I said to him, his lack of a need to inconvenience himself with work was a great boon to me, because he made himself available as my tour guide in DM. I couldn't say whether this was because he was bored and needed a diversion (beyond the amusement of having a pet camel and a helicopter), or because he took delight in his home town and wanted to show it off, or perhaps merely because he'd been instructed to look after me by the Rajah – there might have been elements of all three. But I was happy enough with the arrangement, especially as it became clear very early on that Sammy himself just wasn't available to be my guide.

I had been engaged in my solitary wanderings along the corridors of the palace, filling in time whilst I waited for Ali to collect me, when I happened to stray out of the domestic quarters and into the administrative section of the building. There I found a very large floor of serried desks, some behind informal, glass partitions, at which were sitting more people working at computers than I could count. Everyone looked up at me, and I was about to make an embarrassed exit when one of the staff stood and beckoned me over. She introduced herself – I didn't catch the name because of the hum from all around, but it was something like 'Parveen from accounts' – and led me towards an enclosed space at the far end of the room, where Sammy was sitting behind his own computer. He leaped to his feet and greeted me warmly.

Sammy: Phil, how good of you to come down to the workhouse!

Me: It looks very light and modern to me. Sorry, I didn't mean to disturb you at work.

Sammy: No problem at all. Come, I'll show you around.

I had no idea how much work is involved in being the heir to a minor throne, and I'm delighted to admit that I'd been utterly wrong about Sammy's idleness. He showed me the sections of the office, with people involved in activities such as communications, marketing (they were beginning to develop a strategy to attract tourists, apparently) and so on, plus administrators dealing with legal matters and the day-to-day running of the state; the press team were mainly engaged in fallout from the terrorist attack, I learned, delivering the message that everything was in hand. It was impressive, and all driven by Sammy's clear desire to continue to develop DM, to make it fit for purpose, as he put it, in the modern world. Moreover, he was the big boss, running the whole lot, because his father had handed it all over and retired as soon as he'd returned from Oxford. This I hadn't realised.

I didn't stay long as they were busy, and it was approaching the Ali-hour (I assumed he didn't like to get up too early), so found my way back towards my room. I was even more curious now as to what Arabella did with herself all day, however, because she plainly wasn't spending the time with her husband, and resolved to try to pick Ali's brain on the matter – subtly, of course.

As we left the palace by the front door, on foot this time, to walk down the central boulevard towards the sea (together with our two armed guards), I broached the subject of what people without jobs did around here all day, and Ali immediately thought I was talking about him. Fortunately, he was amused, although not particularly forthcoming. Instead he slipped into blue badge mode, and began explaining the sculpture on the roundabout adjacent to the palace.

It memorialised the woman who had modernised DM's medical provision, a Dr. Vijinalakshmi Bunta, who had come here as a missionary doctor in the early twenties, during Uncle Cat's time, and stayed, becoming the state's first minister of health as the great post-war redevelopment began. To celebrate her contribution to the state, this statue had been commissioned and the main hospital named after her when it was opened on the tenth anniversary of her death, by Rajah Muktbir, Sammy's grandfather, who had himself been delivered by the good doctor, apparently.

She was, I learned, a formidable woman, said to have conceived a child out of wedlock at a time when that was a very big deal, and delivered the baby herself, no less, after which she carried on working, dragging the health system into the modern age, and defying anyone to take exception. She eventually married an incomer called Billy Bunta, who adopted her son and devoted himself to assisting her in her quest to improve the lives of all Dusa Mathavasians. Although I had encountered her name in my researches here and there, I hadn't known any details of Dr. Bunta's life, so was pleased to have fleshed her out somewhat. I thought hers was a strikingly modern story, especially by the standards of what had, in the day, been a very backward place.

There are no references to Dr. Bunta in any of Cat's surviving letters, so it was unclear if their paths crossed whilst he was in DM, still less that they actually knew each other. It was a matter of deep frustration that Uncle Cat was becoming a phantom here in the city, popping up in my imagination, on this corner or in that doorway, as we walked down the boulevard. It was rather as it is when you lose a favourite cat – as opposed to Cat – and for weeks keep thinking you've seen her lurking in the corner of your eye, when it's only ever actually your backpack or shoes. Of course, our surroundings were almost entirely modern, so there was hardly anything around me which he would have seen, but I knew he'd been here, that something of him must have been left behind, and I just couldn't find it.

As we approached the mosque, Ali began to talk enthusiastically about the building, and the good it had brought. He explained that there hadn't been any sort of focus for the ceremonials of state before it was completed, when this site was bare, so no central area where gatherings could be organised or rallies held, and that the plaza in which the mosque now sat had become, as he put it, the Trafalgar Square of DM. But in explaining his family's connection with the building – that is, they paid for it in its entirety – he revealed more than I think he meant to.

For starters, the simple fact of the Qifar family paying for such a lavish building suggested that it wasn't just loaded, but that it had money in the way other families have water. Just how many of the show-piece buildings in the Emirates had the company constructed, I wondered? And there was more than a suggestion that the family was heavily involved in the administration of DM – his father, for example, despite sitting at the head of his business empire, was also the current divan – with all the implications of the possibility that due processes, such as tendering, which were generally the norm elsewhere, might not have been strictly adhered to. I put it no more strongly than that. Ali's tendency to casually adopt the *royal we* as he spoke began to look like it might have had some sort of basis in practice.

The mosque itself was nothing if not an impressive achievement, although I couldn't help but think it was disproportionately large given its surroundings. It was considered to be so important, as a statement of modern intention, that it was due to be slated as one of the attractions being catalogued by the tourism team back at the palace. Ali thought it not a good idea for me to enter, the nature of the building being what it was, and with tensions high after the murder of the engineer, but it was no great loss because it was so open I could see the marbled grandness of the interior from where I stood.

As we walked on, I was aware that those around us were stepping out of our way. I couldn't tell if it was this English academic they didn't like the look of, or the Qifar family member, or the two commandos armed with machine guns.

Me: (puzzled) I appear to be the only foreigner here, Ali?

Ali: Nope, there're loads here.

Me: Where?

Ali: Lots of Pakistanis come here to work…

Me: Yes, well, I mean, they're not really foreign, are they.

Ali: (superciliously) They're from a different country!

Me: Yes, I know, what I mean, I suppose is, uhm…

Ali: (drily) You mean white people. What you're asking is where are all the white people.

I realised immediately that that is precisely what I'd meant, and furthermore that the question contained a number of loaded assumptions. I might as well have asked how the state could possibly operate on a day to day basis without a European present to supervise everything, since it was impossible to imagine that brown people could do it on their own. I wasn't pleased with myself.

Ali: There are some Europeans at the western end, at the oil colony, but that's its own little world over there. But we're going to launch a campaign to attract visitors in the near future.

Me: Yes, I met the team this morning, as it happens.

Ali: (stopping in his tracks) You did?

Me: Yes, I accidentally wandered into a guided tour from Sammy.

Ali didn't reply, and showed every sign of being not pleased, as if I'd intruded into his domain.

We walked on for a reasonable stretch, to the other end of the boulevard, past the newly-opened branch of Khaadi, which was heaving despite the heat of the day, and approached the roundabout with the sculpture I had spotted from his car, the one he'd called *Aerial*. The structure was higher than any of the buildings around (apart from the minaret), and made of shiny metal, like a giant reproduction of a telescopic car aerial.

Me: Ah, so this is *Aerial*!

Ali: You spotted it!

Me: It looks just like an, uhm, aerial.

Ali: (cynically) Doesn't it just!

Me: It's, what should we say, a fairly literal title, then.

Ali: It's actually more literal than you realise, since in addition to being *Aerial*, it's also the main mast for mobile comms in the city.

Me: Yes, I can see how that would work. Why not stick it on top of the mosque, out of interest?

Ali: It wasn't my decision. This is Arabella's baby. She's taken upon herself the task of beautifying DM with art, and she bought this.

Me: (nonchalantly) Who is it by? It could almost be a Claes Oldenburg.

Ali: Ooh, very good! It's actually by Brad Leksak, one of his pupils. Apparently.

Me: Never heard of him!

Ali: No, neither had I.

Me: So that's what she does with herself?

This was my opportunity to talk about Arabella, hoping that Ali's indiscretion would now extend as far as spilling the beans about her. And it did, although he spoke in guarded terms, to be fair. As he had said, she had taken upon herself the commissioning of the new palace, its interior decoration, this piece of public art and the general spending of as much money as she could lay her hands on, in ways which were considered by most to suit her and her alone. She had even attempted to replace Dr. Bunta's memorial with 'something more modern', but had come up against unshakeable public opinion, so put down that particular pet project. I wondered whether she had actually enjoyed the irony of *Aerial* being the mobile mast, whether she had got the pun, or whether it had been merely seemed like a good idea she could run with. I knew she was no fool, but I didn't know that she had much of a sense of fun. I also wondered how she fitted in as a European, spending state money in a place where, judging by Ali's mien, European involvement wasn't openly sought.

Me: Doesn't she get bored here?

Ali: Seems not.

Me: Ten years out here is a long time – I mean…

Ali: Oh, don't worry, I'm not offended.

Me: It's not a big place, and there ain't no opera house!

Ali: That's precisely why I've got the Robinson. I spend quite a lot of time across the water. There's stuff to do there. Oh, by the way, I'm off to Karachi tomorrow, so I won't be able to take you out, soz.

Me: Oh, what're you doing there?

Ali: (flatly) A favour!

Me: To?

Ali: Sammy wants me to bring back some journalists who want to come to cover the murder of the Chinese engineer.

Me: I thought you you said your helicopter was yours, not the state's!

Ali: Well, yes, but what can you do. I think it's a mistake, myself. That's a story which should stay here rather than make headlines across the world, but my father thinks all publicity is good publicity.

Me: Your father?

Ali: (caught out) As, er, divan, of course. Come let me show you the old harbour.

14

‘*The New Mozart*?’ Cat persisted.

‘Look, Cat, I will tell you all about it, you have my parole - it’s an interesting story, as a matter of fact, which relates to my presence here…’

‘Here, in this place?’

‘Veritably, if you can you believe that – but not now, we don’t have time. Lo, we have arrived.’

The unlit edifice of the palace had risen up ahead of them as they passed through the rear range of buildings and into the yard. There was a commotion all around, illuminated by the flickering of countless oil lamps, as laden servants passed between open doors, shouting, engaged in the practical running of a royal residence. Enoch, more familiar with the route than Cat, led the way towards the back door. Cat trailed in the brilliance of his white tails.

‘Who is Willy Poo, by the way?’

Enoch came to a halt, ‘How do you know… Indira, obviously! He was a character I developed for children whilst I was still a child myself. He’s a bear. Juvenilia. I sent the stories to Punch but never heard back. I must return to them at some point.’ Enoch hesitated as he set off again, ‘I should warn you that this probably isn’t going to be a royal banquet in the sense that you will possibly have imagined,’ he muttered confidentially, ‘in fact, it may well be a rather curious affair which will satisfy no-one in any degree, but it’s important that something royal happens from time to time which resembles a state matter, if you follow.’

‘Huh?’

‘We need to be able to demonstrate, if asked, that the royal line is behaving in a royal manner, and that the state is suitably placed to retain some degree of internal autonomy under the present royal family.’

‘If asked by who?’ Cat recognised scheming when he heard it.

‘*Whom* Cat, *whom*! Chalo, let us make ourselves present.’

Enoch stepped into the lead once again. Cat sighed and followed him into the passage which, paradoxically, was more brilliantly lit with lanterns at night than it had been by sunlight during the day. Cat could see now the details of the mahogany-dark wall paper which must have been an ill-judged attempt to decorate the space from the time when the palace was first built, doomed to fail from the very start. They were met by Ajaz, who was more splendidly attired than usual, in his smartest livery and with a stiff, pleated fan rising from his turban. Cat resolved to ask him who in DM had the skills with starch to produce such an effect, since that was plainly where he needed to go to get his collar and bib put into a fit state for a performance. But, on second thoughts, why would he choose to forsake the collapsed comfort of his present state?

They turned to the right, into the door before the drawing room, beyond which was a startlingly large room, the full length of the east front. There were four enormous windows, covered in lavish hangings of an indeterminate dark colour, which were as dusty as they were old-fashioned. The walls which they interrupted were covered in a comparatively brilliant rose-pink sateen, worn through in places where shoulders had lounged for too long, These in turn were punctuated by girandoles, in each of which burned three candles.

Standing on the polished hard-wood floor, in the centre of the room, was the grand dining table, a long and elaborate reproduction of a Tudor table, with massive, turned legs, surrounded by matching chairs, in the darkest of dark oak, with heavily-polished rattan seats and backs. Along the length of the table was a linen runner, of the same darkness as the window drapes, with the bare surface on either side set with linen mats and a full service of porcelain, in a pink which more-or-less matched the walls, once gold rimmed but now worn from the attentions of generations of the dish-washer caste who had cared for it over the years. Positioned equally along the centre of the runner were three very tall, elaborate silver candelabra, each with nine candles, newly lit, the lustres casting dancing pools of golden light onto their surroundings.

Cat was taken aback by the formal grandeur of the room, tired, old-fashioned and worn as it certainly was. From his experience of how glamorous a concert hall looks when prepared at night for an audience, compared to the drabness of the same space under working lights during the afternoon's rehearsal, he could easily imagine that if he were to come back in daylight, when the sharp light of the sun had replaced the burbling glow of the candles, it would seem to be a very different space indeed, but for now he was very happy to enjoy his first experience of a palace looking like he felt it should.

At the far end of the room stood the group of those who had arrived earlier, creating a bubble of conversation, which came to an abrupt halt as Ajaz made his rather formal announcement, 'The Political Agent and Mr Cat Adam.'

Cat was irritated that Enoch had been introduced according to his position, whereas no mention had been made of him being the Master of the Rajah's Music. Still, he recognised that he was cast into a more personal role as a result, more a friend of royalty than its servant.

As they advanced towards the party, Wigly shouted out, 'Oh, look, it's the Brothers Obo!', which gave rise to a chorus of laughter.

'I don't play the oboe,' hissed Cat as they walked towards the group, 'do you? They're barking!'

'Already drunk, more likely, I fear. The Brothers Obo are a comedy variety act, Edgar and Leolin, known as The Popular Laughing Comedians, as I recall. I fear the sots are alluding to the possibility that they have already begun to associate each of us with the other in a comedic manner.'

'Is this because they already know of your background in music hall?'

'Of course it is not!' Enoch's heckles rose, 'This is entirely coincidental. Music hall acts are not something I discuss with anyone – not least because my background, as you most unfortunately put it, was in *variety*, and that only for the briefest period. The only novelty was my youth, which has now passed. I am a serious artist, never forget! Ah, Your Highness...' he segued seamlessly into a deep, sycophantic bow.

'Good evening, old boy,' grinned Hurree, 'so pleased you could make it.'

'And looking so white too,' gasped Wigly, 'at least in the garb! How's that awful brother of yours, do tell.'

'Mr. Wigly, my sincerest greetings to you on this most auspicious occasion.' Enoch smiled with the warmth of a hard-boiled egg gone cold, 'As I believe I've informed you in the past, my brother was a very brave man who perished in the war. I, on the other hand, am terrifically cowardly, and so live on. Now, would you be kind enough to fetch drinks for Mr. Adam and myself?'

Curiously, Wigly complied, despite muttering as he turned that he wasn't the one dressed like a waiter. Since he wore black tie with a rather vulgar short jacket, rather than full evening dress, Cat thought he could in fact easily pass for a waiter.

Hurree acknowledged Cat politely before turning round to continue his conversation.

'What's your brother got to do with anything, Enoch?' hissed Cat.

'He went to your school briefly, and whilst there made himself unpopular, I understand. The Rajah and his friends like to bring him up in conversation now and then.'

'Da Costa – da Costa – I don't remember him.'

'Perhaps as well, old chap. I'll tell you about him another time,' smiled Enoch, 'I'm going to circulate. Catch you later.'

Cat looked about, wondering what sort of people would find themselves in this exclusive gathering. He spotted Barton on the edge of the group, correctly dressed of course, laughing with a man of a similar age who, although dressed as a Muslim in a finely embroidered shalwar kameez and white taqiyah, had within his hand a large, crystal-cut tumbler with a bahot burra peg of Scotch in it. They caught Cat's eye, so he made his way over to them, excusing himself as he appeared to barge people out of the way, the inevitable consequence of squeezing his large form through small gaps.

'Ah, Adam, the man of the hour!' Barton had plainly been drinking, but was not yet at the point of being drunk, 'Allow me to introduce you to Faiq Qifar, a good friend to the court. Faiq, this is Adam, an old, old school friend of ours.'

'Salaam alaikum, Mr. Adam' Faiq was tall, athletic, and had an enormous, rather beautiful smile.

'Wa 'alaikum al-salaam, sir' Cat felt instantly that he might be in the presence of one of nature's very few perfect specimens, and had to be careful not to give himself away with a nervous swallow, 'I shall be delighted if you will call me Cat.'

'Then I will be happy to delight you, Cat,' purred Faiq, 'and please please me similarly by calling me Faiq.'

'What do you do, Faiq?'

'I am a builder, Cat, nothing so grand as being a musician like yourself.'

Barton snorted, 'Calling yourself a builder is a little like the Archbishop of Canterbury calling himself a clergyman!'

'Well, I don't know about that, but thank you, old bean, anyway.'

Cat decided that Faiq's considerable charm was only possible because he was sober, and that the enormous measure of whiskey he clutched was so large only because he'd not drunk any of it. But he demonstrated otherwise, as he downed his drink in one, and deftly swapped it for another as a waiter fleetingly passed by carrying a tray. Cat attempted to do likewise, but missed, and was only relieved when Wigly followed on, begrudgingly handing Cat a glass of Champagne.

Cat attempted to offer his thanks, but the moment was lost in the cloud of ill-humour whipped up by Wigly's sharp about turn and retreat.

'That man will be a problem,' opined Faiq, 'you wait and see!'

'I know,' assented Barton, 'but it's difficult to know what to do about the situation. We can't just – you know...'

Cat did not know, and was not a little taken aback that this fragment of a conversation was being had within his hearing. It was true that he had known Barton for a long time, but they had never been friends of any sort, and they had had no contact with each other since school days, so functionally he felt like he was listening in on the conversation between two complete strangers.

'What is it that makes you an archbishop amongst builders, Faiq?'

'All things are relative, Cat, as you know – my family merely owns the largest construction company in this very small place. That's all. Hardly an archbishop. Let's settle for a dean!'

'Is it an old company?'

Barton, believing that his inestimable social skills had done the trick, took his leave, in order to seed a conversation elsewhere in the group.

'It is. In the glory days, my forebears built the palace we're standing in now, although you will have spotted, I'm confident, that the glory days have slipped by somewhat since.'

'It's fairly obvious!'

'Whilst our prominence within the State for so long has meant that my family have often been guests here in the palace we built, we have had to look on as the neglect of its maintenance has taken a hold, only able to step in to perform remedial works of an urgent nature (often at very reduced rates). However, we have survived as a company, exactly at the point when we might have found it difficult to continue here, because of the fortunate decision to build the new church.'

'Aha, so that was you,' Cat nodded, noting privately that this meant that Faiq was now in possession of what little money the State had had left. His perfection suddenly seemed a little tarnished.

'Well, someone had to complete it, I suppose. And it seemed fair it should be us, since it was the family firm which laid the foundations back in the fifties.'

'Mr. Qifar! I want a word with you...'

'Oh, lor'!' They were interrupted by a lady of ample girth, bearing down on them with a formidable sense of purpose. 'Watch out, it's the doctor,' Faiq muttered urgently.

'Yes, by god, it's the doctor, Mr. Qifar! And what is that doctors do? The treat sick people. And where do they treat sick people? In the clinic. And what does the clinic need? It needs beds and medicines. And where do the beds and medicines come from, Mr. Qifar? Huh?'

Faiq sucked in his cheeks and cast his eyes up towards the dark ceiling.

'Beds and medicines come from the simple conversion of money into goods, Mr. Qifar. And where does money come from? It comes from the zakat of the wealthiest person in the State. And where is the wealthiest person in the State right now? He is standing in front of me. And where is his zakat? It is still in his pocket, despite the promises he gave me several months ago. What do you have to say for yourself, you wretched little man.'

Cat was more than a little impressed by this lady, although he didn't feel able to agree that Faiq resembled anything close to being either wretched or little. He had watched her as she had torn a strip off him, and thought she was magnificent, dressed in a salmon-coloured sari over a blouse of broderie anglaise, which revealed beneath it hints of underwear such as a lady might wear on a whaling ship. She had on her forehead the customary tilaka of a Hindu woman, but not the perfectly formed circle of vermilion usually seen, rather she had an orange splash of what looked like dried tincture of iodine, carelessly administered not as an antiseptic, but as an adornment. And she was – Cat searched in vain for the right term, the correct, polite word to describe her most obvious physical quality – she was just extremely large.

'How do you do, Mr. Adam!' she turned on Cat as if he were the next duck along in a shooting range, and he found himself unable to respond in a timely fashion. 'I'm Doctor Rajmani, Vijinalakshmi Rajmani. You can call me Vij. You may not call me Vaj. What shall I call you? Come on, cat got your tongue?'

'Yes, that's right.'

'What's right?

'Cat.'

'Don't be silly, only a metaphor. It would be clinically very difficult if a cat actually got a man's tongue!'

'No, no, my name...'

'Yes yes, your name?'

'...is Cat. I'm Cat, Cat Adam.'

'Oh, I see. Well, I'd not expected that! You're not exactly feline in appearance, rather more elephantine, if you ask me.'

'Well, madam, if you don't mind me saying...'

'Oh, I know, I know. We fatties need to stick together. Take me to the drinks – let me take your arm. I'll see you again later, Mr. Qifar,' she hurled over her shoulder.

Cat was smitten.

'Is that shamps you're drinking? I'll have the same. Now, tell me all about yourself, Cat, and don't spare my blushes.'

If Dr. Rajmani had ever in her life blushed, it seemed to Cat that it would certainly have involved the telling of more scandalous tales than any he could draw upon in an account of his simple life. In any case, something about her suggested that candour was the order of the moment, that she would be able to discern the slightest falsehood, the most trivial overstatement, and that she would take far less kindly to this than to any historical moment of carelessness or moral lapse. So, as if involuntarily, the first thing he told her about himself was that he had eloped with his double bass, whereupon he unexpectedly found himself relieved of a burden of guilt he'd not even known he'd been carrying.

Having listened carefully to Cat's tale, Vij took him by both hands, drew him close toward her and looked unblinkingly into his eyes. 'I like a man for whom passion is life's great imperative. Without really *believing* in what we do, there's no point doing it, wouldn't you say?' she whispered confidentially.

'I, er, oh crikey… I think, er…' Cat was overwhelmed by the enveloping closeness of the contact he was enjoying as the doctor pressed against him. Her bosoms formed a welcoming cushion, and she smelled lightly of fenugreek, his favourite spice; he found not just that he had developed an erection, but that it was pressing firmly against her pudenda.

'Oh!' the doctor took in a short gasp of air, smiled slightly and spoke even more confidentially, 'that's very kind of you, Cat.'

'Y-y-you're welcome, I'm sure!' sweated Cat.

'And I perceive we are about the same height!'

Ajaz commanded the assembly to take their seats at the table, and Cat didn't know whether to be dismayed or relieved. He was, however, astonished to realise that he had forgotten he was hungry, despite it being his permanent condition. Vij turned him out of her clutch and re-took his arm, at a more appropriate distance, in a single action, as a mother might manoeuvre a small child. 'Lead on, dear Cat,' she instructed, 'I hope we can continue our tête-à-tête later.'

As Cat escorted his new friend to her place at the table, the candles appeared to burn more intensely, and the whole room seemed brighter. He all but shouldered a waiting servant out of the way in order gallantly to assist with her chair himself. And whilst he was to be seated beside the Rajah in the centre of the table at one side, she had been placed on the far end of the other, so that he felt as he left her that he was the pebble in his old catapult, that the stretching rubber might at any moment propel him back towards her y-shaped stick.

The table stood as it waited for the Rajah to take his seat. 'Oh, do sit down, stop all that fuss!' he insisted, sitting first anyway.

Opposite Cat, partially obscured by the central candelabra, was Enoch, who leaned sideways to catch Cat's eye, before casting a look to Dr. Rajmani and back again, with his eyebrows raised in high arches. Cat shrugged, tried to look indifferent, became hungry, and introduced himself to the older gentleman sitting to his right, without hearing the name, which was lost not so much in the hubbub of the table, but in the lustful pounding of the blood in his ears.

'We've got something a bit different for you this evening,' said Hurree on Cat's left, 'seeings how you like your grub, what, Adam. Bet you've never eaten this stuff before.'

The room had been filling with servants, carrying small, domed serving plates, who each took up their stations beside one of the diners. Cat was impressed so far, and had high hopes for whatever new delight was about to be revealed. He glanced at the doctor, who was busy tucking her serviette into her cleavage, disappointed not to see his glowing smile reciprocated; he would try again later.

The room grew silent in anticipation. 'Voila!' commanded Ajaz, whereupon the lids were withdrawn synchronously, high into the air in an arc which took them away from the diners, and the plates advanced for admiring first glances to be taken. But for a slight snigger from Wigly, some way off, there was complete, uncomprehending silence.

Sitting on each plate was a small bread bun, which had been cut in half horizontally. Between the halves was a rectangle of what looked like a thin slice of grilled compressed minced meat, and a piece of pickled gherkin. Cat had never seen the like of it, and thought it might make a tasty morsel with which to start the banquet proper, a single mouthful at best. He hoped very much indeed that it was either that, or that it was a joke, because it certainly wouldn't do for dinner.

'Ta-da!' announced Ajaz, drolly and without enthusiasm, obeying an order with which he didn't agree. Cat looked across at Enoch and saw in his face puzzlement; this was something truly remarkable, an object about which he didn't know anything.

'The palace is pleased to be able to introduce you to *hamburgers*,' Ajaz continued, with a perfectly judged hint of insolence, at which he bowed solemnly and left the room.

After a pause, with some awkward looks exchanged, Hurree laughed loudly, and was joined distantly by the hyena Wigly. 'Oh, you chumps, don't look so dismayed! These are the latest thing in America - we discovered them on our trip last year, and we've been waiting for the right moment to introduce them to you all.'

'Why?' asked the anonymous gentleman to Cat's right, sternly.

'Because they're modern, uncle, they're the new thing, and we need to find the new thing in all we do from now on.'

'So this is what they call a hamburger,' nodded Enoch, revealing that he did know something about the subject after all.

'It is.'

'Hamburger?' interjected Faiq, 'you're giving us haram meat because it's modern?'

'Don't be crazy, Faiq, it's not pork. Obviously!'

'Then why's it called a hambugger?' objected the uncle.

'I believe, your highness,' interjected Enoch, 'that the term is a corruption of one applied formerly to an American dish which is presumed to have been first developed in Hamburg, and so it is more correctly burger than bugger.'

Wigly snorted hilariously at this, and caused heads to turn in his direction momentarily.

'Well that's a bloody silly thing if I ever heard it,' complained the uncle, picking his hamburger off the plate and eyeing it disdainfully. 'I hope it's not beef either?'

'No, of course it's not, uncle, we're not complete idiots!' objected Hurree.

'Well, what is it, then?'

'It's, uhm, I think it's lamb. Or is it goat?' Hurree turned to the servant beside him, who, in turn, felt unable to answer.

Prince Shankarrao, sitting beside Enoch, spoke for the first time, coolly and with an air of precision and authority, 'The introduction of misappropriated cultural novelties to provoke the illusory happiness of the people is the demand for their real happiness...'

'...hamburger as the opium of the masses,' assented Enoch, enjoying the Marxist reference, as it passed others by.

'Whatever's in it, I'll be damned if I'll eat it,' harrumphed the uncle, throwing his hamburger back, 'take it away, bearer.'

The uncle's servant hesitated, still holding the exposed plate before him, looking for a lead from the other servants,

'Didn't you hear me, you damned dolt, take it away!'

Barked at so fiercely, the servant replaced the dome and backed away from the table.

'You heard my uncle, take them all away,' commanded Shankarrao, 'take them all away instantly!'

'Oh, you chumps,' laughed Hurree nervously, 'we've got proper food, of course – go on, you men, take the hamburgers away and bring the next course out. Really, you asses, did you seriously think that was going to be dinner?'

One by one the servants returned the domes to their plates and withdrew from the table. Cat, during the distraction of Shankarrao's interjection, had managed quickly to down his morsel, and thought it remarkably tasty, but was pleased when his dome covered the empty plate lest it be considered that he had behaved inappropriately. He glanced over at the doctor, who was dabbing her mouth with her napkin, clearly also having just managed to down hers in the nick of time. She glanced back at Cat now, nodding her approval of the new-fangled food as she pouted at him.

15

During my short time in DM, I came to confront a commanding but simple truth, one which had been eluding me simply because I'd been looking the other way; it was like an over-energetic child playing hide and seek whom nobody comes to find. It was that, whilst I had proudly considered myself an expert in the history of DM, I was in fact a historian of the place around 1947, and only then, when the Republics of India and Pakistan were founded and this tiny spot was dusted off the map. In every other respect I was largely in the dark. The seed of this realisation had been sown subliminally in the helicopter, and it began to sprout later as I pondered further my ignorance of the existence of an early-modern fort on the western edge of the chersonese. It is the inevitable consequence of doctoral research that you come to know more and more about less and less. That's well known, but it hardly excuses the arrogance of my initial response. The only small comfort that I could find in this self-awakening was that it was perfectly acceptable for me to know so little about Uncle Cat's time here.

Rudge: How do I define history? It's just one fucking thing after another.

Thus Alan Bennett nails it in *The History Boys*; you can't know a historical period without knowing something of the period which preceded it. And, indeed, I did know something about the state of Dusa Mathavasi before 1947, but not much, and only by way of background to the period I had been researching. Looking back now, I can see that the reason why I didn't come here to find out more, during my doctoral studies, was because of my personal insecurities, and yet my youthful cockiness. Frankly, I was all thought and no action – a coward. It had seemed then that it was a far away and dangerous place which I would be better to avoid, and that it was possible to do that because I was able to mine the archive remotely, thanks to Sammy's people being so cooperative. And, let us be quite clear about this, I knew that what I was doing was going to be satisfactory for the purposes of my doctorate, because I was sure that no-one knew any better, so wouldn't question the evidence I was producing.

I'm not the only person to feel that his doctorate was a bit of a fluke – this is a commonplace, I have found – but, by the simple fact of being here, I had been confronted with the realisation that, as flukes go, mine was amongst the flukiest there had ever been. (This is an admission which I make here, at least in part, to prepare the ground to reveal how my unearthly stupidity was shortly to be exposed, with life-changing consequences.)

So, with a day wholly to myself coming up, I decided that it was time to dive into the palace archives, to learn something of the history of the state before 'my period', with the hope especially that I would find there the shade of Uncle Cat, perhaps some empirical evidence of his appointment as a court musician, the circumstances of his contract, his remuneration, and so on.

That the DM archive existed I knew, obviously, but I didn't know where it was or who was the archivist, so I did the simple thing and asked the Yuvraj, up on the roof the evening before, whether I might have access and how to gain it. Now, Sammy is an amiable bloke and, as I had witnessed, a competent organiser of the world around him, so I had expected him to say that I would be welcome to look at anything I wanted, and that I would find it situated in room *x* on floor *y* of the palace. In fact, he became quite blank, being himself unable to think where it was. He consulted Arabella (who for a moment seemed to fit the stereotype of the wife who knows where her husband's socks are), who said that there was a room set aside in the palace, where new documents were being filed already, but that none of the old documents had been transferred over from the original site. Indeed, she thought it possible that so completely had everyone's attention been directed to the commissioning of the new palace, that very few people could have even entered the old archive since I had been asking questions about it for my research, nearly ten years before. I was welcome to look at anything I wanted, Sammy confirmed, but he would have to find out where it was and would let me know in the morning.

Thus, I awoke fearing there was a danger I would have nothing to do that day should Sammy fail to send the information I needed. I was fully aware that, in the scheme of things, this was a real possibility, as it was an unimportant matter for him compared to the task of running DM PLC. Mildly panicked, I was confronted with the possibility of being a long way from home with no diversion, and it occurred to me that low level anxiety such as this might well be the basis for what we know commonly as homesickness.

Lakshmi was attentive and helpful, as usual, bringing me a fine breakfast, which I stood to eat, looking again over the wooded area around the reservoir. Since first seeing it, I had decided it was inconceivable that I had ever claimed to have known really anything at all about DM, without understanding this as a physical feature. Its presence spoke so eloquently about the history and development of the place, about how the water it had brought must have changed into the beginnings of a city what can have been nothing more than an encampment, how agriculture could have flourished, how the first palace could have existed only because of it, how the British were interested in DM (which gave rise, presumably, to the practise of educating the Rajahs in England and creation of an Anglophone upper-class, and why, in the spirit of Rudge, I was here at all).

I will make it the object of further researches in due course to establish why the British walked away, and left the Rajah to his own destiny. But today, looking over this land-far-from-home, I was feeling diminished, both academically and personally.

I began to develop an emergency plan-of-action, to walk westwards to see the site of the fort and take some pics, before the airport development obliterated everything. I knew it would be hot, but I reasoned that if I walked through the side streets off the main boulevard, I could keep mainly to the shadows, and I might also expect to see some of the local colour which, perhaps, Cat could have known. The whole city couldn't yet have been turned into a living, breathing Bicester Village? I was also mindful of the armed guards which Ali insisted we had with us at all times, but thought that he was much more likely to be a target for terrorists than me, given the lifestyle he was known to enjoy as a playboy Muslim, and that I could pass more or less anonymously through the back streets, even if I was perhaps the only white face amongst the crowd. Whatever the difficulties, I knew that if I didn't get out and do something – anything – I stood a very good chance of finding out more about my insecurities than I felt I needed to know.

So, having made what felt like a momentous decision, that it was time for me to be brave, I was almost disappointed when I received a WhatsApp from Sammy, giving me the info I needed about the archive. This very quickly gave way to delight, joy even, because I could concentrate on doing history, the thing I knew I was good at, and save being brave until later. Lakshmi returned soon afterwards with a key – the key to the play chest! – and a hand-drawn map of how to find the building which housed the archive.

I left the palace by the front door, very grandly, but wondering briefly whether I would need some sort of a pass to get back in. The guards all seemed very relaxed and informal, as if being tough was for them something of a mask they wore. One of them even pointed me in the location shown on my map, with a smile and what I took to be words of encouragement.

I walked a short way down the central boulevard before turning right, to the west, where the world around me changed dramatically within half a block. Behind all the new-build lining the main drag was exactly the sort of urban space I imagined Cat could have known, with narrow, shadowy lanes separating buildings in what I will describe as a vernacular style; low-rise, flat-roofed, the more recent ones roughly made in block work, others made from what I took to be locally-made bricks, and all of them with a tendency to wear a patina of dark mould. I will aim one day to research the hypothesis I formed as I walked, that the clay for the older bricks came from the excavations for the reservoir.

Many of the buildings were live-work premises, with open frontages, where it looked like every trade and service could be found, from a haircut to a re-bore, and many of the shiny-plastic-covered things you might buy from the stores along the boulevard were available here straight from the sack/barrel/crate. The bustle, the noise, the crowding were all remarkable and, in their own way, rather exhilarating.

When I reached it, I found that the archive was in a building in wretched condition, and that this was characteristic of the square on which it stood. The alleyway I had walked down emerged into this relatively open space, where dereliction had reached the point when someone had begun to do something about it. In particular, opposite where I had entered was a long hoarding, the full length of the square, with, according to the developers' board, work going on to convert the shell behind it into modern apartments. And the someone who had made this beginning? It was Ali's dad; the developers in question were the Qifars. They were going to turn this neo-gothic facade into *Zee House*, a suite of ten yuppy flats, complete with gym and indoor swimming pool. Where were the buyers going to come from? It had to be the case, surely, that the other buildings around the square would follow in short order, if these apartments were to make good money? It was the dynamic process of redevelopment in practice, laid out for all to witness, local history in the making.

The door to the archive creaked open, in a manner as gothic as the facade opposite, and I found myself alone in a dusty, shadowy, exhausted space, with rough, creaking wooden floorboards, spiders' webs, lizards and, well, I chose not to worry about what else lived there! It had clearly once been a respectable house, laid out in separate rooms accordingly, each one packed with ancient, rickety, wooden shelving units, loaded with bundles of documents in parchment folders tied with ribbons. I hesitated to throw back the shutters, in case they fell off their hinges, but it would have been too dark otherwise to read. Disorientated by the sudden quietness, I sat at the wobbly desk in the front room, causing a puff of dust to rise around me, gazed around at the disorder, thought of the un-mined knowledge which it contained, and bliss descended upon me.

16

Eyes firmly closed, Cat lay uncomfortably in his bed the next morning, his barely-wakeful state a reminder-to-self that, with only a moderate amount of effort, further sleep might still be had. He grunted as he rolled onto his front, onto the great bulk of his form, and pressed down with his forehead and feet so that he could create an arc of sorts with his body, which would in turn allow his engoncé manhood to hang vertically downwards. Thus he could unsnarl himself from the surrounding folds of tissue formed at the confluence of belly and legs. It was a familiar, practised manoeuvre which, he had always assumed, was known to all fat men, and one he could complete whilst still nearly asleep. Further snoozing tended to follow, enhanced by the greater ease of disentanglement.

As he arched, the unexpected cupping of his testicles by a hand which was not his own shoved him unambiguously out onto the open plains of wakefulness, with an accompanying cry which came from the old brain, combining the shock of the unexpected with a primordial dread of castration. The first fully-formed thought which he could identify was that there was now no chance of further sleep, the second was that he must have got lucky last night, and the third that it was with the doctor that he'd drunkenly wandered back to his bungalow.

'Good morning, big boy,' purred Dr. Rajmani beside him, in confirmation.

Cat could maintain the extreme strain of his arched position no longer, and felt Vij's arm trapped beneath him as he gave way, her hand relaxing its grip just in time to avert an disaster. He turned his head and opened his eyes, to see beside him a woman smiling broadly and happily, and he felt a surge of joy wash over him. Glimpsed memories of the night began to return.

'Crikey,' he grinned, 'and good morning yourself!'

'Well, I must say, Cat Adam,' continued Vij in pillow-tones so intimate that she might merely have been thinking what he heard, 'you're a very fat man, and I'm a very fat woman, and together we had a very fat fuck.'

'I seem to think...' Cat could get no further momentarily, whilst a broad grin spread across his face as the memory of the night returned more fully, '...that we were engaged in passionate love-making for most of the night.'

'You can call it passionate love-making if you wish, Cat, but I call it a big fat fuck, and as I lie here beside you,' she brought her ample leg up over him and drew herself closer to him, 'I feel utterly fucked in the most gorgeous fucking way.'

Cat tittered, 'Is this the formal medical term?'

She grinned and pecked him on the lips, 'you need to get off my arm, you great lump, because I have to inspect your facilities.'

With some effort, they negotiated their separation and Vij slid out from under the mosquito net and off the bed. Cat watched her folds bounce as she eased herself into the upright, noticed that her enormous breasts were astonishingly self-supporting, observed the thick, black bush of her pubic hair, glistening a little with sweat, and felt a surge of desire overcome him. She was the most wonderfully womanly woman he'd ever seen, he thought, watching her disappear in the direction of the thunderbox, as naked and unashamed as the day she was first squeezed into this world as an oversized baby.

Several minutes of very audible ablutions followed, which caused Cat to reflect on some of the very few words of wisdom to come from his peculiarly buttoned-up father, that 'you're not properly a married couple until you can fart in front of each other'. How quickly this uninhibited woman had arrived at this point, he mused, not a little excited, and as she returned he announced that further fat fucking would be a very good thing, casting back the sheet to reveal his readiness.

'Uh-uh, big boy,' she smiled, 'not now.'

'Aw, come on!' he whined.

'No no no! I've got a clinic to open, and you've got to start rehearsing with Mr. da Costa.'

'I'd rather you come back to bed than...' Cat stopped short. 'What do you mean I've got to start rehearsing with Enoch?'

'You don't remember?' laughed Vij, 'Well you really were laced last night, weren't you!'

'Apparently so!'

'You agreed to give a recital together when the bishop comes from Karachi to consecrate the church. Do you really not remember?'

'Oh, lor, I do, slightly. Oh cripes. When is it?'

'Twenty-somethingth.'

'At least that gives us a bit of time, I suppose. What are we going to play?'

'I don't know! You were going to discuss the programme this morning, over breakfast. Look, I've got to go, dear Cat...'

'But I want breakfast with you!'

'I'll have to pick up something from the kitchens, I'm late. But we can have dinner if you like?'

Cat beamed, 'Yes, I like very much.'

'Bhavya! Come and meet me when my clinic finishes. Five o'clock.' Vij, having thrown on her sari as they talked, paused as she reached the door, 'It's too early to be sure, Cat Adam, but I have a feeling about us – and I'm not talking about the one between our legs.'

Cat was well aware that love, like chamber music, needs practice, so that players can learn to play *in d'accordo*, and it would be a very foolish musician who declared himself ready for performance after just one session. But he felt a strong sense that here was music worth the rehearsal.

And he was also becoming aware that there was a fart-within which had developed a life of its own, and wouldn't be contained for much longer.

Under circumstances such as these, with almost any other woman, he would at that moment have clenched hard to prevent its release, but he felt emboldened by Vij's extravagantly uninhibited noisiness on the thunderbox, and let it go, a great, rasping, bubbling release. It was, by any standards, a magnificent fart, but so loud that he worried that he'd gone a little far, that it might have been better to have hung on just that moment more until Vij had left the bungalow fully.

'Thaar he blooows!' roared the doctor, as she stepped over the threshold, 'In both senses, better out than in, kya!'

He listened to her untidy foot fall as she walked away towards the palace, and found that, with each tread, a flush of anxiety washed through his gut. The calm of being not alone, which he'd last felt the day before Mariah walked away, had woken with him this joyful morning, yet already it began to fade as he peered up into the gloomy vault of his sagging mosquito net. It came as some paradoxical relief, therefore, when he became distracted by the growing certainty that that fart had been the start of a process, not the end, and that the need to reach his thunderbox was pressingly urgent. He cast back the net and made his own naked dash for the veranda, hoping both that he would get to it in time, and that there would be no-one about – especially not Indira – to see him in this exposed state.

In his haste, he caught a final, thrilling glimpse of Vij's wide back as she disappeared through the entrance into the palace yard, and as he pulled Parvati's case around him and slumped on the thunderbox, his head was full of her. At first, he didn't hear Enoch singing *Rejoice greatly, O daughter of Zion*, but the music filtered through eventually, followed by the sound of the splashing of water, and Cat realised that it was bath time once more. He tidied himself up and crept back into the bungalow to prepare to meet his friend at the water's edge.

'Aha, good morning, you rutting *Hippopotamus adamibus* you,' Enoch broke off in the middle of a florid run, 'in you come, wash those sins away!'

'I don't believe I've sinned in the slightest,' sniffed Cat as he dropped his kaftan to the ground and waded into the lake, 'I had, in fact, a very beautiful night with a very lovely woman.'

'Well, I'm very pleased for you, my dear friend. It wasn't an outcome that I'd anticipated, she being, what shall we say...?'

'Let me say now, quite clearly, that I am going to require you to say only good things about her. I can't stop you thinking what you will, but I don't want to hear it. Is that clear?'

'Oh, Cat, how could you! I am a great admirer of Dr. Rajmani, a selfless woman dedicated to the care of her patients, and a woman of clear intellect who has no need to be in this wretched backwater. What I was going to say was that you and she getting together wasn't an outcome I'd anticipated, because she's a woman of great discernment. My intention, which I now see was inappropriate, was only to josh you in a well-natured manner. If you had a good time, then no-one could be happier for you than myself.'

'Gracious of you to say so,' Cat gulped, moved. He resisted the urge to blurt out that he was wholly in love, a confession which seemed likely to result in a second attempt to tease, and one with more justification. 'Anyway, to change the subject, I understand that we are to perform when a bishop from somewhere or other comes to bless the church, or something like that?'

'My my, Cat, we did have a skin full, didn't we!'

'Yes, we did, don't remind me. Well, actually, you better had remind me!'

'To be precise, the Bishop of Karachi will be arriving on the twenty-third, resting the night and consecrating the church the next day, Sunday the twenty-fourth. It has been decided that there should be some entertainment for the poor, hapless man on the Saturday evening, and that that entertainment should be provided by you and me.'

'So what are we going to do, put on red noses and oversized shoes? I can't juggle!'

'I rather think that's something like what Wigly was implying when he made the suggestion.'

'Wigly!' Cat frowned, 'What's he got to do with it?'

'You might very well furrow your brow,' nodded Enoch, 'especially as I think he made the suggestion as a jape, confirming that he considers you and me to be mere entertainment. He expected to create a moment of great amusement and, I daresay, to garner eagerly sought plaudits from his *special friend*, but His Highness instead thought it a jolly good idea. He has, in short, commanded you – he seems to be warming to the idea of having a Master of Music – to perform.'

'Oh lor!'

'Oh lor, indeed. It was your idea that I should join you in this venture, and that together we should give a short recital in the church.'

'On a harmonium and double bass? Seriously?'

'Ah, but of the finer things in life these people know nothing - *omne ignotum pro magnifico*!'

'Tacitus?'

'My dear Cat, well done!'

'Don't patronise me, Enoch - it's always Tacitus with you.'

Enoch paused, unsure if this was true, and troubled that he might be becoming predictable. He rinsed his hair, shaking his head like a drenched dog as he surfaced. 'So, we will get to do the Dittersdorf, then.'

Cat sat heavily down in the water and contemplated for a moment. He adored playing the Dittersdorf, and would enjoy the preparation very much. So would Parvati, he thought; it was a piece they'd played together several times. And this would cement his role as Master of the Rajah's Music, without question, thus arming him further against the advances of the Trustees. So, in itself, it seemed to be a reasonable proposition, assuming that *The New Mozart* was as good as he claimed, that he could actually reduce the orchestral score in his head. But a single concerto didn't make a recital.

'What else are you suggesting we play?'

'Well, I thought I might compose a piece for double bass and harmonium…'

'Harmonium, for god's sake!' tutted Cat.

'Might I remind you that Rossini, a composer of infinite wit and clarity, scored his great *péché de vieillesse*, the exquisite *Petite Messe Solennelle*, for harmonium.'

'As it happens, Enoch, that is a piece I know well, and it *also* has two pianos.' Cat remembered watching Mariah playing one of them in a performance early in their relationship, wondering at the strength of her playing as she competed with the bloody harmonium. 'Two!'

'Indeed, indeed. I am found out! Nonetheless, we have at our disposal a harmonium and a double bass, and we need to make the best of it. Oh, and I thought I would sing a couple of arias as well.'

'You're going to sing? What are you going to sing?'

'If you were able to accompany me, I thought I'd sing the *Königin der Nacht* arias - you brought them to mind when we were in the church.'

'Look, Enoch, singing as a male soprano is one thing,' Cat complained, not entirely sure it was actually a thing at all in the real world, 'but the Queen of the Night? You can't be serious, you just can't have the notes, surely?'

'I specialise in high coloratura parts, as it happens.'

Cat took a deep breath, 'You can't be a specialist in everything, Enoch, it would make you a generalist.'

'Well, that rather depends on your frame of reference. Anyway, in answer to your question, yes, I have got the notes…' upon which Enoch expanded his puny ribcage and launched into an ascending scale which took him into the highest range of the human voice.

Birds in the trees fled their perches, creating a flurry of movement in the canopy above which disturbed Cat, as it appeared almost that Enoch's voice had given rise to a great, unearthly wind. And to add to the effect, as he held the highest point in his scale, he raised his arms to the horizontal, dripping water, whereupon the reflection of the sun on his wet skin made him look like he'd been rendered in marble, that he had become a baroque fountain.

'There, see, no problem,' grinned Enoch smugly, as he relaxed his position.

Indira came running round the corner from the bungalows, breathlessly, fearing some terrible event had given rise to what she evidently considered to be a dreadful scream. 'Sahib - oh, Sahib - you ok - oh, Sahib!'

Cat fell back onto the water to conceal his torso from her sight.

Her voice trilled in panic, and it was all Enoch could do to command her with gestures not to enter the water to save him.

'Oh, Sahib,' she continued, 'you make bhayahnak shor!'

'Bhayahnak shor?' Enoch was clearly hurt by this lay assessment of his high coloratura, 'terrible noise, indeed!'

Cat's feelings about Indira took a sharp turn for the better, as he stifled his grin. 'We'll be fine now, Indira,' he swallowed a chuckle, 'Mr. da Costa and I will take breakfast together on my veranda this morning. We have things to discuss.'

'Oh, yes, Sahib, yes, I bring now. Oh, Sahib - oh, Sahib,' she continued muttering, shaking her head, as she scurried away from them.

'So we have two weeks, then,' Cat returned to the subject of the moment. 'It should be enough, if you're sure you can play from the orchestral score.'

'I am sure,' Enoch was still puffing indignantly over Indira's reaction, 'quite sure! And how about you, Cat? Can you play the Queen's arias on a harmonium?'

'What does it matter? As you said, omne ignoramus magnificent sunt!'

17

Situated within the delightful surroundings of a rickety old house full of dusty documents, unread for decades, I found myself in a reflective mood about the origin of the word *archive*. I had Jacques Derrida's *Archive Fever* to thank for a piece of information which, until now, I had considered useless, that the term derives from the Greek *ἀρχεῖον*, the dwelling place of an *arkhon*, the person who governs, who makes the law, circularly by dint of being in possession of the archive.

The term *mon-archy* ('rule by one') derives from the same source, and it dawned on me that far from sitting amongst merely a cacophony of primary sources, I was in fact located within the very seat of power for the rajahs of DM, the pedigree for their absolute, monarchical rule. It was their equivalent of Yggdrasil, the sacred ash tree in Asgard, which keeps Odin in the top job.

In practice, this positioned the archive as the authoritative, material source of law, the place where precedents were established in a system of rule without any other form of judicial establishment, and it seemed paradoxical, negligent even, that the Yuvraj hadn't known where it was. I suppose the Rajah himself probably knew, but as a functioning part of government it had apparently fallen into abandonment before Sammy had taken up the reigns. It would be the right thing to do, at least as a symbol of power, to relocate it within the new palace, DM's own *arkheion*.

But where was I to begin? I didn't know what was important because I didn't know what was there, yet I couldn't possibly read everything here in order to find out, given the short time I was going to be in DM. I knew I was interested in the creation of the reservoir, in the transfer of power from Hari to Shankarrao in Cat's time, in Cat's presence itself, and the Qifars. It was self-evidently a family which exerted some influence in the state, whether formally, like Ali's dad as divan, or informally, as in the way the young people seemed to defer to Ali. In addition, just minutes before, I had seen plain evidence of its involvement commercially, in the ongoing development of the city's infrastructure. And its cultural importance in building the mosque was beyond doubt.

My starting point was to be 1924, however, when I knew Cat was here, that being my reason for being in DM at all. If I learned nothing else in this web-strewn treasury, I needed to glean all that I could about him. And it became a rivetingly brief search, since there was nothing about him to be found. It crossed my mind that if my great-great-uncle had wanted to 'disappear' with his double bass (which is essentially what he did), he could have done worse than pick the most remote of all the Indian princely states, written letters which purported to have come from there (and who back then in Surrey would check?), and headed off in the opposite direction. As red herrings go, this would have been a magnificent kipper.

But there was a problem, in the form of the absence of evidence for the lack of evidence. It's wasn't just that I could find no trace of Uncle Cat, there was nothing about the actual Master of Music, the real post-holder at the time. I could find no record of a Morris being registered, neither was there any mention of anything or anyone else who was here because, for a period of three years, there were virtually no records of what had happened at the court, dating from the death of Rajah Gurvir to the accession of his second son, Rajah Shankarrao. You can never completely eliminate the trail of a human life in history, as shadows are always cast, and the reality of Hari's existence could be seen in his birth record, some school reports and, crucially, a document which referred to the decree declaring him rajah, but beyond that his adult life was gone and, with it, any trace of his brief rule. In other words, Rajah Hari was missing from the archive, he had been rendered absent, condemned to *damnatio memoriae*, along with all the people who served him. If Sammy hadn't told me about his existence, one night all those years ago down in The Kiln, I would never have known anything about him.

This was an extraordinary discovery, which, as discussed above, I would later find was mirrored by the erasure of Enoch da Costa from the ICS records. It raised very serious questions about what had actually happened in those three years – there must, I presume, have been an unconscionable occurrence, so dreadful that the culture of 1924 couldn't bear it. It goes without saying, naturally, that this historian intends to return to this area of research at a later date.

Meanwhile, unable to decide which of the Qifar family or the reservoir I was more interested in, I tossed a coin and it fell in the water. This meant that I had to go to the oldest part of the archive, supporting my hypothesis that it was the water that made the state.

The very earliest records were in Persian/Urdu, as they would be in a place where the English connection was yet to be forged, and I was obliged to place those aside as yet another regrettable example of the limits of my scholarship. However, what I did find in English was lucid, and explained both the water *and* the Qifars. The British, looking to establish themselves in DM, sought permission from the owners of the chersonese to develop the reservoir. The owners were a noble Rajput family who had been given this useless, arid spit of land a century before by the Mughal Emperor as his very modest reward for their Hindu loyalty. This was the same family who now claimed royal descent, Sammy's forebears; that much I knew already. What I didn't know is that, in exchange for concessions (historically, how they had always operated), the British turned over a large sum of money to that family, who put out to tender the task of digging the reservoir, which tender was won by one Mehmet Qifar, an enterprising but otherwise undistinguished individual from Lahore. He moved west, organised the labour he needed and, physically, created the state as we know it. So the Qifars and the Rajahs are both founding fathers, both going back to the origins of of Dusa Mathavasi in the first quarter of the nineteenth century.

The first Qifar, I learned, already had on his shoulders a very astute head for business because, in addition to the large amounts of money which passed through his hands as he dug the reservoir, the contract specified that his family would have the exclusive development rights in DM *in perpetuity*! Whilst this was undoubtedly a visionary clause from his point of view, it looks like stupefying carelessness on the part of the first rajah who, I have to assume, had neither the wit nor experience to realise what it meant. The effect was to set in place the potential for a dislocation of power in a manner which brought to mind the rocky dealings between King John and the Barons, but for the reduced scale and the fact that I could find no trace of DM's equivalent of *magna carta*. In a state where governance is still by *vis et voluntas*, it paved the way for the *force* to come from a different estate than the *will*, with the Hindu rajahs wholly dependent on the support and money of the Muslim Qifars, monarchy v. monopoly.

This was an astonishing discovery, made all the more remarkable by one of the earliest post-WW2 documents, from 1946, in which one Faiq Qifar writes a letter of reply to Rajah Shankarrao, stating that he is prepared to return to DM now 'on the same terms as existed before you exiled me in 1924', with the assurance that he will be a loyal servant of the rajahate. It seems this return became a possibility only after the death of Prince Airavata, the Rajah's uncle, all of which rather suggests that the Qifars were in some way implicated in the dark deeds which led to Rajah Hari's downfall.

I note also that the full modernisation and development of DM, which began in earnest only after the war, happens, then, to coincide with the return of the Qifars, and I am sorely tempted by the error of considering the *post hoc ergo propter hoc* fallacy a certainty!

It was growing dark and there were no lights in the building (indeed, there was no electricity). This had been my best day in DM by far, and I wandered contentedly back, knowing no more about Uncle Cat but at least beginning to understand the materiality and substance of the streets through which I walked.

On the palace roof that evening, I was surprised to find a cluster of four older men amongst the jolly youth, all of them looking rather serious. Three of them were white, making the group stand out even more. And when one of them addressed me directly I suppose I should have taken that as a sign that I knew him; it was the neighbour I'd been drinking gin with on the flight to Karachi. I realised when I recognised him that these must be the journalists whom Ali had gone to collect.

Alban: (cheerily) Hey, Philip – Dr. Adam – great to see you!

Me: (failing to remember his name) Good heavens, er, what's a nice boy like you…

He had the good grace to laugh at this patently ridiculous gambit, which would certainly have needed us both to have been pie-eyed to have been even slightly amusing for real.

Alban: Work, as usual! Pleased to see you, been wondering how you'd been getting on.

Me: You didn't say you were coming here?

Alban: Didn't know myself, suddenly got word from the office that the situation'd changed.

Me: (remembering his name) Yes, Alban, I see.

Alban: Given us very nice rooms here in the palace.

Me: Us?

Alban: Yeah, other guys're hacks too.

Me: What situation has changed?

Alban: (distracted) Oh, we're being summoned. Come and meet the others.

I followed him over to the journalists, where introductions were made, and to the fourth member of the group who was none other than Razi Qifar, Ali's dad. I thought him very severe indeed, very sober. His son, in a cluster opposite, was very merry. I was intrigued as to why Qifar *père* was here up here with Alban and his colleagues, and would have made enquiries had I not been called away (irresistibly) by Lulu, who emerged siren-like from Ali's group and beckoned me over.

Thereafter, the evening passed in a very jolly manner, with much laughter, and before I could return to the glum bunch, they'd all disappeared, destined for their grown-ups' early nights.

18

Cat was distracted.

He had agreed with Enoch that they would travel down to the church together at two o'clock that afternoon, in order to begin rehearsing for the bishop's recital. That would give him time to organise himself after breakfast, and to eat lunch-part-one at least, before setting off.

Parvati was Cat's greatest worry for the time being, and at the heart of his concern was the matter of how he was going to transport her to the church. There was no question, realistically, of moving her in her plywood case, any more than there once had been on a day to day basis in London; whilst a student, Cat had managed to move her around in her soft case with *merely* the greatest difficulty, because his walk to and from the Tube was short at each end of the journey, and between stops she nestled comfortably in the space by the connecting door at the end of the carriage. But the problem with the soft case was that its handles were badly placed, unsurprisingly given the impossibility of enclosing such an awkward shape in what was essentially just an ill-fitting canvas bag, never quite right to establish an equilibrium, to find the centre of balance. Cat had learned that the easiest way to carry a double bass, by far, was uncovered, when it became possible to carry her on edge, passing his carrying arm between the strings and the body and hooking his fingers under the C-bout. But he had never carried her outside through the streets of London in that undignified manner, and he certainly wasn't going to do it here, in addition to which the direct sun, away from the moderating effect of the lake, would undoubtedly put her in danger of splitting.

There was no choice, therefore; Parvati would have to travel in the soft case, and she would have to do so with minimal exposure to the midday sun. But it was, without question, too far for Cat to carry her alone, and he would have to enlist some help, so he asked Ajaz to provide him with a pair of lackeys.

'I perceive problem, Sahib,' nodded Ajaz, 'yes, can send coolies to carry, will also send kittysol bearers.'

Cat, not knowing what Ajaz had meant, concluded that the servant had somehow confused his name, cat for kitty, and that he was going to have some special mode of transport provided solely for him, but didn't seek further explanation since it hadn't appeared to have been an act of deliberate insolence. English, after all, wasn't the poor man's first language.

He took Parvati into his arms, checked her tuning, and began to play mournful minor scales. 'You see, my love, I think I'm going to have to leave you locked up in the church between rehearsals,' he ground the bow into the open E string, making her boom, 'I know, I know, but it won't be safe for you to move through the city every day, and I'll find a shady corner where you can stand. And I'll be back every day to be with you. I promise it's for the best.'

But for the first time in their lives together, Cat wasn't being wholly honest with Parvati. Whilst it was undoubtedly true that remaining at the church, in the shade, was absolutely the best thing for an antique wooden box of delicate construction, it was also true that he was anticipating spending a lot of time with Vij, to be spending it intimately moreover, and that he felt embarrassed to have to account, even to himself, for his relationship with two female entities. To divert himself, he rooted through his pile of useful stuff to unearth his dog-eared copy of the Dittersdorf concerto, the heavily-used condition of which gave him much satisfaction, and he went to the veranda where he extracted the soft case from where it lay in guard over his pile of cash, wondering briefly what secure alternative arrangement there might be.

As he struggled to squeeze Parvati into her case, there was a delicate knock at the door, and Indira announced with her vanishing voice, 'I bring food for you, Sahib, burra plate you ask for.'

Cat was very hungry by now, and so he sat on his veranda to eat lunch with some urgency, despite being a little disturbed by the breeze coming off the lake, which carried with it wafting reminders of the close proximity of his thunderbox. He realised that he had never seen it emptied, although every day it clearly had been, and concluded that it must be a matter of palace etiquette that privies were never dealt with in the presence of the principal user. It was all very well, good practice to be sure, enabling a chap to forget about all that sort of stuff, but a nuisance when he'd been in all morning, thereby delaying the carrying out of this vital service. But what a horrid task it had to be for the poor wretches whose duty it was; best not hang around the bungalow all morning again.

Enoch emerged from the palace yard, in his work uniform, the customary white suit and sola topee. He was grinning to himself, walking jauntily.

'What ho, old chap!' Cat greeted him, 'Why are you looking so pleased with yourself?'

'I've had a good morning at work, my dear Cat, is why.'

'Work? What have you done for 'work' this morning?'

'I've been to the telegraph station, whence I sent a communication.'

'The telegraph station? What telegraph station? Where is it? Who runs it?'

'Eastern Telegraph, obviously. Down to the coast road and turn right, it's right at the far end, way out of the city, by the river. A tonga ride.'

'Ooh, can I send cables home?' Cat became excited, having it in mind to send details of the upcoming concert back to his parents and to the Academy, as a means of underlining the veracity of his claim to be Master of the Rajah's Music.

'It's not really a proper station as such, just a relay base, and it's not available to the general public to use.'

'I say, steady on, I'm not the general public, you know!'

'No, sorry, Cat, I have special access because of my position. That's an end to it.' Enoch was unexpectedly firm on the matter.

'Well, I think you're being a cad! Anyway, what sort of a message were you sending?'

'I sent a diptel, of course.'

'A what? What's a dip tell?'

'I think you can work that out yourself, dear Cat!'

'But I thought the whole point of being diplomatic,' Cat peered over the top of his glasses, 'was that you didn't tell!'

Enoch sighed. 'The engineer there tells me the mail ship will be docking in the next day or two, so if you write in time, you can post a letter home.'

'Well, that's just beastly unfair, if you ask me. Anyway, who is this engineer? Why haven't I met him?'

'Old Mr. Davidson. He lives alone. Very alone. By choice. But that's a story for another time.'

'You keep doing that!'

'Doing what?'

'You keep starting to tell me stories, but never finish. It's always for later!'

'What do you mean? What stories have I not finished?'

'Well, how about *The New Mozart*, since I'm about to rehearse with him? You said it was a story which had something to do with you being here.'

'Ah, yes, so I did. But lo, here come the bearers to help you take your double bass to the church.'

'How did you know I'd asked for help?'

'Oh, come now, Cat, you do know that I know everything, don't you?'

The bearers were, in fact, four of the decrepit guards who generally loitered around by the front gate, recognisable from their livery, although having left their ancient rifles behind. Two of them carried large canvas umbrellas, but of the special transport Ajaz had mentioned, Cat could see no sign.

'H'm,' grumbled Cat, 'Ajaz said something about transport or something, except he referred to me as Kitty, which I thought strange. Anyway, I don't see anything.'

Enoch peered at the bearers, wondering what Cat was referring to. 'Kitty? Ah, kittysol, by any chance? Did he say kittysol?'

'Might have done...'

'Oh, it's fascinating how antique words persist when they become loan words in another language,' Enoch beamed with delight. 'Kittysol is an old word from the Spanish for 'escape the sun' and listen, I'm going to define it by reference to another loan word, parasol, from the Italian, noting that both terms derive ultimately from the Latin for sun, *sol*, and reminding you that, as the great William Jones of Bengal established, Indo-European languages have the same root, so that it can hardly come as a surprise to you that the hindoostani word *suree* is clearly connected. How marvellous!'

'Um, Enoch, before you carry on...'

'Yes?'

'...are you saying that Ajaz was just talking about those umbrellas'?

'Well, yes, in the simplest terms, yes he was, but just consider...'

'Enoch...'

'Yes?'

'...do shut your cake-hole, there's a good fellow.'

Enoch pouted, cut off in full flow, whilst Cat slid Parvati's bow into the pocket which ran the length of the fingerboard, buckling the strap and making sure everything else was ready to go. Two of the bearers were instructed as to the best way to carry her – flat – whilst the other two created an effective shield with their kittysols, and the party set off.

'So, you were saying,' Cat broke the silence between him and Enoch, as they stepped out into the glare of the sun.

'Well, I was trying to say that William Jones...'

'Yes, Enoch, but moving on from that! You were going to tell me about *The New Mozart*. What's your appearance as a variety artist got to do with you being here? I'm very curious.'

'Oh, if you insist, then I will elucidate – *hwæt*! It's a tale of prejudice and privilege, a story of fervour and favour, a narrative of...'

'Get on with it, Enoch, we haven't got all day!'

'As you wish, I shall strip out all the grand rhetorical flourishes which make an anecdote worth listening to, and bore you with the bare facts of the matter. Are you ready?'

'Yes.'

'This won't take long, so pay close attention.'

'All ears, old boy!'

'Very well, then. It happened like this: I was asked to perform at the first Royal Command Performance, as I have told you.'

'*The New Mozart*!'

'Just so. Her Majesty the Queen graciously spoke to me after the performance, and took a liking to me. She invited me to become a friend and companion to her youngest child, Prince John. He was a sickly child, but an interested individual, and he enjoyed the music I played for him. I spent a lot of time with him at Windsor, and we became friends. I went up to Cambridge at the age of fifteen, just as the war ended, my progression undoubtedly aided because of my royal connections. During my first year as an undergraduate, Johnnie came to his end, peacefully and not unexpectedly. Queen Mary wanted to thank me for being his friend and companion, and so, when I graduated, she enabled me to obtain my first appointment in the ICS. That's about it.'

Cat had been bobbing along beside Parvati, nervously protecting her as the party left the safety of the palace for the bustle of the city, and Enoch wasn't sure that he had been listening to the story. Not many people had had the benefit of knowing this part of Enoch's past, and, in general, those who had tended to react in a startled manner. Enoch couldn't imagine what was preoccupying Cat that he had failed to listen.

Several minutes later, as they reached the church, the details of Enoch's story finally filtered through, and Cat, his face dripping with sweat, suddenly stopped. 'Wait a minute! I'd wondered why someone... er, someone like you... how you'd got a job in ICS. Are you saying the Queen fixed it up for you?'

'I take it you mean a brown person? Yes, that's correct, Her Majesty assisted me. She insisted that the ICS gave me a position, regardless of my background and their prejudice. It helped that I had obtained the highest double first ever awarded by the university, so there was the additional matter of them being simply unable to ignore me!'

'But then why, if you're such a clever-clogs and also a royal crony, are you here in this lost little place?'

'That's how they had their revenge. The had to appoint the brilliant little brown boy whom the Queen supported, no choice, but they got their own back by sending me here. The most junior senior appointment of all. Will I advance from this posting? If I achieve the impossible, then possibly. You'll have spotted the catch.'

'Aha, speaking of catches, I need to talk to you about a little engineering problem.'

'Cat Adam, what have you done with you brain today? You're only half listening, your thoughts are all over the place, you're bouncing around like a medicine ball, you have resiled from every conversation you have started!'

'But, you see, Parvati's case is very old, probably Dragonetti's original, and it needs an upgrade to make it safe to use.'

'That monstrous sarcophagus is not Dragonetti's original case, of that we can be quite certain!'

'How do you know? I'm sure it is. Medicine balls don't bounce, by the way – even I know that!'

'I know because it's made of plywood, which didn't become available until about twenty years after Dragonetti's death. Now, can you please cease your intellectual saltation.'

Cat paused by the church door, reflecting on Enoch's plea. 'I'm sorry. You're quite right, I find myself preoccupied. I apologise.'

'And might I enquire as to the cause of your preoccupation? Could it possibly be the little lady?'

Cat grinned, embarrassed.

'Very well, why don't we do the following; we rehearse as planned, paying attention, and then you'll be free to join her for the evening. I'll show you the way to the clinic. Do you think you can concentrate long enough for us to achieve that happy outcome?'

'Oh, yes, yes, oh yes,' Cat laughed gleefully, 'yes, let's do just that!'

The interior of the church was customarily cool, despite the brilliance of the sunlight cascading through the windows, and Cat was happy that this was a suitable environment for Parvati, an improvement on the bungalow for sure. As he undressed her, however, he noticed that the rubber ferrule on the tip of her end-pin had fallen off at some point on the walk, which was going to create a problem, since the rounded bare metal of the peg would slide on the encaustic tiles. As Enoch set up the harmonium, taking his first look at the full score of the Dittersdorf, Cat experimented with various makeshift ways of stabilising Parvati, and found that laying down a cushion made from the folded bag was the most effective.

'*En vivit* Sir Walter Raleigh!' quipped Enoch, peering over the harmonium.

'H'm, it's a serious matter. Is there anywhere where I can buy a replacement? Perhaps a walking stick vendor might have something suitable?'

'There are no walking stick vendors in DM, Cat. Those who can't easily walk unaided don't walk at all. They sit and decay, like everything else in this benighted place.'

'That's ridiculous! You must be able to buy a walking stick?'

'There are artisans who will make you one, but they'll only bend the bamboo nicely to shape. They won't dress its end with a nifty rubber *capote*. There is no colonial branch of James Smith & Sons, alas. I think your best bet is to visit a blacksmith.'

'What, to have Parvati shod? That's not amusing.'

'No, you ass, to have a new end pin made up. If you get one with a splayed end, flattened, you could safely place it in a grout line between the tiles.'

Cat thought for a moment, 'It would have to be quite sharp, cos the gap's not big.'

'That is true, but it needn't have a razor edge to it. I think that would be a good solution.'

'If you draw me a catch for the case, I could get that made up at the same place. Do you know somewhere?'

'I do. I'll take you.'

Enoch began to pump the harmonium more vigorously, and launched into the opening bars of the concerto. Cat had twenty bars of introduction in which to watch his hair bobbing around once again, and to be mildly irritated that Enoch seemed to be every bit as good as his word, reducing at sight the full score at the keyboard with apparently no difficulty whatsoever. In fact, there was a moment when he produced a more complex rendition than the standard, printed reduction offered; he really was an extraordinarily competent keyboard player.

Cat whacked into his opening arpeggio with a strong down-bow, ripping through an ascending thirteenth to arrive at a spectacular high A on the up-bow. Parvati sounded marvellous, and he winced deliciously as she crescendoed through the semi-breve in the second bar, slipping tantalisingly from deadpan stillness to a saucy vibrato.

'Wait wait wait, can we do that again, please,' Enoch stopped them before even the upbeat was complete, 'we need to agree on how staccato the opening phrase is. You didn't match me at all.'

Cat took a moment, breathing deeply, before responding. His view was that it was not the harmonium player's rendition which needed to be matched, this being a double bass concerto, and that it was the direction of the Master of Music which needed to be heeded, not that of an irritatingly-gifted amateur.

'I think you'll find that harmoniums – or should that be harmonia, do tell!? – are less capable of nuanced performances than string instruments, particularly those as ancient and noble as this fine *da Salò*. Do try your best to accompany rather than lead. I will gladly return the compliment when I am at the keyboard and you are singing.'

Enoch raised his head above the harmonium and looked tortured, as the word *sorry* formed painfully on his lips. Cat had long ago come to learn that tension of any sort had a positive effect on musical performance, as long as it was kept under control, so he smiled back gracefully, calmly, and said, 'right, then, from the top, old chap.'

The thought of going from the top with Vij wandered into his head as he waited through the twenty-bars, and he set about his solo fully fired up, with enhanced, manly vigour.

19

My head was thick and pounding the next morning, despite awaking from a sleep so deep that not even a righteous man could have deserved it. Lakshmi was in attendance, of course, busy opening the blinds remotely before I pleaded with him to stop.

Lakshmi: Ah, good morning, Sahib. You sleep very late.

Me: Urgh, really? All the more need to wake up slowly!

Lakshmi: (tolerantly) Yes, Sahib!I bring breakfast.

By the time he'd been and gone, I was in a fit state to focus on the world around me, and had remembered that I had thought, at one point the night before, I was going to achieve a degree of intimacy with Lulu such as might be described as getting lucky. It was not to be, alas, and I realised now that it had only ever been wish fulfilment, but it did explain why my thoughts hadn't been on the situation which Alban had said was changed, and so hadn't asked the question.

Me: Lakshmi, why are there journalists here? What's going on?

Lakshmi: Here for hanging, Sahib.

Me: (after a jaw-dropping pause) Hanging? What hanging?

Lakshmi: Hang terrorist this week.

Me: Hang?

Lakshmi: Haa, hang, Sahib.

Me: They're going to hang the terrorist? This week?

Lakshmi: (patiently) Haa.

Me: The one who killed the airport engineer?

Lakshmi: (not so patiently) She only terrorist.

Me: (incredulous) SHE?

Lakshmi: Haa, Sahib, terrorist kill engineer is lady hang this week.

I was overtaken by a strong sense of revulsion, made considerably worse because, to my horror, I couldn't help but picture in my mind a noose around Lulu's delicate little neck, the object of so much of my attention the night before.

All the anxiety which had accompanied my realisation that I was living in a fortress, with the certainty that that meant there were enemies at the gate, returned to me. I was in a small Muslim-majority state, a very long way from home, where the Hindu rulers were going to hang a female Islamic terrorist, and I couldn't imagine how that could pass without there being a real possibility of serious trouble amongst the people. On top of that, my belief has always been that capital punishment is the most barbaric practice, so I was immediately placed in opposition to the regime upon which I would have to rely for safety if everything did kick off. If someone had offered me the chance to go home at that very moment, I would undoubtedly have taken it.

This sent my brain spinning, and I knew I had to get out of the palace, couldn't possibly stay put. Since no arrangement had been made with Ali the night before, I decided my emergency plan still held good, to walk to the airport site to see the remains of the fort – apart from anything else, if I didn't go now, before the riots occurred, I wouldn't get there at all.

There was no chatting with the commandos at the front door as I left this morning, despite their attempts at friendly greetings. I was absorbed, entrapped, in the unpleasant world to which I felt they belonged, where suddenly the very idea of absolute rule seemed not just removed from the imperfect ideal of democracy, but anathematised my long-held view that every culture was entitled to its own practices, beyond the rightful place of outsiders to question. There was no doubt in my mind that the wilful, calculated killing of a human being, even one who had done likewise to another, was repugnant in the extreme, no matter who did it, or where.

I hurried to the boulevard, knowing that if I headed back toward the archive, I would be going westward, in the direction of the airport. And I recalled from flying over it that there was nowhere else to go, as it was at the end of the chersonese, so that all I had to do was find the coast road and keep walking. Having got up late up this morning, the sun was already high, and I realised that I was going to have to cover my head once I'd left the shade of the city, so I stopped at Kaadhi to buy a hat, not knowing that they didn't have a menswear section. I left feeling rather foolish, and bought one in the shop next door.

Oh, it was a long walk, and it was damnably hot. I'm not a churchy sort, so don't generally give much thought to biblical matters, and yet what I perceived as the absence of anything even approaching godliness in the hanging of people in this place of religions commanded me, ironically, to contemplate the divine as I went. I began to develop irrational thoughts, which grew from a curiously remembered bit of scripture (one of the Wedgwood chaplain's favourites): *His going forth is from the end of the heaven, and his circuit unto the ends of it: and there is nothing hid from the heat thereof.* I imagined the justice of the divine heat, from which nothing is hid, beating down on the head of Sammy.

I was appalled that he was going to allow an execution to happen on his watch. Of course, it might have been his father's edict, the older man being possibly less liberal than I had thought his son to be, but Sammy was the *de facto* ruler, and could, I'm sure, have argued against the Rajah's will. He was a kind and decent fellow, a friend, or so I had thought. No, I was not appalled, I was disgusted.

The only person the sun beat down on was me, as I left the limits of the city and began to trudge along the coast road, where shelter was very limited and the dust plentiful. I'd never understood fully the nature of the dust in India, referenced by so many writers, but it was the same as the heat when I'd encountered it in Karachi, familiar and yet abundant in a degree which is unimaginable unless you've experienced it. My new hat was soon wringing, and sweat poured over my eyes, stinging them, whilst what was beginning to feel like an endless trudge caused chafing in the areas where flesh rubbed on flesh. Had I been religious, I could have dedicated the endeavour to god, as an act of penance for the wrongs of the rulers of this place, my pilgrimage through the pestilence of sunshine. But I was not, and I loathed every awful minute of the hike.

It took me nearly an hour and a half to reach the end of the chersonese, and I was as red as a lobster. It was obvious that I should have turned back, realistically should have stopped at the point when the city came to an end, but I'd entered into that state of mind when it becomes a waste not to make use of the effort-so-far, when the goal is always *only a little bit further.* And the promise of the academic plaudits which describing the fort was going to bring spurred me on to beyond the point of no return.

The airport construction site was visible from a distance away across the flat land, and it was massive. To the north of it there was a development of what looked like housing, where I supposed the people who worked here lived, in what Ali had described as a different world. The oil storage facility must have been on the other side of the development, by the water, as I couldn't see it from ground level, whereas the airport site itself was buzzing with activity, with large cranes turning to lift loads from there to here and back again, and macho vehicles rumbling along rough roads, all behind a high fence of wire netting.

I kept to the coast road, which was heading straight to the south of the site, directly to where I thought I would find the fort, in the narrow strip which was all that remained between the security fence and the water. As I got nearer, the odd truck lumbered past, and the sound of the works became clear, as they rattled and clanged through the burning air.

Finally, the road turned right, to the north, at the point where it met the fence, and I was able to walk straight ahead onto what amounted to little more than barren scrubland, as I closed in on the fort.

However exhausted and overheated I was, however miserable about being in DM, my day was about to become immeasurably worse.

As I walked up to what, from the helicopter, had looked like the remains of a star-shaped fort, I saw actually two long, angled, walled, concrete channels which ran into the water. They were plainly modern modern, as opposed to early modern. I was devastated, realising immediately my error. I vaguely recalled that there had been a remote telegraph relay station left in DM by the British, which had closed down just after the war, and realised that this must have been all that remained of it, the protected means of ingress and egress for the submarine cables.

My physical condition was dire, and my disappointment so great, that the fury I felt towards my grotesque folly and embarrassment overwhelmed me. I'd lost the promise of a rich reward at the end of my struggle, and, with no possibility of feeling religiously purified by the torture I'd inflicted on myself, I collapsed and sobbed, the victim of wish fulfilment yet again.

My pitiful convulsions were what must have prevented me hearing the approach of four commandos, whose guns were pointed at me, and who were being very fierce. They dragged me to my feet, and hauled me brutally across the scrubland to where their four-by-four sat, threw me into the back, and headed off in the direction of the city. I pleaded with them to be gentle, begged them to understand that I'd not been doing anything wrong, but they spoke only amongst themselves, and only in Urdu.

We turned into the palace drive, and I was mightily relieved because here would be people who could explain who I was, and I'd have the opportunity to tell the commandos what I'd been doing. But the car turned left and drove, at speed, round the side of the building, to a separate entrance, where other commandos stood on duty. I hoped that one of them might have been at the main entrance earlier, and would be able to identify me, but no.

I was bundled – shoved – out of the car, and frogmarched into the building, where, with the rattle of keys and much commotion from the commandos, I was taken through a grey steel door, into a barely-lit room and thrown roughly into a cell.

I lay on the floor face down, trying to catch my breath, scared beyond my ability to think straight. My brain seemed to have decided that this would all go away if I stopped looking at it, so I squeezed my eyes shut, and shuddered as I heard the cell door slam shut, followed by the sound of the commandos marching out to beyond the steel door, which made a sound like a steam hammer as it sealed me within.

20

Enoch led Cat in the direction of the zenana hospital after they had rehearsed, as promised, diverting along the way to a small, hidden blacksmith's workshop where, for no reason Cat could imagine, he was known. After exchanging warm greetings, he had handed over Parvati's endpin, giving instructions, in Urdu, about making something similar but with a sharpened end. And he quickly sketched out the two parts of a lock for Parvati's case, with instructions to attend the veranda of 2nd Bungalow and fit it at the earliest opportunity. Moreover, Enoch paid for the work in advance, a gesture which was bound to please.

Cat had described fully his desire for a self-fastening device for Parvati's case only as they had placed her securely under lock and key in the vestry, and, amazingly, Enoch seemed to have designed a suitable device in his head as they had walked from the church.

'Dum diddy dum dum da da daaaah,' hummed Cat as he approached the clinic, taking his leave of Enoch, who had winked knowingly at him.

'Diddly dum-de dum,' came the response from an unseen person, tunelessly.

'Wha'? Who said that? Sang that, rather. Come on, show yourself, you cheeky blighter!'

'You think I am a cheeky blighter?', came the reply, in a starched, upper-class English accent, such as could suit a fifth baronet.

'Yes, I bally-well do! Show yourself.'

'If you so command, my imperial overlord, then I must obey.'

'Why, you've got a chee...'

Cat was reduced to stony silence as his interlocutor stepped out from behind the flight of blackened stone steps which rose to the clinic's entrance. There stood an elderly Indian with long, matted, white hair and an untrained beard, carrying a trident, and, apart from a smears of red and white paste across his forehead, as naked as he undoubtedly had been at the other end of his life, long ago. Covered in dust, he was no sort of athlete, with a pot belly, spindly limbs and, thought Cat, a reduced penis of such smallness that most public schoolboys would have sought to keep it to themselves.

'Good day to you, young man,' the sadhu extended his hand in greeting, 'I am a penitent, and my name is Denis.'

'Denis? Seriously?'

'Indeed, most seriously. I was Sir Denis Aloysius Clough Selveratnam, to give me the whole bloody shebang, but we don't need all that. Do you doubt my word?'

The notion of a man presenting himself in this way and needing to lie about his name seemed so wildly improbable to Cat that he just shook his head incredulously. He was less keen on shaking the hand, not knowing where it had been, but was overtaken by convention and so exchanged greetings.

'My name is Cat.'

'How do you do, Cat. I'm very pleased to make you acquaintance.'

'Likewise, I'm sure,' Cat lied, 'but, but why do you sound like an Englishman?'

'Is that really the most striking thing about me, Cat? How very curious!'

'Well, I don't know that it's the most striking thing, exactly, but it is one of them.'

'Well, you can blame T.B. Macaulay for that. I am exactly the Englishman he wanted us Indians to be.'

'Well, whoever he was, I'm not sure you're exactly what he had in mind...'

'Oh, but I am! I was brought up speaking English, won a scholarship to a major public school, graduated in law from London, returned to India and, in due course, became a high court judge, still speaking English, delivering judgements in an Anglophone legal system, and generally being the right sort.'

'I see,' muttered Cat, confused, and wholly more interested in seeing Vij naked than Denis, 'well, if you'll excuse me, I'm here to see Dr. Vijinalakshmi, so I'll just...'. He gestured his intention of climbing the stairs to the clinic.

'Ooh, no, you can't go up there.'

'Why not?'

'Because that's the women's entrance, and since this is the zenana hospital it seems only fair that it should stay that way.'

'What's it to you?'

'Aha, a very good question. Do you suppose that, even though not one of the women who enters this building know that I am their protector, I am anything otherwise?'

'You're protecting the clinic? From who?'

'*Whom*, Cat, *whom*. I've been protecting the clinic from you.'

'But I've only just arrived! How can you have been protecting it from me?'

'Every moment is part of the eternity. You have always been here, yet you have always been elsewhere.'

'Really?'

'Most assuredly.'

'Oh, I see… Well, how do I let the doctor know I'm here? She's expecting me.'

'Come, my son, I'll lead you round to the back entrance. There men can linger.'

Cat thought this a most suspicious offer, with smutty innuendo such as he'd not heard since he was at school, but decided he would be safe from the advances of this little old man, especially since he considered he'd been forewarned.

The clinic was housed in what looked like a miniature Victorian hospital such as could be found in most largish towns at home, although not painted this colour. The arrival of nineteenth-century neo-Gothic, so common elsewhere in India, had passed DM by on the whole and, apart from the new, anachronistic church, this cherry-red building was the only one with lancet windows and lofty aspirations which Cat had noticed on his walks. It was in very poor condition, with crumbling stucco and rotten windows in addition to the usual black mould. Around it were several women in small groups, impoverished, drably covered, many with babies held tightly, all ignoring completely the extraordinary presence of Denis amongst them. Some climbed the stairs to the clinic, with the assistance of others if they were sick or very heavily pregnant, some walked gingerly down again, whilst others sat together on flimsy, bentwood chairs, evidently put out for that purpose. Other than

Denis, there were no men, except occasional passers-by, and Cat was reminded of the quayside, where there had been no women. How did the sexes ever meet each other, he wondered? What social mechanisms could there possibly be for making introductions, when those making them would themselves have needed to have been introduced?

'Please walk this way,' beckoned Denis, stepping out of his corner into plain view of all those around. Cat was in awe of his lack of shame.

He followed Denis down a shadowy alley at the side of the clinic, too narrow for the sun to reach the ground, in which there were free-roaming dogs living their quiet lives alongside a handful of derelict people; the way was strewn with turds, not all of which were canine. The humans were tired, too worn out even to stretch out a hand in the hope of a coin or two from the well-fed white man, and the dogs likewise seemed to lie in a torpor. This, surely, had to be the very poorest part of this impoverished city, where hope had moved on, and only decay remained?

Unexpectedly, there was a cat, a tabby, which strode straight up the middle of the alley, apparently in command of the dogs, which would all have formed a guard of honour if they could have been bothered.

'That cat is the good doctor's own pet,' remarked Denis, seeing Cat's reaction to its presence. 'The dogs listen to the cat, like the humans listen to the doctor. The difference, of course, is that the doctor looks after everyone else, whilst the cat cares only for herself.'

'What's it called?'

'She has a name, but I choose not to remember it. She is only passing through, after all, like the rest of us, and I don't think she needs to be burdened with the residual memory of a name to which she has never willingly answered anyway.'

They had arrived at the rear of the clinic, where there was a sweat-soaked workman mending a door which lay across a pair of trestles, replacing the wood in its lower panels, which had become beset by rot. He glanced up at the visitors as they emerged again into the sunlight, and nodded casually. Cat acknowledged the gesture with a smile.

Denis stood by the back door, positioned so as to make it clear he wasn't trying to see inside this forbidden place, and raised his rich, resonant voice to a plummy bellow. 'Doctor, you have a visitor. A man.'

One of the dogs howled in response, as if Denis wasn't also a man, and the others picked up the cue and bayed, so that Cat felt as if he'd just been introduced at the court of Count Dracula. Even the aloof cat, who was making her way inside, stopped to peer at the intruder, flicking her tail to indicate just the right degree of displeasure.

Shortly, there appeared at the door a young nurse, very properly turned out, crisp and clean in contrast to all around. She spoke in Hindustani to Denis before disappearing inside.

'Oh, I do wish these damn natives wouldn't assume I'm one of them,' complained Denis. 'I'm really not very sure what she said – I think it was that the doctor is busy and will be out with a stick, but I suspect I may have misheard.'

'I believe I heard *minat*, which would be minutes.'

'I say, you've got a bit of the lingo! That's very good indeed, shames me completely.'

Cat resisted the temptation to observe that he was pleased that at least something did, and shortly Vij appeared at the door, in a white coat, looking rather stern, as if she hadn't wanted to be disturbed at work. Denis bowed low before her, too low, leaving nothing further to Cat's imagination, but distracting him from the dismay he felt upon witnessing the reaction his arrival seemed to have elicited.

'Good evening, doctor,' crooned Denis, as he stood upright.

'And good evening to you, Denis-ji. Have you passed the day well?'

'I believe I have, doctor, in atonement for my sins and reflection on my rebirth. Yourself?'

'Oh, you know, same really, but I have been dealing with today's batch of rebirths, rather than those happening in a time yet to arrive. I hope we can speak in the morning, Denis-ji.'

'As do I, doctor, very much, but now I must leave you in the company of Cat, your charming new friend. Cheerio both.' Denis turned on his heels and exited by the same route, hopping nimbly from dry patch to dry patch.

Still looking stern, Vij surveyed the scene around, whilst she decided that no-one was looking (the carpenter had his head down taking a measurement), then allowed her face to light up with joy. 'Why, hello, big boy! Glad you could make it!'

Cat grinned back, but was slow with his response, 'My dearest Vij, I've been thinking about you all blinking day, and now I'm with you again...'

'Do I sense a *but*?'

'No, well, yes, but no, not really, it's just that...'

'Spit it out, big boy, what is it?'

'This place – this place where you spend your days… it's, it's just terrible!'

'I know!'

'And is this where you live too?'

'It is, mera dost, I have a room on the top floor, beside the nurses.'

The attractions of 2nd Bungalow were manifest by comparison, and Cat was dismayed for Vij. 'How do you stand it? How do you, y'know, put up with being here when, well, you're a doctor, you could work anywhere, live in a lovely home, have servants?'

'Darling Cat, can you imagine how much worse it would be for the women if I was not here?'

Cat hadn't anticipated this answer, and felt a rare tear well up in his eye.

'And you might recall that when we first met, I was chastising that appalling fellow, Faiq Qifar, for not supporting us. He has all the money in the world, but these women – women in general – don't matter enough to him to do the decent thing.'

'Who could forget!'

'So, here we have it! This is my mission. The very nature of it is that I can't really share it with you, but life isn't about a single purpose, and I would like to share the other part of my life with you.'

Under the blistering sun, Cat felt a wave of warmth spread over him. He took off his cap and made to step towards his great love. But she stopped him with an upheld hand.

'No, don't come near, don't come to me, because – I swear – I want you so badly that I'll have your clothes off your back before you can say *sun burn*. And that would never do on the back doorstep of the zenana hospital.'

'Then what?'

'Then go and talk with Denis whilst I tidy up here. Our lives together, Cat, are going to be spent in your bungalow, if that suits you?'

Cat could imagine nothing which suited him more. 'Uhm, talk to Denis? He's, uhm, a bit weird!'

'He's not what you think, whatever that might be. And he's been very important to me. He'll lighten your burden. Go, go – I'll be with you as soon as I can.'

Cat nodded and turned, just in time, as the tear rolled down his cheek. He paused, gathered himself, waved backwards over his shoulder at Vij so she wouldn't see it, and trudged back, past the dogs, past the lost souls.

Denis eyed Cat silently when he emerged from the alleyway, unmanly tear wiped away but clearly affected. 'She's a remarkable woman!' he said eventually.

'Yas!' Cat could think of nothing to add.

'We are often to be found in intercourse.'

Had anyone else made what, on the face of it, was this preposterous claim, then Cat would have been instantly riven with jealousy. But it was abundantly clear that intercourse meant something different to Denis, a generation older, than it did to him.

'What do you talk about?'

'We talk about our spiritual progress, the difficulties of living in this imperfect world, the nature of reality. What I think you would term hindoo stuff.'

'Why are you naked, Denis?' Cat felt he should just ask the obvious question straight out.

'Oh, that one's easy. It was five years ago I became sanyasi. Nineteen-nineteen! I felt unable to carry on as a puppet of your nation, unable to support the imperial overlords by administering their justice in their courts in their language.'

'But you don't speak the local lingo?'

'There's nothing wrong with English – it's a very good language indeed – and whilst it's not the language of my countrymen, it is the language of their laws. Nor is it the language of my god, but that's a different matter. I had a choice, either to become a nationalist, or to seek purification of my soul and pray for the future of this land. I would be a ridiculous freedom fighter, more ridiculous than I am as an elderly, wrinkled fellow walking around naked. A simple choice, you see. You see.'

'Can't you seek purification of your soul with your clothes on?'

'Curiously, no, it's not the same. You should try it.'

'Fat chance of that!' Cat realised instantly that he had embarrassed himself, and tried to recover, 'I, I mean, I don't jolly-well think so!'

The front door opened and Vij emerged, wearing a saree, and with an extraordinary lightness of step descended the stairs, almost as if floating. The women stood as one, and greeted her, forming a huddle, reaching out with bony hands to touch the doctor, making light, happy noises. Vij laughed with them, exchanging words with some individually, to all collectively. As she stepped off the bottom step, she said to Cat, 'you can't touch me here, obviously, it's a cultural impossibility, you understand.'

'Yes, it's clear enough. I'll walk beside you, at a respectable distance!'

'We can close the gap when we're alone!' she grinned.

'Madam,' interjected Denis, 'Tilak took issue with inter-caste relations, and you and Cat are most definitely inter-caste!'

'Denis-ji, if you don't mind me saying so, bollocks to Tilak, he was an old goat!'

'That he was!' agreed Denis, 'Imagine that, Cat, the father of the independence movement was an old goat. Can you see how much work needs to be done?'

'All I can say is that it's just as well none of these women can follow the banter between the two of you,' said Cat, with raised eyebrows.

'They wouldn't care, they have other things on their minds!' Vij palmed some money into Denis's hand, which he took without being in the least troubled. She turned to Cat, 'Come along, big boy, let's go and eat lots,' and set off in the direction of the city centre, like a galleon picking up the wind.

'Yes, right. Good idea. See you again, Denis, old boy – er, old boy-ji.'

Denis smiled gently, wisely.

21

I haven't a clue how long I lay on the floor of the cell. It could have been moments, it could have been hours. I was hurting all over, because of the physical hardship of the walk, because of the roughhousing at the hands of the commandos, because my face and arms were beginning to burn from over-exposure to that awful sun. The experience was so far removed from anything I'd ever anticipated that I'd never rehearsed it in my imagination, and it seemed like a terrible hallucination.

Beyond the chaos within my head, curiously, the only sense of the external environment I recall was how clean the glossy, grey-painted floor was, as if no-one had yet walked on it. I remember thinking rationally that the goal I'd had in mind when I set off in the morning, was not to be the inaugural occupant of a gaol cell, but a different sort of first altogether, an academic coup, which added further to the unreality.

After who-knows-how-long, I heard the steel door open and a pair of boots march in. A voice commanded me to stand, whilst keys rattled and my cell door was swung open. I assumed that the terrible error which had led to me being in that horrible place had surely been uncovered, and I was about to be set free? But, no, a hand reached out and grabbed me roughly by the arm to drag me back out, beyond the steel door. I kept my eyes averted until we were in the interrogation room, casting them downwards so as not to make real my presence here.

I use the term *interrogation room* to describe the place I was dragged to, not because I have any sense of what such a room looks like, beyond the shabby-chic warehouse interiors MI5 always used in *Spooks* (which this shiny new space didn't resemble in the least), but because it was literally a room in which I was interrogated. Nor were there a good cop and a bad cop, instead there was just one highly-disagreeable commando of, I assume, senior rank, who shouted a lot and asked questions in English which was so poor I could hardly understand him, particularly given the resonance of this bare, hard chamber.

Repeatedly, whenever there was a pause, I stated my name and that I was a guest of the palace (if I'd had a rank and number, I would have given them too, frankly), that if he contacted the office of Yuvraj Samaba my identity would be verified. This seemed to infuriate my interrogator, who, as far as I could tell, was insisting that I was a European terrorist plant at the oil colony, intent on causing further disruption to the airport because I was a dastardly saboteur. And, it turns out, it's difficult to assert strongly that you're no such thing, because denying the accusation is exactly what a dastardly terrorist saboteur would do, wouldn't he?

Realising he was getting nowhere through these means, I was duly frogmarched back to my cell, relieved for the second time in not many days not to have been caned. On the other hand, what was it about the commandos I encountered in this awful episode that made each and every one of them behave aggressively toward me? It must have been perfectly obvious to them that I wasn't about to offer any resistance, yet still I was thrust back into my cell as if I was the Incredible Hulk.

I looked around me for the first time, and found that the walls on three sides were painted in the same grey gloss paint as the floor, with not a single piece of graffiti, not so much as a set of tally marks left by a previous inmate. There was no window, just a low-power light fitting high overhead. Against the left-side wall was a bed, opposite a small desk and plastic chair, and at the end a stainless steel toilet (without a seat) and a basin. There was no adornment whatsoever, which made the white bottle of hand-wash stand out like a gem, and the towel on its hook seem like a tapestry. The fourth wall consisted entirely of bars, from floor to ceiling, also in stainless steel, in which the door was set, like a two-dimensional Russian doll.

I went to the bars to see if there was someone I could speak to, to ask if it was safe to drink the water, since I was parched. I called out a couple of times, but no-one came, so I shouted loudly and was peremptorily told, in English, to shut up. I was speechless.

Looking across from my cell, I could see opposite there was another, identical to mine, in the middle of a row of three. And as

I peered into its depths, beyond the bars, I could see a person within, lying on the bed,

Me: Hello – you speak English?

Yelda: (with a Manchester accent) Course I bloody do.

Me: Why?

Yelda: I'm from pigging Bolton.

It is probable that I wouldn't have believed it, except that anyone who could speak the name Bolton here must have had some knowledge of that distant place, and you just wouldn't make it up, would you.

Me: Goodness, I work in Altrincham!

Yelda: Posh twat, are yer?

Me: Blimey, not at all. I lecture at the university.

Yelda: Might've guessed. What y'do to end up in here, then?

Me: ABSOLUTELY NOTHING!

Yelda: I would say they all say that, but there aren't any others. Dead boring.

Me: There are no other prisoners?

Yelda: No, it's just been me for over three weeks now, all on me tod. Really, really tedious.

Me: Well, what did *you* do to end up in here, then?

Yelda: I shot a bloke. Killed him.

It still amazes me how long it took me to put two and two together. I know I wasn't in tip-top condition and all that, but still, I was engaged in conversation with a woman who was admitting killing someone, in a place where someone had just been killed by a woman, and where there was no other prisoners. It reminded me of a story that my Nan told me once, about a famous old comic called Arthur Askey, who was in a lift at a hotel somewhere or other when a woman next to him told him he looked like himself, and that that was a great coincidence since the real Arthur Askey was staying in the same hotel.

Me: Oh my god, you're the terrorist!

Yelda: (feigning a yawn) That's not the word I would use.

Me: (cynically) Oh, sorry, freedom fighter, then?

Yelda: It's not funny, pal, and you can fuck right off if you're going to start getting cocky with me.

Me: (wrong-footed) I, er… sorry. I'm Philip – Philip Adam.

Yelda: Eh up, Philip Adam. I'm Yelda Shirani.

Me: How do you do, Yelda.

Yelda (laughing) At least you didn't say 'pleased to meet you'!

Me: No, well, I don't know the etiquette of cell-to-cell meetings, sorry.

Yelda: No, mate, neither do I. You'd think that's what cell phones're for, ta-da!

I managed a smile.

Yelda: What do you teach at uni?

Me: History. I'm here on a field trip. What do you do?

Yelda: Me? I'm a global jihadist, obviously.

There was a tiredness in her voice which she failed to disguise despite her attempts at being upbeat, more world-weary than worldly-wise.

Me: Are you? Really?

She got up and came over to her bars where I could see that she was astonishingly young, just a girl, and pretty. But she was also worn out, her skin had a pale cast to it which matched the grey of the jumpsuit she was wearing, her long hair was bedraggled and she had a nervous tic on one side of her face.

Yelda: Apparently.

All I knew of Islamic terrorists had come from the same source as my knowledge of interrogation rooms, and it didn't include the possibility of someone like this girl being one.

Yelda: Well, any rate, I killed someone, so I must be.

Me: Did you really kill the Chinese engineer?

Yelda: Yep.

Me: What with?

Yelda: Me gun.

I couldn't think of anything to say.

Yelda: Shot him through the head.

Me: Please, I'd rather not know.

Yelda: (sadly) Yeah. Yeah, me too.

Me: What do you mean?

Yelda: I didn't set out to be a killer. But I am one now, and that's that.

Me: I'm not sure I get any of this. Start at the beginning – why are you here at all?

Yelda: (sighing) Again, eh! OK, pay attention…

I nodded.

Yelda: My family are Pakistani originally, and we came over two years ago to visit relatives in Quetta, they said, but really they were going to marry me off to some spotty git who I'd never met. When I found out, I ran away, and accidentally ended up with the Taliban, who took me to Kandahar. They were a fuckin' terrible bunch, held me prisoner so that the blokes could use me when they wanted. I got pregnant, lost the baby. You still listening?

Me: Jesus!

Yelda: Anyway, one day they left me alone, so I got away – picked up a pistol I found in the house before I left, and that's all I had apart from the clothes on my back. I got back into Pakistan, and discovered that the whole world thought I'd run away to join a bloody terrorist group from choice. I couldn't go back to England, I wasn't safe in Pakistan, didn't know what to do or where to go, so I wandered, living from hand to mouth. Ended up here.

Me: Why here?

Yelda: Walked in by accident. I'd found a nice little place to hide away in a shed by the building site when this Chinese geezer comes in and tries it on. He was going to rape me… I'd had it with being raped, so I shot him. Didn't try to run away, thought they'd believe it was self defence.

I wasn't sure I believed any of this tale.

Me: How old are you, Yelda?

Yelda: Nineteen. How old are you?

Me: Me, oh, I'm thirty.

Yelda: So it all ends here. Some bloke decided I should be hanged cos I am obviously a terrorist. They're just waiting for the hangman.

Me: (gobsmacked) Why are you so calm?

Yelda: Y'know what, Philip, I'm so pigging tired that I don't care any more. I've got no family, no home, no friends. I just don't care any more. Let them kill me.

Me: But that's manifestly unfair!

Yelda: (mockingly) Ooh, manifestly unfair! The only thing which annoys me is how sexist the business of seventy-two virgins in paradise is. I mean, what good are seventy-two virgins to me? Eh?

Me: I don't understand how you can be so glib?

Yelda: No, Philip, neither do I. I don't know why I've given up. But I have.

Me: But you've not had a proper trial! Have they even listened to your defence?

Yelda: *The Rajah's the law*, they keep telling me! I have no rights. They're just waiting for the good Christian hangman to arrive from Islamabad.

I certainly wasn't about to tell her about Alban and his pals turning up to report her execution, or that their presence supported Lakshmi's information that the hanging was likely to be any day now. And then I had an awful insight, that what I had thought was the scaffolding those men were working on behind the palace was, in fact, *the scaffold.* Worse, that was the reason they'd cleared the space behind the palace, the reason they'd found the huts, the reason I was here at all. I welled up.

Yelda: Don't you start blubbing! This ain't a pigging episode of Corrie!

Me: I'm going to explain this all to them. Who was it decided you should be hanged? Who told you?

Yelda: Dunno. Does it matter?

Me: Yes, Yelda, it matters to me very much. I'm not going to let this happen.

Yelda: You're doing a good impersonation of someone who cares.

Me: I do! This cannot happen. It's a travesty. I'm friends with the son of the Rajah…

Yelda: Told yer yer a posh twat!

Me: STOP IT – BE SERIOUS!

She looked at me through her sad eyes without blinking, whilst the muscles in her cheek and forehead twitched uncontrollably. Finally, she turned round and went to the back of her cell, where she unzipped her jumpsuit, perched on the toilet and had a pee.

There didn't seem any need to look away, modesty being superfluous in this place, and she didn't appear to care.

Yelda: (washing her hands) The water's OK to drink, by the way, since you ask.

Me: Yelda – I promise you I'm going to sort this out. Do you understand. I PROMISE!

Yelda: Good luck with that one, pal, stuck in here.

She sat on the bed and reflected for a moment before lying down again.

Yelda: But thank you anyway.

22

Dawn was breaking and Cat, awake unusually early, was enthroned on his thunderbox. The lake was silent, and the mosquitoes had retreated to their slumbers, so he was listening to Vij's snoring from within the bungalow and, when a caesura allowed, to Enoch's bizarre night-time noises from next door. They still sounded like fragments from an incomprehensible, ecstatic, soprano aria, but he had become more familiar with Enoch's extraordinary singing during rehearsals over the past week, and wasn't now convinced that that was what he was hearing. It was altogether more fractured in nature, reaching for extremes of pitch, both low and high, and dynamic, with whispers and loud cries, albeit muffled. This was a commonplace occurrence, almost nightly, and it was this plain evidence of the acoustic transparency of the bungalows that had led to Cat and Vij making extreme efforts to keep their sexual activity quiet and private, no easy task for two such amply-proportioned and eager lovers.

The rehearsals for the recital had gone rather well so far, for all the oddity of the programme, and Cat had enjoyed them very much, for the music-making, and for the sense of purpose, of routine. A week in, Enoch had truly mastered the reduced Dittersdorf, and Cat was reaching the point where his own accompaniment of the Mozart arias was becoming acceptable. After much argument, he had persuaded Enoch that the best interests of the audience would be served if he sang in English, despite the idea seeming to wound his very soul. And yesterday morning, Enoch had produced his composition, an extraordinary piece which he had entitled *Sonata for Harmonium and Double Bass*, a plain and unimaginative choice in Cat's view (not to mention the wrong way round again).

Enoch's writing was impossibly neat, both the alphabetical and musical, so that Cat had momentarily thought the sheets he was handed had been printed. There wasn't a single error, not a crossing out, not the wobble of a hesitant nib, just perfection in laying down clearly what the composer had in mind. It was in three continuous sections (Cat had been told off for calling them movements), structured through a complex system of all-pervasive serialism in which every element was pre-ordained from the start, but brilliant in its execution so that the mechanical process of composition hadn't resulted in obvious failures such as, for example, the double bass playing pianissimo high harmonics inaudibly against fists-full of low, discordant notes on the harmonium. It was as if Enoch's brain had been able to know the end before he'd written the beginning.

The problem, as far as Cat was concerned, was that it was twenty minutes of brilliant boredom. There wasn't so much as even a moment of excitement, of dynamic surprise, of a memorable motif, it was just very, very clever. And as for tunes to whistle, well, there wasn't the slightest chance. Enoch was pleased with his endeavours, that much was plain, and Cat was interested in the challenge of what was, actually, a technically difficult double bass part to share with Parvati, but he couldn't find any greater enjoyment in the piece beyond that; he had deflected questions about his first impressions of the piece by claiming that only second impressions counted. He worried what the audience would make of those twenty minutes too, but supposed that, in the presence of a rajah and a bishop, those few people attending would effectively be entrapped, disinclined to get up and leave, and that if the da Costa came first, before the audience had tired, followed by the Mozart and the Dittersdorf, then it would become near enough to being a decent programme.

There being no music shop stocking manuscript paper in DM, chief amongst the various elements which made the *Sonata* unusual, in addition to the very curious instrumentation, was that Enoch had produced it on the backs of his official foolscap letter head, on which he had had to draw the staves by hand. These flimsy sheets tended to fall off the church lectern, which Cat had brought into service as a music stand but which didn't have the benefit of the extendable arms. On the other hand, Parvati's modified end pin was working very well, Cat found. The blacksmith had fashioned something which had a splayed, chisel-like end, which fitted neatly into the grout lines of the floor tiles, and which was very successful in giving Parvati a good foothold.

The only problem with this solution was that the sharpened tip tended to produce chips in the edge of the tiles, unless it was very precisely placed and, as far as possible, not rotated. Of course, Enoch had seized the opportunity to explain that pressure was something to do with weight divided by area, and that the area of the chisel-ended spike was tending either to infinity or nothing – Cat couldn't remember – as a result of which the sharp end was especially sharp. Or something like that. Anyway, apart from a few chips in the shiny new floor, it seemed to work very well.

At some point during the week, although Cat hadn't noticed exactly when, two self-closing locks had made an appearance, attached to Parvati's case. He had had it in mind that one would have been sufficient, but was happy that two were better, top and bottom, particularly as they were strong and highly effective, involving pivoted pins which fell under gravity into holes in the tapered pegs attached to the door, after they had closed into their corresponding staple on the body of the case; it was one of the projecting pins catching on Cat's kaftan, during the usual process of drawing a screen round himself, that had alerted him to the new fittings. The blacksmith had made something functional, rather than pretty, in blackened iron, which Enoch had described as being 'delightfully hand-made', but the important thing was that they worked, and if the case was shut, it locked automatically as desired, and stayed locked until, with some difficulty, both pins were simultaneously held open. They were an enhancement to the case, to be sure.

The pile of cash in the bottom of the case, which Cat felt had been inadequately concealed since he'd removed the soft case folded on top of it, now had a new home. The mail ship had arrived, as Enoch had said it would, and on it was a small parcel from Cat's mother, containing a tin of Huntley and Palmer biscuits bought as a special treat for him at an exhibition in Wembley. They were delicious, and devoured within moments by him and Vij (despite their mutual protestations that they should keep some for later), leaving just the empty tin, which was exactly the right size and shape for a stack of bank notes. Pleasingly, it also fitted very neatly into one of the small drawers at the bottom of Parvati's case.

The purr of Vij's snoring drew Cat's attention. He relished the sound for the human presence it described, the insistence that he was not alone. He was beyond happy about how completely they had fallen in with each other's way of being, their appetites, and their openness with each other. Every evening this week, he had wandered over to the zenana after rehearsals, to meet her as the clinic closed, and they had walked together back to the palace. They had eaten at the bungalow on some evenings, occasioning raised eyebrows from Indira not because of Vij's presence, but because of the extraordinary quantity of food they managed to consume together. And twice they had eaten in the town, after Vij had been delayed by a case at the clinic, when they were just too hungry to wait. On one such evening, Cat had been delighted when young Salma appeared from nowhere, to walk with them, and dismayed when she explained with stoic great sadness that Osman, her little brother, was sick with dysentery. Vij had been very kind and gentle, telling her that little girls were never too young to attend the women's hospital, and that little brothers could come too.

Some evenings, the lovers chatted to Enoch on the veranda, which seemed to amuse him. Sometimes they did not, according to how urgently they felt the need to retire to the bedroom. And in bed, they had found a passion and enthusiasm for each other in which not only were they matched, but which seemed always to take them somewhere much further than they might have reached otherwise.

This night, there had been an urgent knocking on the door at one-thirty, a messenger having been sent to ask Vij to attend an emergency at the clinic. Cat had helped her dress, and then managed to return to his slumbers, but upon her return, with the news that she had lost the patient, Cat was unable properly to sleep again. Whereas the doctor seemed able to accept the necessity of death, the musician could not, so whilst she curled up to sleep for what remained of the night, he was upset and tossed restlessly. Illness, degradation, violence shocked him, not least the consequence of having attended a school where beatings were common and lonely boys cried themselves to sleep, silently, beneath the blankets, lest they were overheard by the bullies in the dorm. Death seemed to be the next stage down the line, the ultimate affront to the gift of life, and so he had contemplated rebirth as an idea, thinking about the conversations he'd had with Denis, wondering at the marvel which was having another go at *being*, repeatedly, until you got it right. If you believed in karma. Vij believed in it. She had been brought up and educated a Christian, but had converted (she said *reverted*) to Hinduism, aided by Denis's counsel.

She snorted magnificently, and there was a pause of some seconds whilst she stopped breathing, during which Cat could hear that the sound from 1st Bungalow had suddenly changed. It was no longer from an incomprehensible single source, but plainly two different voices, and they were engaged in hushed dialogue. He was startled. This was not expected.

He quietly pushed the case away from the wall, expanding the thin gap which was always there so that he could see the front of Enoch's bungalow, and waited. There was no question that Enoch was talking to someone, although Cat couldn't hear the second voice clearly, and it occurred to him that the nocturnal noises had seemed so odd only because he had thought they'd come from one person, not two. It all made sense now, it was obvious, and Cat admitted to himself that the problem of perception had arisen because he'd had no expectation that Enoch could have had a lover. It had crossed his mind, and Vij's, that the noises were Enoch masturbating, but they happened too often, too regularly for that to seem probable (although with Enoch, who could say). But no, he had a lover.

Noiselessly, the door to 1st Bungalow swung open, and Enoch, wearing a diaphanous white kurta, stepped out onto the veranda to peer into the half light, looking out for any potential witnesses. Once he was confident that there was none, he beckoned to his lover to emerge. Would the lover be a boy or a girl? A girl, surely, since Enoch was so clearly unsympathetic to the Rajah and his personal arrangements? But, with the exception of his funny little goatee, Enoch was himself so feminine that Cat felt unable to be sure. He clenched hard on a fart which had been about to escape, raspingly he feared, and suddenly there on the veranda was Indira – Indira! – who had clearly taken upon herself the duties of chamber maid to a degree which couldn't be considered typical. But they didn't embrace as she left, they merely whispered a good night and an acknowledgement of a job done, very coolly, before Enoch handed her what, Cat assumed, was a wad of money. Cat was dismayed for both of them that here, in this place on the edge of the world, this was as far as they had been able to travel together. They might as well have parted with a handshake.

Cat's fart escaped just as Enoch turned to go back inside, and it was heard. Enoch stopped, looked towards the double bass case and knew, even though Cat had ducked forward out of sight, that his secret was out, that he had been seen. Knowing there was no point pretending, Cat sat back, looked through the gap, and his eye caught Enoch's.

'Good morning, my friend!'

'Morning, Enoch!'

'A little more sleep, I think. I'll see you later, Cat.' said Enoch, drily, as he turned back into his bungalow.

Cat waited for a respectable moment, then hurried inside, naked, to tumble back into bed with Vij.

'Hello, big boy,' she mumbled, sleepily, 'where've you been?'

'Thunderbox.'

There was a slight snore before Vij grunted an acknowledgement.

'But listen, guess what...'

Another snore.

'Vij, Vij...' he shook her until she snorted.

'I've got to sleep... big boy... I can't do it again... not now… please. Shhh-hh-h-h...' Her voice drifted away.

Cat curled up tightly against her, feeling her warmth as he tucked in as closely as he could. Of course she must sleep, and so should he, but, boy, did he have a tale for her when she awoke.

He managed to snooze some more himself, and emerged onto his veranda a couple of hours later. Indira had laid out the breakfast which it had become her practice to leave, piled high on plates covered in light muslin cloths – so fresh, so delicious, so sustaining, enough for both Vij and him. How little sleep the girl seemed to need!

Before he'd pulled on his kaftan, he'd lain in bed and told Vij of the events during the middle of the night. Her reaction hadn't been what he'd expected at all, to the extent that he'd pressured her into saying more than she thought, professionally, she should. And the gist of it was that Indira was known to Vij as a patient, one with, she would only say in loose terms, a 'communicable disease', which Cat took to mean VD. Vij took pains to suggest that he should make it clear to Enoch somehow that he ought to get himself checked out, to get on a boat down to Karachi for a couple of days, where he could find properly trained medics rather than the pirs which abounded in DM. But Cat could think of no possible way of raising such a conversation, for any number of reasons, including that he just couldn't be that close to Enoch. Anyway, he wasn't sure how relations between them would stand after last night, and certainly shouldn't reveal Vij's professional indiscretion in this matter.

Vij had been out to the thunderbox already, and was now inside, dressing, when Enoch sidled over from his bungalow.

'Good morning, Cat – again!' he began.

'Yes, good morning, Enoch, uhm...'

'Concerning last night...'

'No, no… I was going to say... there's nothing to explain, no need to say anything. Nothing at all. What you do in your own time is completely your own business.'

'And what *I* was going to say is that I know that, and I know you're sympathetic to that position, but I would ask you to be respectful of Indira's reputation in this place, and not speak to anyone of what you might have seen. I'm fond of her, you know.'

It flashed across Cat's mind that passing on VD to an innocent was hardly respecting her reputation, and not an act of fondness. But then the situation might have been the reverse, in which case Indira's reputation in this masculine culture might be under question anyway.

'It is obviously not my place to talk to anyone about any of this, Enoch, and I do hope you didn't think otherwise,' Cat's indignity rose with the tone of his voice.

'Including...' Enoch gestured with his eyes that he was referring to Vij, inside the bungalow.

'Enoch!' Cat feigned deep indignation, 'What sort of friend do you think I am? I wouldn't dream of telling anyone,' he lied.

'Thank you, *dear* friend.'

'I will say that I'm relieved, just between you and me, because I thought you had been singing in your sleep, and it was all a bit strange, rather disturbing. I thought perhaps you slept horribly, whereas I know now that you don't seem to sleep at all!'

Enoch smiled. 'You really thought the exchange of auditory signals of sexual satisfaction between Indira and me was, instead, me singing in my sleep? My somnucanerism? How amusing!'

'What did you just say? What was that word?'

'Eh, oh, what, somnucanerism?'

'Yes, that word.'

'What of it?'

'I want you to look me in the eye and swear you didn't just make that word up...'

'Wha', I mean,' Enoch looked away, 'it's a perfectly good coinage – based on somnambulism – or somniloquy – wouldn't you say?'

'You're a bounder, Enoch da Costa, you know that, don't you. I'm getting the measure of you, you know!'

'I have no idea what you're talking about, Cat. And lo, the imago appears!' he deftly changed the subject, as Vij emerged from the bungalow.

'Good morning, Enoch,' she hesitated momentarily, before stepping into the conversation, 'I trust you are implying I'm more butterfly than moth! Will you join us for breakfast?'

'That would be very pleasant, thank you. And I have an outing for you this morning, if you wish it, Cat, after our bath.'

Cat panicked, casting his eyes towards Vij, who understood exactly what was in his mind. She smiled and nodded reassuringly, 'You're very lucky to have a large body of fresh water in which to cleanse yourselves, you two, very healthy. I have to make do with the bucket or two of larvae-infested slop my maid can produce each morning.'

Cat looked surprised.

'I'm joking, big boy! The one thing we have got at the hospital is a very large boiler! Hot water and towels, the two things you can never do without!'

'I am expecting a reply to my message last week, so I'm going out to the telegraph station. You'll be welcome to join me for the ride.'

'That'd be terrific, old bean, thanks, but I'm afraid I'm already spoken for this morning.'

Enoch paused, attempting to work out exactly what Cat meant. 'You have a prior commitment?'

'I do.'

'What is it, if I might ask? What can you possibly be doing in Dhoosar Mathavassee that is more interesting than taking a tonga ride to the very limits of the state?'

'I've got an appointment at the palace. I am commanded to appear.'

'Commanded by whom? For what?' Enoch seemed disturbed by this news.

'By the Rajah.'

'For what reason?'

'To discuss the arrangements for the arrival of the bishop.'

Enoch sat back, his eyebrows in a high arch. 'Well, I advise you strongly against accepting any involvement whatsoever. Do not be part of it.'

'Enoch, can I point out that I am appointed to serve the palace – it's why I'm here!'

'You may, but might I point out that the only payment you have received, to my certain knowledge, has been as a courtesy from His Majesty's government – from me! – and that the question as to whom should be the recipient of your loyalty is moot?'

'No, it is not! I am here as Master of the Rajah's Music, and that's what I've been all this week in rehearsal with you. If I can contribute in some way to what is intended to be a grand spectacle...'

Enoch snorted derisively.

'...a festive occasion, then that is what I shall do.'

'You are a British subject, are you not?'

'You know jolly-well that I am,' Cat was becoming defensive.

'Well then, you have a duty to the Crown, which I represent, and I require you to keep your involvement in the bishop's visit to the minimum. For your sake and mine!' Enoch insisted, unusually sharply.

Vij rose, 'Gentlemen, I'm sorry to break into this tête-à-tête, but I must go to my clinic before it gets too hot.' She kissed Cat on the lips and rubbed noses, then, to Enoch's surprise, bent over and pecked him on the top of his head as well. 'Be good, you two.'

Cat waited until he and Enoch were fully alone before continuing, 'What do you mean *for your sake and mine*? What's going on? What are you up to?'

'I'm being a dove, of course,' he grinned unpleasantly.

'Cats catch doves...'

'Is that so!' sneered Enoch.

'Yes, and we need less doves of your type, if you ask me.'

'*Fewer*, dear Cat, *fewer*. It's time I bathed. Will you be joining me?'

Enoch rose decisively and marched back to his bungalow. Cat followed him with his eyes, wondering what was in his mind that had made him so aggressive this morning. He was always elusive in his manner, always given to skirting round points of discussion, deferring the telling of anecdotes, but generally without being sharp in his manner. It was as if he had decided that Cat had joined his team, and that together they had an obligation to stand against everything in this little, downtrodden state, so that neither of them should have any dealings with the palace. But what was the point of either of them being here at all, wondered Cat, perfectly clear that, insofar as he had anything to do, it was his job somehow to make things better. And he desperately needed to remain the Master of the Rajah's Music, for Parvati's sake, so serve the palace he would.

He heaved himself out of his chair, sauntered over to the water's edge and pulled his kaftan over his head, just as Enoch emerged to join him. The two men faced each other, naked aside from their modesty coverings of baggy underpants and loincloth, one robustly fat and white, the other punily skinny and brown, in a moment of implicit acceptance that they were stuck with each other.

'There are differences between us, Cat Adam...'

It was now Cat who snorted.

'...but what do they matter, hey?'

Cat wanted to expound on some of the differences and explain why they did matter, but realised there was no point in questioning the limits of a relationship that neither of them had sought, but from which both had benefited, if only in terms of neighbourliness. He waited for Enoch to enter the water, mindful of Vij's view of what was likely to be his diseased state, and joined him at a greater distance than previously.

'Come now,' observed Enoch, 'no need for gelidity! I'll have to shout to converse with you over there.'

'Just give me a moment, Enoch, please. I just need to take a moment.'

They bathed in silence.

23

Can you have an explosion without a bang? That's what it felt like when everything in and around the cells changed. The air fizzed, and there was a tremendous kerfuffle from the other side of the steel door, with shouted commands and the stamping of feet, followed by the hurried opening of the steel door with a great rattling of keys. A pair of commandos marched in very stiffly and, for a horrible moment, I thought that this was it, they'd come to take Yelda away. Like her, I had been lying down, and we both jumped to our feet as if spring loaded.

Behind the two commandos followed a scurrying old man, who looked around him desperately, looking like he was fleeing from a swarm of bees. I thought for a moment that we were about to be joined in this pristine dungeon by a third person, but then I recognised him. It was the Rajah, and his desperate fidgeting was in fact the consequence of his abject rage, which seemed to be so great that it could find no other way of releasing itself.

The Rajah: (shouting) WHERE?

One of the commandos pointed at me, somehow both hanging his head in shame and remaining at attention.

The Rajah: UNLOCK THE DOOR! IMMEDIATELY!

The commando did as he was told. And so would I have in his boots, since the Rajah was incandescent. He paused for a moment, caught his breath, before speaking (a little) more calmly to me.

The Rajah: Philip, I don't have words enough to apologise for what's happened here. I am devastated that one of my guests has been treated in this appalling way. I will be investigating, and I can tell you that heads will roll.

He glanced threateningly at my interrogator, who had entered the chamber behind him. Despite my relief at seeing him, which was almost as great as my amazement that he was actually here in the cell block, I couldn't help but think that his choice of words was regrettable.

Me: (bowing slightly) Your highness…

I could think of nothing to say. What could I have said which wasn't obvious?

The Rajah: Come, let's get you back.

He gestured with his hand for me to lead the way out. I hesitated, looking over at Yelda, which he spotted, when he cast his eyes to the ground and continued, embarrassed.

The Rajah: Come, Philip, let's go right away. We must not stay here.

Yelda nodded at me, bade me go, her face quite impassive. I made a fist and struck my chest softly, which I meant to be a gesture of intent, of strong defiance, but she smiled her weary smile again, and I felt that she was amused by my lack of street-cred.

I was led through a column of shame-faced commandos standing to attention, straight out and into the Rajah's car for the three-minute drive round to the front entrance of the palace. I've never received such a mighty bollocking as I got from him on that short journey, and it was clear that he was as cross with me as he had been with the commandos. The essence of what he had to say was that DM was in a state of emergency, that I had known this, yet I had still wandered off on my own, without a guard, to more or less the precise spot where the engineer had been shot, and that there was a very real sense in which the misfortune which this had occasioned was as much my fault as the commandos'. Put this way, I have to say that I agreed with him, so I made a grovelling apology, which he was kind enough to accept, and that's where the matter rested.

For him.

It was already dark, and Lakshmi having been forewarned of my return, had run me a bath by the time I entered my suite. I had to let some cold water into it because my sunburned skin couldn't take the heat. He brought food too, and I was famished, so it disappeared in very short order. And that should have been my day, as I was exhausted; I should have hunkered down and had an early night. But there was Yelda, and I couldn't get her out of my mind.

The roof crowd would have started assembling by now, but I knew Sammy usually joined them later on, so assumed he would be down in the living room where I'd first seen him. Thanks to my meanderings in the palace, I knew exactly where that was, and so descended one floor in the posh lift, and knocked on his door. Sure enough, he and Arabella were sitting together, watching the Pakistani news channel.

Sammy: (leaping up) Oh, Philip, thank god! Are you OK?

Arabella had been sitting beside him and he nearly sent her flying, which made her scowl.

Me: Yes, Sammy, I'm fine, and I can only apologise for what I did today. It was incredibly stupid of me.

Arabella: (acidly) Yes, it was.

Sammy: Oh my god, you're like a lobster! Y'ok?

Me: (self-deprecatingly) Yes, I appear to have caught the sun!

Sammy: Come, sit down, let's have a drink.

Arabella: Must you, darling? You'll be drinking on the roof later, I suppose?

Sammy: I think under the circumstances, a stiff gin wouldn't go amiss. Yes, Phil?

I nodded, and bells were rung, drinks brought, seats settled into. I searched for the correct way into the conversation I wanted to have.

Me: I would say that that's the smartest cell block I've ever been in, except…

Sammy: ...you've never been in one before! It's only been finished a couple of months, part of the gradual gathering of civic functions under the one roof.

Me: Like the Doge's palace!

Sammy: Yes! Spot on, that's exactly what I had in mind!

Me: But there is another person being held in there, you know.

Sammy: (struggling for the words) Indeed, one who committed a dreadful crime.

Arabella: We don't have crime here – we don't tolerate it.

Me: Yes, fine, but have you heard her side of the story?

Arabella: Whatever she said, a story is what it was, a pack of lies.

Me: Well, I'm no expert, but it seems to me that she might have been acting in self-defence?

Arabella: She shot him! Would you say that's proportionate?

Me: Well, no, of course not, but given what she'd been through, and the fact that she had a gun to hand…

Arabella: Yes, exactly, she had a gun to hand! And we know what she's been through. We know she's a radical Islamist, that she ran away from England when she was seventeen, that she was with the Taliban, then she turns up here, armed, and shoots a senior member of the team working on the airport. And you're telling me you believe her sob story? Seriously, Philip? You always were gullible.

Sammy: Steady on, darling.

Arabella: No, seriously, Ess! We can't afford anyone to be in any doubt – we won't tolerate acts of terror here, and that's that.

Sammy: All Phil's saying is that there is at least a case to be examined. That's all. Do you not think that judgement was arrived at a little too easily? It's a girl's life at stake!

Arabella: She shouldn't have been here with a gun. It really is as simple as that. If we're ever going to bring this fucking place into the modern world, then we're going to need tourism, and tourists don't go to places where there are terror cells. Look just next door! No-one goes to Balochistan, despite all the natural fucking wonders they've got there.

I didn't stay long, lest Arabella's fascist fantasies ran away with her, and Sammy's embarrassment became my embarrassment. I was astonished by her attitude, the glibness with which she seemed content that a girl's life was on the line, but I had seen at last what she did all day; it was clear that she had spent the last ten years hating every minute of her time in DM, that marrying the heir to a minor throne hadn't been the compensation she had snobbishly thought it would be, and that her solution to the problem was to spend lots of other people's money, to dream of creating a fantasy land all of her own.

I went to the roof, at the end of his dreadful day, and had every intention of getting drunk. But I was invited to sit with Alban; he had been hard at work all day, getting interviews with anyone who would talk to him. He had one compelling story to tell, about the rift in government which the 'terrorist in the cells' had created.

It seemed that neither the Rajah nor the Yuvraj wanted to execute Yelda, yet their hands had been forced by others around them, most notably the Divan, Ali's dad. Alban had been wondering how an absolute monarch had been cajoled into making a decision he didn't agree with. The penny dropped!

I hinted that they should look into who was financing the airport construction, said that I would bet it was a joint project between the Chinese and the Qifars. Alban had assumed that the airport was an extension of the *China-Pakistan Economic Corridor,* beyond Gwador and into DM, and a state initiative, therefore.

I said no more, and went looking for whiskey and Lulu.

24

In order to attend his audience with the Rajah, Cat had had to walk around the lower part of the lake towards the opposite bank, where Ajaz had told him he would find the royal family's private temple. Having never been on this side of the water, he wasn't sure what he was looking out for, but in his mind he imagined that it would be something like the Vadapalani Murugan temple which he'd visited in Madras, en route to DM. That was a shiningly modern structure, like the church here, and had a brand-spanking, lavish rajagopuram guarding its entrance. The difference between the new temple there and the new church here, however, was that the one was heaving under the pressure of crowds at any time of day, whereas the other lay desolate in its pristine, deserted state.

Not having considered the matter too closely, he was half-expecting to spot an ornate, tiered tower overlooking the lake, just as the one in Madras overlooked its tank, so that when he first caught sight of the temple he thought it was merely some sort of annex, an outhouse, a shed. It was standing alone in a small clearing amongst the trees, the facade about twenty feet wide pierced by a central door, in turn flanked by two avatars, one of Sri Ganesh and the other not known to Cat. Across the length of the front was a cornice decorated with scallop shapes which, it could just be seen, had once been brightly painted, and on top was a central protuberance, a mere pimple, which was intended as the gopuram. The entire building, standing so near the water's edge, was damp-blackened with mould.

Cat stopped by the door to remove his plimsolls, listening to the chanting of a single voice from within. The singing was poor, there was no denying, but he could make out with his Westerner's ear what he would have described as the flattened seventh of the mixolydian mode, which, he knew, would have been an inadequate simplification of Indian music. Parvati would love playing some of those ornaments, he thought, and could bend a tone with the best of instruments, so he made a mental note to make sure he learned more about the ragas.

By and by the chanting stopped, and Cat produced a measured cough.

'Oh, you're here, Adam! Don't stand out there, old boy, do come in,' the Rajah commanded from within.

Cat lowered his head as he entered, not so much out of reverence, but because the door frame was imposingly low and it wasn't clear what obstacles, if any, would be encountered once across the threshold of the dark interior. The main source of light was the open doorway, most of which Cat filled as he stepped through, but there was a suspended oil lamp burning over a central, stone lingam, and the priest held in his hands a lantern from which a burning wick sent spluttering flashes of yellow. The priest and the Rajah were both bare-chested, seated on either side of the lingam, in a fug of smoke from the burning incense, and behind them, as Cat's eyes adjusted, he could see a small statue of Sri Shiva dancing within a ring of fire.

'Your highness, I hope I'm not intruding,' began Cat.

'Nope, I reckon we've about finished here. We done, Denis?'

'I believe so, Hurree.'

Cat was startled when he realised it was Denis clutching the lantern, not an unknown priest; wearing just a saffron dhoti, he was more fully dressed than Cat had seen him previously. 'Denis, I didn't recognise you at first! You didn't say you're a priest – I thought you were just a penitent sanyasi?'

'I'm not a priest, my friend, but priests are hard to come by out here – they've always had a better offer! – so I stand in and assist the Rajah and his family with their pujas when I can. I am, at least, a Brahmin, if that helps?'

'Do come and sit down, Adam, if you would. I'm afraid I'm going to have to ask you to take off your shirt.'

'Huh, wha'?'

'It's the tradition in this temple that men are bare-chested.'

Cat wasn't in the least comfortable with this as a tradition, but accepted that he didn't really have a good enough reason to complain. Who could count how many times Sooty had seen Cat wholly naked when they'd been at school (the reverse being equally true had never lessened the shame), and it seemed preposterous to be coy about being stripped to the waist in front of Denis, given his own particular habit. He pulled his shirt over his head and clutched it securely to his chest as he sat, relieved to rest his ankles after walking a distance on soft, irregular ground.

'I will take my leave so you two can discuss the matter in hand,' Denis stood and began to unwrap his dhoti.

'No no, please stay, Denis-ji, your opinion will be most welcome.'

'Yes, your highness, of course,' Denis sat down again, the trail of his half-undone dhoti falling over the lamp where he had set it down, extinguishing it. 'Oh bugger and damnation!'

'Thank goodness we're not in church, eh, Denis,' quipped Cat, pleased at first with his quick irony, then not so sure he might not have given offence. The otherness of the situation he found himself in had taken away any sense of what was appropriate, but he felt no anxiety, no desire to be elsewhere. 'Uhm, on the matter of language, I thought you said you didn't speak the lingo round here, Denis? What were you chanting?'

'That was Sanskrit, my friend. I am an excellent Sanskritist, even if I say so myself, but that's as far away from the vernacular as Latin is to, shall we say, Cockney rhyming slang.'

'Oh, I do enjoy a bit of the old Cockney rhyming slang!' the Rajah was enlivened by the reference, and offered after a moment's thought, 'So here we are in the old *nation*, saying our *think-you-ares...*'

'I regret to inform your highness that I haven't encountered those particular examples before,' observed Denis, drily.

'Oh come on, you men, work it out,' grinned the Rajah, 'don't be dense!'

Cat made a pretence of working out what the Rajah was saying, but it was nothing more than that, as he didn't have a clue. Denis didn't even try.

'Oh, really, you're both so dull! *Nation* rhymes with *station* – Temple Station – temple – so here we are in the old temple … yes, come on…'

Further silence.

'Oh, dash it all, you're not even trying! Saying our *think-you-ares* – think you are – *who'd'ya think you are – who'd'ya puja*. Brilliant, what!'

Hurree's youth and inexperience, whatever else they might have excused or justified, meant he just didn't command sufficient respect from either of the other men that they were able toadily to laugh and extol the great wit of a high and mighty ruler. Quite the reverse, and Denis leant forward to ask, 'Do you really insist upon me staying longer?' an implied threat that he might be about to leave on the grounds of having much better things to be doing than listening to that sort of nonsense.

'Well I do think you might give a man credit for trying, at least!' moaned the Rajah. 'Anyway, if you want to be businesslike, then that's perfectly fine, so let's get on with it.'

'What is it we're getting on with, exactly, Sooty? Ooh, sorry, I mean your highness...'

'You can call me Sooty if you want, Adam – I know old habits die hard. Not in public, though, ok?'

'Yes, of course. Thank you.'

'I want to sort out how we're going to welcome the bishop when he arrives, put on a bit of a show, y'know.'

'What, festoons around the quay, that sort of thing?'

'He's not coming by sea. Can't stand sailing, apparently, so he's motoring up from Karachi instead.'

Denis winced at the thought of the overland journey. 'Being an impoverished bishop, I don't suppose he'll be chauffeur-driven in a Hispano-Suiza either. Poor bugger!'

'Yes, well, that's his choice. The last leg will be from Gwador, so I suppose we could greet him at the quay, before he turns up the palace road, but I think it would be better if we dolled-up the palace instead. Perhaps he can make a progress up the road in a convoy?'

There was a heavy silence for a moment, before Denis spoke up, 'A convoy of what, Hurree? Of camel carts?'

'Eh? Oh, yes, I see. No, that would never do, obviously.'

'I'm going to suggest that we wheel out the military band to play...' began Cat, quickly aware that he needed to stop developing this absurd idea, '...in the palace yard as he arrives, but… but I don't suppose...'

'We haven't got a military, really, let alone a military band.'

There was further silence, during which Cat decided that this wasn't so obviously his problem that he had a given duty to speak up. He would help if he could, but had no idea what to offer.

'Oh, dear, we're in a jam, aren't we,' murmured the Rajah, 'this is why I wanted your help, you chaps.'

'What is it we're trying to achieve?' asked Denis, tactfully adopting the first person plural, 'If we concentrate on what the aim of this enterprise has been, then perhaps we'll discover a means to do it sufficient honour.'

'The enterprise, Denis-ji, is to welcome a bishop to the state of Dhoosar Mathavassee for, I believe, the very first time.'

'I actually meant the greater enterprise, the whole bloody shebang – the church! What's it for?'

'Oh, that, it's to prepare DM – my impoverished little state, my subjects – for the future, which I firmly believe will be in the hands of western powers. If I can make DM a more attractive place to live and work, then I can attract the foreign investment we need here. That's what it's for.'

'Wouldn't a hotel have been a cheaper, more obvious start?'

'No no no, Barton and I have talked all this through! Land here is so cheap that any hotelier could come in and build exactly what he wanted, whereas the church is meant to show that we are an open state, where all religions are equal, and everyone can live side by side in peace. We got the idea from our trip to America – freedom of religion, first amendment, all that – and it must matter here because we're already religiously divided. So if we make it plain that this is a tolerant, liberal state, then people are bound to come and invest.' Hurree paused before continuing, sotto voce, 'We think there's oil here, you know!'

Cat admired the aim of the Rajah, who seemed to be so much less silly when sober, not clinging needfully onto Wigly, but he felt the thinking behind the decision to build a church, as described, was quite as bonkers as Enoch had made it out to be. Nonetheless, understanding that they weren't in a position to seek an ideal outcome, he felt he should contribute something positive towards finding at least the best possible. 'Look, we can't do much to welcome the Bish, because we haven't got much to welcome him with, but what we can do is greet him warmly, so that he can go back to Karachi and tell everyone what good eggs we are up here.'

'You are wise beyond your years, Master Adam,' observed Denis, 'because you have the courage to speak the truth plainly – and I shall take my lead from you. The palace is falling down, Hurree, there's no denying it, and there's no possibility of dolling it up in time. So we have to make it plain that that doesn't matter, that the people of DM are rubbing along perfectly well, and are eager to welcome outsiders.'

'Clearly, we'll have to get the imams out in their best whites...'

'No, Sooty, I think you're missing it. We don't need to put on a show. We need to demonstrate that we're ticking along in good order, despite having no oof, and that this is a well ordered state. The imams can turn up in rags, honestly, so long as they do turn up, look like they're doing their job properly, and that everyone seems happy.'

'I believe Cat to be correct, Hurree. I think the concert in the church is the key...'

Cat wrinkled his brow, wondering what Denis was going to suggest.

'...because that's where you can do the stuff of state, with all the toffs around. Otherwise, just get Ajaz out in his best bib and tucker to meet the bishop and bring him to you in your drawing room, where you'll be waiting, ready to give him tea.'

'Waiting with Barton,' Cat added, 'no-one else.'

The Rajah plainly understood the implication of Cat's remark.

'Then, when he's settled into his room, washed his hands and all that, you can walk together through the city to the church, so that he can meet the people, whom he will find charming, erudite and appealing.'

'How can you be so sure, Denis-ji?'

'Because I will station myself on a convenient corner and waylay him with my refined English and exquisite manners.'

'But you'll be bloody starkers, Denis!' complained Cat.

'So I will, but don't worry about that, these Anglicans take some shocking, I can tell you!'

'What shall I do with Political Agent in all this?' wondered the Rajah, 'He's so starchy and negative about everything I do!'

'I'll make sure Enoch's busy, Sooty, don't worry.'

'Thanks, Adam. You're actually a good sort, y'know! I'm glad your here.'

Hurree rose to his feet, preparing to leave, and waited for the others dutifully to stand with him, but Denis was too old and too detached to be bothered with all that, and Cat's ankles would trouble him if he were to stand now, so they both remained seated. Not sure what protocol had to say about seated insolence in his realm, Hurree nodded briefly and left, as powerless merely as a half-naked mortal.

'Well!' commented Denis, after a moment.

'I say!' responded Cat.

'What a conundrum.'

'Why oh why, do tell, Denis, are you in DM? Your life was in Delhi, you said. What made y'come here?'

'I should have thought that would be obvious!'

'It's not at all obvious why anyone would come here, not given the choice.'

'You came here! You didn't have to.'

'I had my reasons,' sighed Cat, seeing in his imagination Parvati loaded into the back of a black Maria, 'but surely, given how you live, you could've gone anywhere?'

'*In this dark cave I am alone, merged in myself, and the eternal night is still, like a mountain lake afraid of its own depth.*'

'Tacitus?'

'Don't be foolish, Cat! It's my old friend, Rabindranath Tagore.'

'You know Tagore?'

'We overlapped at university. But!' Denis raised a finger of admonishment, 'He only gave up his knighthood after Amritsar, whereas I gave up my life. I chose to come here because it was the act of penance; some ascetics stand on one leg for years on end, others walk on broken glass, but I chose to come here, the worst place in India, where I am in a dark place, solitary, and I have entered the infinite, the eternal annihilation, with Shiva, the great God – the mist has lifted, my fear and longing have gone, my consciousness glows clearly and brightly.'

'Yes, that's all very well, but you didn't give up *your* knighthood, did you!'

'I gave up the name to which it was attached,' Denis batted away the objection, gazing with apparent rapture at the statue of Shiva Nataraja.

The mention of Tagore brought Cat to remembrance of the evenings he had spent with Mariah, when they had lain together and she, resting her head on his shoulder, had read to him from *Gitanjali*, in the time before his heart had been broken. He joined Denis in a moment's silence, but without the benefit of the divine for companionship.

'Would either you or the gods be offended if I put my shirt back on now, Denis?'

'Only if you would be offended if I remove my dhoti.'

'That's a deal, then!' nodded Cat, suddenly overtaken by pangs of hunger, 'I'd better go and prepare for rehearsals, if you'll excuse me.'

25

Uncle Cat was no longer the first thing on my mind when I awoke the next morning, as I had become wholly preoccupied with Yelda. I see now that I was in a state of denial about the horrific end facing her, which seemed far, far removed from anything which could possibly happen in a modern(ising) state; I felt in my gut that it would surely all go away. What would bring about the moment when her narrative changed I didn't know, but my wishful thinking led me to believe it was inconceivable that the execution could go ahead, that the dread of hanging was her punishment alone. It just *had* to be the case the reprieve was already signed and waiting to be issued as soon as it was felt she'd suffered long enough.

I WhatsApped Sammy from my bed and asked him for permission to visit Yelda in her cell. I didn't attempt to debate with him further the wrong which was intended, but simply said I thought it was appropriate for someone to spend time with her to relieve the boredom she'd spoken about. He came back to me very promptly, making it clear that his reply was personal, intended only for my eyes, and stating explicitly that he was tormented by the fate which awaited Yelda. I was annoyed, frankly, because it seemed to me that if his sensibilities were so disturbed then he should do something about it. No-one was better placed than him to redirect the course of events, and simply grieving about it all was no substitute for action.

He gave me his permission, but was very keen that I was discreet about my visit; I think he must have meant primarily that he didn't want me to talk about it over drinks on the roof. And he sent word to the cell block that I was to be allowed access to Yelda as and when I wanted it.

I found her dozing on her bed when I arrived. She looked peaceful, her face relaxed, as I peered through the bars, and there was no sign of the tic which had been present the day before. I spoke her name, quietly at first, but she was in deeper sleep than I'd anticipated and I had to speak quite loudly to waken her. Maybe I should have left her to her slumbers, because she leapt up with her face a mask of terror, conditioned to expect the worst every time someone came in. She looked bedraggled, like someone the cat had dragged in backwards, as my Nan used to say.

We exchanged greetings in a ridiculously ordinary manner, as if we we'd bumped into each other in Boots, and she was interested to know what had happened to me after I'd been *sprung* (she joked) the day before. I told her about my dressing down by the Rajah, but didn't go into details about my conversation with Alban, or my hypothesis about the extent to which the absolute power which had condemned her probably wasn't as absolute as all that. She told me my skin looked much improved on yesterday, which reminded me about my too-hot bath, which in turn prompted me to ask when she'd last been allowed to shower.

The guards, it became plain, had received instructions that what I wanted was what I got (with the exception of Yelda's release, I'm sure), so that when I insisted they make provision for her to shower, they jumped to it immediately. She was led out of her cell, towards the end of the corridor (away from the steel door), where there was evidently a shower room, and I was furious that something so straightforward, so easily achieved, should have to have been asked for.

Fifteen minutes later she emerged, freshened and in clean clothes. Her long hair hung wet in bedraggled rats' tails over her shoulders, but it would dry in time. I insisted that they leave the cell door open, so that I could sit with her, to talk, to be some company, which caused a bit of a commotion. But I pointed out that the steel door still stood between her and her liberty, and the guards acquiesced eventually.

As I sat with her, I sensed she was anxious in case I was there to take advantage of her, as she became much more defensive in the way she interacted with me without the separation of bars. I assumed that two years with the Taliban had taught her to flinch emotionally any time a man came near, which must have made her time in this cell block a nightmare, since all the guards were male. I deliberately distanced myself by, for example, leaning away in the chair, in an attempt to show that I had no interest in her whatsoever, beyond being a friend when, I feared, she most needed one.

In at least one respect I failed as a companion, since she was greatly interested in knowing what had happened in the television soaps over the previous two years, information which I was entirely unable to provide. I could have told her about the rich and varied cultural experiences which I'd had in Manchester, my passion for theatre principal amongst them, but it was a complication-too-far to go into the business of whether or not soap opera should be counted in such company. I did promise myself, however, that I would watch an episode or two of 'Corrie' or ''Stenders' when I got home, to give them a go.

As I left, an hour or so later, and despite knowing that she'd thought the gesture silly the day before, I tapped my chest with my fist again. This time her smile was different, and I thought (hoped) she realised that I meant it, whether it was cool or not. I was inwardly terribly upset, as an hour of my time seemed too small a thing to give her, after all that she had endured. Whilst it was ridiculous to think of her as an innocent, because she was very definitely not that – and I don't mean in terms of shooting someone (oh, heavens, what a terrifying experience I thought that must have been) – it was impossible to think that she was sagacious in any ordinary sense of the word, and her mind must have been in a state of dreadful turmoil, regardless of how brave she tried to be.

I repeated my visit the next day, made sure she was showered, sat with her and chatted. We talked about Jodrell Bank, which I'd visited not long before I came here, and which was one of the last outings she'd had with her family in the weeks before her life had been ripped apart. She mentioned a younger brother, wondered how he was, reflected that he would just have left school and might be going off to uni in the autumn. That made her cry, for the first time since I'd met her, but only a little, and she was soon back in control of herself.

That's when she delivered her thunderbolt, for which I couldn't possibly have been prepared, and which, I swear, caused my heart to miss a beat. She asked me to be present at her hanging.

I protested that it wasn't over yet, that I was still working on getting her a reprieve. But we both knew that was untrue. There was nowhere to go to, no mechanism for overturning the Rajah's legal judgement. This place – where shiny new buildings were going up all over the place, flawless roads being laid, the internet ubiquitous and oil flowed freely to fill the treasury with cash – was, at heart, a brutal mediaeval state, kept that way by the corruption which had been made institutional from the get-go. Fur coat and no knickers, as my Nan would say. There was no possibility of me doing anything about Yelda's plight, no court of appeal, no parliamentarians, and, I guessed, no-one on her side; it was one thing not to want to see her hang, but something quite different to want her released and sent back to Bolton to pick up the pieces of her life.

She asked me to be present at her execution because she was afraid of being brutalised, either physically or at least in terms of being able to maintain her dignity. She wanted me to look after her interests, in so far as she still had any left. There was nothing at all in the whole world I wanted to do less than attend a hanging, any hanging, but I had committed to being her support and, with great reluctance, I promised I wouldn't let her down. I've never regretted an unintended pun as much.

I tapped my chest again, and she told me not to be a silly ha'p'orth.

As I left the cell block, tears welled up in my eyes, so I looked upwards to stop them falling, and saw across the city Ali's helicopter coming in to land. I wondered if he'd been running another state mission in his private machine; there was little doubt in my mind whom he'd gone to collect this time.

26

Cat arrived at the church before Enoch, having slogged through the extreme torridity of the afternoon, which was exceptional even by the standards of DM. The streets were utterly empty, the city having retired defensively to the darkness of its bedroom, which is where he would have liked to have been as well. He dragged himself from shadow to shadow, dodging as best he could the beams of the sun as they roared through the gaps between buildings, driven on by the strong sense that he shouldn't allow Enoch any opportunity to kick up a fuss, such as not turning up for a pre-arranged rehearsal.

As he made his pitiable progress, he was startled by an unexpected thud nearby, astonished when he saw that a kite had crashed from the sky, dead, in the middle of the roadway beside him. He'd heard of days so hot that birds expired on the wing – when the temperature topped 120°, he had been told – but never quite believed it, and never been able to imagine what that would be like; fine distinctions between one sort of too hot and another he found difficult to conceptualise. Well, here it was, the dreaded day of unbearable, deadly heat, and there he was, right in the middle of it. He cursed Enoch, at whose threshold he was happy to lay the blame for this torture.

He hesitated, knowing that it would cause offence to nobody if he simply walked on, allowed the twisted corpse of the kite to lie where it had fallen, but couldn't fail to respond to the urge he felt to retrieve it from the middle of the road, to lay it out in a more dignified pose in the shade. He thought perhaps that he should dash into and out of the full sunlight quickly, so as to avoid being rendered as lard. But any great exertion, on the other hand, could result in him too falling dead in the road, so there was a case to be made for undertaking this self-imposed mission slowly, casually. In the event, he half dashed and half meandered, with the average amounting not to a single, smooth action, but rather to significantly less than the graceful sum of its parts.

Close up, the once-beautiful kite was a big bird, heavier than Cat felt probable for a creature which soared so easily on the wing. And it was hot to the touch, poor thing. What a terrible way to come to your end, he thought, cooked in your own feathers, and he hoped the creature had been dead before it had hit the rough street and broken its neck; he imagined the horror of being a bird as magnificent as this suddenly unable to fly, tumbling chaotically towards the ground, to a certain death in the place of lesser, earth-bound beings. He carried it tenderly into the shade, where he laid it down, arranged it on its back, with its wings folded neatly, and legs sticking up in the air. He didn't want to wonder what it would taste like, an ignoble thought which he regretted, but lying there like that, it looked very like the sort of fare you'd see in a game shop during the shooting season back at home.

He trudged on until he was opposite the church, when he knew he'd have to cross the road in full sunlight, finding no more shade until he was safely inside. The recollection of maths lessons hadn't been one of his great pleasures since leaving school, but he did at least remember that the shortest distance is always a straight line, so he stepped out purposefully in the direction of the shimmering, hazy, white building. There were usually men at work on the tower at this time of the afternoon, but there weren't any today, and the crows which roosted alongside them in the scaffolding had all gone elsewhere too. The silence was eerie; oh, if only it was chilling. For a moment, as a wave of super-heated air wrapped itself around his face, he felt he couldn't breathe, wouldn't be able to carry on, but being certain that not carrying on would place him in real peril, he determined that the best, easiest, quickest way to deliver himself from dread was to continue, despite every bubbling cell in his body demanded that he return instantly to the shade.

It was touch and go whether he would reach the church alive. Or, at least, it felt that way. The haunting image of the dead kite had put him in a bit of a panic, and so he was relieved when he reached the door. The black iron latch-ring had been dangling in the full glare of the sun, and he burnt himself by grasping it too urgently, letting out a brief cry before pushing the door with his shoulder so as to tumble inside. The church interior was always a few degrees cooler than the city outside, and so it was today, although that was only relative and today it was jolly warm. The sunbeams radiating from the windows sliced through the white void, causing the air to shimmer even inside the building, and lighting up brightly the dust which danced in the thermals they created. Cat wondered how Parvati had been, resting in the shade of the vestry, and guessed that she wouldn't be at all happy.

Perhaps Enoch wouldn't actually be foolish enough to attempt to come to rehearse today after all, and having decided that he himself was staying put until the evening brought some respite, it occurred to Cat that he might actually have the afternoon alone with Parvati. What a rare treat that would be, and he could begin his adventures in Indian music with little steps, away from the prying ears of others, trying to mimic some of the scales and ornaments he had been hearing ever since he had arrived on the subcontinent. Away from the ears of Enoch in particular. He had no doubt whatsoever that, whilst he would be learning to play the sounds, regardless of what they were called or when they should be used, Enoch would know all the technical details, and probably value that knowledge more highly than the fact of being able to play them.

Retrieving his ancient, treasured, hot instrument from the vestry, it appeared to be just Parvati's tuning which had been affected, thankfully, so Cat steadied her on the chisel-ended spike, and began to twist the keys back and forth as he plucked the strings. Interestingly, now he thought about it, the oscillating microtones which this produced already had something of the Indian ornament about them, it couldn't be denied, although he had always in the past despised his coarser friends at the Academy when they had made such observations disparagingly in the presence of Mariah. Finally, Parvati was ready for him, so he stood for a moment, his face against the scroll, communing with her, before he picked up the bow and prepared to warm up, with glissandi through an octave on each of the strings.

There was a sound, a tiny sound, from amongst the pews, slight enough that Cat thought for a moment Indira might have followed him to the church. But that seemed so improbable that he dismissed the notion and lifted his bow again, only to hear the sound once more. If this was Enoch playing a trick, he'd be furious, and would certainly stripe the bow across his backside if he could get to him. But he heard the sound again, a sob, a child's cry.

'Who's there?' asked Cat, gently, fearful that he might scare the child out into the deadly sunlight if he was too abrupt. 'Hello?' he repeated, in response to the silence, 'salaam alaikum, me dost hain.'

There was a long pause before a vanishing voice squeaked, 'Me dost *hoon*, Cat-ji, nahi *hain*!'

Cat laughed. It was Salma, correcting his Hindustani. He carefully rolled Parvati onto her side, and went to find his little friend, curled up miserably as she was, on one of the pews. She looked dreadful, and not just from the heat. He studied her, then knew what had happened to his favourite friendly mite.

'Your brother? Osman?' he asked.

'*Murt.*'

Cat went to her side as she thrust out her orphan's arms needfully, longing for a moment of tenderness. He held her tightly, a tear dripping onto the inside of his glasses.

'Oh, you little thing, I don't have the language to tell you how sorry I am,' he sighed.

Salma hung onto him, convulsed with grief.

Cat struggled to think clearly, trapped in a moment of emotion without the means to respond, to find a fitting response, some way to enable him to make real the sharing of Salma's great upset. 'Wait, little one,' he blinked and another tear ran down his face, as he sat back to look at her, 'come with me, come, let's listen to Parvati together.'

Salma didn't understand, but she followed Cat, still holding his hand, back to where the double bass lay. He patted her shoulders to root her in place, and took Parvati up into his arms. The little girl's mouth fell wide as the strings resonated with the echoing sound of this giant wooden box. It might have contained a monster, for all she knew. Cat picked up the bow, and she flinched reflexly at the movement of a stick through the air. He gestured that she shouldn't be afraid, that all was well, held a finger to his lips inviting her to listen, and quietly played a sustained note on the open G string; she gasped. Cat pressed into the bow and crescendoed to forte and back again to piano; she smiled. He began a slow chromatic scale downwards through a fourth, to the open D string, then suddenly plunged a major third to the B flat below, returned through the intervening C to the D before dropping to the third position G on the bottom string. Salma stood with her eyes popping out of her tiny, still-wet face, her breath taken away by the richness of a sound she'd never imagined.

Cat paused for a moment, smiling at her. She smiled back, so he played the descending scale again, allowing it this time to become the ground bass of the lament from *Dido and Aeneas*, the last piece he had shared with Mariah, when she had played the harpsichord continuo. The chromatic descent of the scale dug deeply into his heart and, as he played, he started to sing the aria, '*When I am laid, am laid in earth...*'

Salma listened, tears filling her eyes once again.

'*...may my wrongs create no trouble, no trouble in thy breast...*'

Cat choked momentarily, which Salma echoed with a whispered *ahh*.

'*...remember me, remember me, but ah! forget my fate...*'

Cat stopped, gathering himself, as he tried to fight back more tears.

'*...remember me, but ah! forget my fate...*'

Parvati sang the chromatic scale plaintively again, and Cat sobbed, his hand shaking, the notes developing into a wide, pleading vibrato.

'*...remember me, remember me...*'

Salma had heard the ground bass, understood it, started singing it as Cat played, four octaves higher.

'*...but ah! forget my fate!*'

Together they repeated the scale, once, twice, thrice, when Salma began instinctively to improvise around the figure. Cat gasped when her voice soared like a crystal bell against Parvati's deep song, introducing the very ornaments he'd been hoping to learn. He began to introduce similar effects, copying her, to which she responded in full measure, and in a short time they were making music together, bound up in their curious variations on a ground bass by Purcell, immersed in a response to grief which had become an expression of the value of existence, here, now.

The moment was shattered when Enoch, who had entered unseen and unheard, added his shrill soprano to the ensemble, singing a descant like an unwelcome reveille from the most brutal bugler. Salma and Cat winced as one and ceased, united in the soul of their music, cast out of it together. Enoch held his arms horizontally, as if to take a bow, grinning with satisfaction.

'Ah, the passus duriusculus rendered passingly ridiculous,' he cried. 'May I ask what *she's* doing in here?'

Cat wasn't in the mood to explain Salma's presence, and felt, in any case, that no explanation was due. 'We're making music together. I should have thought that was obvious!' he replied curtly.

'H'm, very touching. Well, good, that's been a useful warm up for you on this very hot afternoon, so she can go now.'

'Are you serious Enoch? Are you suggesting we throw this child out onto the street on a day like today?'

'I'm not suggesting, I'm insisting!'

'Insist away, pal,' snorted Cat, 'but if she goes, I go!'

'You can't possibly, we have to rehearse – there isn't much time before the recital.'

'Fine, so we rehearse, but this little girl will sit in on our rehearsal. That's an end to the matter.'

'I won't allow anyone, particularly not a street urchin like *her*, to sit in whilst we rehearse. We have standards to maintain, you know!'

'Yes, we do, we certainly have standards to maintain, standards of decency towards a distressed little girl who needs shelter for the afternoon, and to be in the company of other people. Friendly people.'

'You just can't be serious, Cat!'

'I am absolutely serious. It would be inhuman to turf her out in this heat. She stays, or I take my chances with her and, frankly, that would be the end of our duo for good. Take it or leave it, Enoch.'

The political agent did what he did best, apparently, pondering rationally the situation as he found it, and he acquiesced with a shrug, suggesting that it hadn't really mattered in the first place. Cat was infuriated, but retained his composure both for Salma's sake and in order to protect for now the musical partnership, to salvage something from the afternoon. He laid Parvati down again and took Salma by the hand, leading her to a front-row pew, where she could watch the rehearsal. He gestured that she had to be very quiet, and she nodded, understanding.

'Right, shall we start with the concerto,' insisted Enoch.

'As you wish,' hissed Cat.

Cat took up Parvati, settled himself, cast a grin over towards Salma, whose eyes twinkled back as the introductory bars played out, and began to bow. Looking up from time to time, his delight in seeing the reaction from Salma was all consuming, and he had to check himself once or twice, finding that he was concentrating on her and not Dittersdorf, playing merely by rote. She was the perfect audience, soon humming along to herself, he could see, when the harmonium echoed his line, dancing along in her seat.

They spent about half an hour on the Dittersdorf, clearing up those few details which remained to be agreed. Then it was time to move on to the Mozart. Cat found his seat, squeezed into position, and began to pump. Enoch took up his position beside the harmonium and began, on cue, to sing.

'*Hell's vengeance boils in my heart, death and despair burn around me!*'

Cat snatched a glimpse at Salma, and saw in her face a look of awe, of horror, of dread that this was what the world of adults might involve routinely. She grimaced, and discreetly plugged her ears with her fingers, so Cat winked at her but she scowled back. Enoch battled on, hitting the high notes like a screech owl, and the next time Cat looked up, she had vanished, preferring the lethal heat to Enoch's soprano. Cat stopped playing.

'What? Why have you stopped?' snapped Enoch, irritated.

'Salma's gone. I'm worried for her in this heat. She didn't say she was going.'

'You stopped for that! I was right in the middle of the run – you've wrecked my breathing!'

'Crikey, Enoch, what's wrong with you? The girl was in a bad way. Couldn't you see that?'

'These feral kids survive, that's what they do, they just get on with it. Leave her alone. You'll never tame someone like her.'

'I'm not trying to tame her,' shouted Cat, wondering whether Enoch considered he'd tamed Indira, 'and they don't all survive. It seems they just don't.'

'From *my daughter nevermore*, please, if it's not too much trouble.'

27

I had told Lakshmi that Yelda had asked me to attend her execution and that I feared the hangman had arrived. It wasn't a great surprise, then, when he woke me early, rocking me gently by my shoulder. The servants' grapevine was alive with the information that this was the morning and, despite his calm manner, he insisted there was an urgent need for me to get up. The hanging was going to happen at six o'clock, and it was already five-thirty.

I've never wanted less to get up and face the day, yet a speedier awakening isn't possible. He was himself wired with anxiety, but helped me dress and escorted me down and through the back door, across the lawn towards the clearing in the woods, where he took his leave, making it plain that he had no desire to watch someone hang.

It was early, and the sun was only just reaching up above the top of the trees, casting long, red shadows across the clearing. The darkest shadow seemed to be that of the gallows itself, angular, static, man-made amongst those of the soft trees all around. There was a small group in attendance already, standing within a circle of armed commandos, which I could see included both the Rajah and the Yuvraj. I couldn't identify the half dozen people with them, but notable by their absence were any members of the Qifar family, likewise, Arabella. Forming their own little huddle at the rear of the protected ring were Alban and his colleagues, each with a notepad to hand, like reporters from a bygone, pre-digital age. On the scaffold were two men in black balaclavas and someone I took to be an imam, wearing a long, white robe.

Two of the commandos attempted to block my path as I approached, only to be called off by Sammy, who signalled I should join him.

Sammy: (whispered) Phil, what are you doing here? This isn't for you.

Judging by the pained look on his face, I guessed he wished it wasn't for him either. I acknowledged the Rajah with a nod of my head, noting that he too looked as though he was about to pass out.

Me: (also whispered) Yelda asked me to be her witness. Please don't stop me – I promised her, and it wouldn't take much to make me turn round and break the promise.

He began to make it clear that he was as grief-stricken as anyone by what was about to happen, that it was beyond his control, but I just couldn't bear to listen to what amounted to a whining admission of political impotence.

I looked up at the scaffold, which was about three metres above the ground, constructed largely of steel members painted in red oxide. There were waist-high railings on the front and sides, with a smaller area, an echo, similarly enclosed in the middle. Running from side to side overhead was a large H beam, the sort of thing you see in factories with a hoist and chain running along it, except that here there was a central, fixed ring, directly over the smaller enclosure. From that hung a long, thick rope, which looped down to the floor of the central area and back over the railing on the right side, where it was hooked over the end of a long lever projecting from the decking. At the end of the rope was the noose, made by tying the rope back on itself in the way we've all seen in films, except that the knot was much larger than I'd expected – but the word 'expected' is quite, quite wrong, because I had never dreamed of seeing such a knot in real life. At least the noose wasn't hanging loose in mid air, in the manner of the Hollywood version.

The sight of it made me shiver, as if there was a chill in the warm, moist air; Sammy stopped talking for a moment as I whimpered.

The central enclosure clearly had to be the trap, to be operated by the lever alongside. The thought which had gone into enclosing it, indeed the entire structure, with railings, to keep safe all those except those whom it was specifically designed to harm seemed too literal, too ironic, and the labour which had gone into this piece of engineering, its design and construction, was mind-blowing. I can imagine, I suppose, that it might just be possible to kill someone in a fit of temper, but not to coolly plan the end of someone's life, with engineering drawings and the importation of the steel stock necessary to weld into this structure. The lever even had a rubber handgrip on it. Such detail. And all for the sake of killing a helpless young stray from Bolton. This world seemed mad.

Me: (interrupting) This structure looks permanent. Is it going to be used again?

Sammy: Oh god, I hope not.

Me: Then why's it built like this. Why not just hang her from a tree?

Sammy: This is the design the Pakistan prison service sent us. It's supposed to do the job humanely.

I chortled sarcastically.

Sammy: I know what you're thinking, Phil, I really do, and I'm ashamed. No-one here can remember the last time anyone was executed in DM, and I regret that it's happening on my watch more than I can tell you.

Me: Then do something about it, Sammy!

Sammy: What!?! What do you want me to do?

Me: You're the heir, you run the place, put your foot down!

Sammy: But I'm only the Yuvraj, and my father has sentenced her to death. I can't go against the Rajah!

I glanced at the Rajah, who looked grey and anxious, fidgeting again, and simply couldn't believe that he was responsible for the decision which had led to us being gathered here this morning.

Me: It's the Qifars – I know it is. I know that they run this place like their own mafia fiefdom. I know that they're interested in protecting their investment in the airport. That's the reason why Yelda's being hanged today. *Pour encourager les autres.* It's nothing to do with justice. I know it – and you know it!

My whispers were becoming emphatic and harsh.

Sammy: Please, Phil, keep your voice down…

Me: *If you would know who controls you, see who you may not criticise.*

Sammy: Tacitus. Here, now, you quote Tacitus!

There was a flurry in the trees as a breezy gust caught their crowns, and the lingering smell of the felled trees mocked us with its sweetness, presaging the terrifying arrival of a jeep, coming round the track from the side of the palace. It was open, containing four commandos and Yelda. I saw immediately that they'd shaved her head, before it disappeared behind the scaffold, where it was hidden from our view by the black boarding covering the lower part of the structure. We fell into a deathly hush.

There was a substantial wait before we began to see activity on top of the scaffold, and I don't mean a moment which seems to last an eternity, but a real pause of two or three minutes. Then the first two commandos appeared, ascending the steps up to the deck, followed by Yelda, and then the third and fourth. Immediately, one of the commandos handcuffed her, and I concluded that the pause at ground level had arisen because it had been necessary to release her hands in order that she could safely climb the stairs.

One of the men in the black balaclavas took her by the shoulders and led her to the central enclosure where, her back towards us, he made her lift her feet in order to take off her trainers before pinioning her ankles. Her shadow struck out across the deck and mingled with the sharpness of the steel on the ground. He swivelled her around so that she faced us, and I could see plainly her eyes find me, when a smile came to her face. I thought she was pleased I'd kept my word, that she had at least one friend with her at the end. But she raised her manacled hands, made a fist with one of them and struck her chest with it, in a gesture which was contemptuous, mocking me, fixing me with her eyes, telling me I'd been duped. She continued to smirk at me even as the hangman wrapped a short fabric scarf around her neck. The imam approached her and she sent him away with a curl of her lip.

What followed happened very, very quickly, occupying the moment when I was still vainly trying to construct an expectation of what would happen next. The hangman slipped a black bag over Yelda's head, followed by the noose, which he tightened under her left ear – really tightened it – so that when Yelda began to repeat *Allahu Akbar Allahu Akbar* her voice cracked. And suddenly she was gone, dropped out of sight in an instant. The rope, from having been casually draped in a great loop, now hung straight and tight, disappearing through the decking, twitching briefly before swaying gently from side to side. The Rajah vomited, became suddenly crippled with frailty, and was led away promptly to his waiting car by one of the attendants.

I was incapable of clear thought, standing rooted to the wooded ground watching the gentle swaying of the rope. It looked like it could belong in a children's playground, that a kiddy had just finished playing on it. I watched as the hangman and his assistant disappeared down the steps, presumably to check that their work was done. I watched as the commandos patted each other on the shoulders, their job well done, but more, I suspected, that their stress was lifted. I saw Sammy led away to his waiting car, and watched as our ring of guards dispersed. I stood alone in the forest clearing, willing the ghost of Uncle Cat to return to this place and take me in hand, a kindly old male relative to be gentle, wise and generous.

Alban: (softly) Come on, Phil. Let's take you away from here.

Alban took me by the arm and led me around the scaffold towards the palace. I could have looked back, into the darkened space where Yelda's trussed body was hanging, but I closed my eyes to make it go away.

Alban: I've seen people hanged before and, if it's any consolation, that went pretty well as they go.

It was no consolation whatsoever.

28

Tremendous excitement surrounded the Right Reverend Jacob D'Souza's arrival on the 23rd. His dust-covered, open, bullnose Morris Oxford approached DM, bouncing along the dirt road from Gwador, with the bishop at the wheel, his wife beside him and a servant behind, at around two in the afternoon. This was usually a time of repose amongst the population in general, but the cry had gone up that that there was a motor car – a motor car! – nearing the city, and very quickly a large crowd of both men and women had turned out to witness this spectacle.

Being as unused to bishops as they were to cars, no-one was able to make any sense of the strange man in front, wearing inappropriately heavy black clothes and with a bright purple shirt beneath his jacket. He and his behatted wife, sweating profusely, smiled and waved at the crowds, as if they were the King Emperor and Queen Empress arriving at the Delhi Durbar, attempting to seem charmed and relaxed. It was plain to Cat, however, that they both looked like they'd endured forty days in the desert, with not a single temptation by way of relief.

Cat admitted to himself reluctantly that Enoch's intelligence gathering was extraordinarily impressive, as he had been able to tell the palace exactly when the bishop would be arriving, almost to the minute, and that Mrs. D'Souza would be beside him in the motor car. He had volunteered to be at the quayside, to be the first person to greet the party (rather as he must have done when Cat had arrived, it was clear), and was standing in the square, looking like a Roman policeman in his white suit and sola topee, ready to flag down the car and direct it towards the palace. Cat had agreed to accompany Enoch in order to keep him busy, as promised, by diverting him into the church as they left the quay, for a final run-through of the evening's programme.

The car pulled to a squealing halt as Enoch raised his arm. Cat was certain there was a brief moment when the bishop actually thought he was being detained by the local force, until Enoch made his introductions, politely, acknowledging Mrs. D'Souza with a raised topee and bow. He spoke for a moment or two before inviting Cat to come over and introduce himself.

'Good afternoon, my lord, madam,' began Cat, always ill at ease around a bishop, 'I trust your journey was pleasant?' This was so clearly a ridiculous gambit, made worse when Mrs. D'Souza's response to it revealed that she was on the very edge of weeping, that Cat felt rightly dismayed by what was a disastrous start. He had only one piece of information he wanted to share with the visitors anyway, and the conversation wasn't going in the right direction for him to reveal it, as it were, organically, so he opted to just to dive straight in, 'I am Cat Adam, the Master of the Rajah's Music.'

The bishop raised a disbelieving eyebrow, whilst his wife observed, untruthfully, that she was charmed. Enoch directed them up the road to the palace, and they disappeared through the parting crowd and swirling dust, the Morris complaining bitterly of the treatment it was receiving.

'Ah, you see, that'll be the eleven-point-nine horsepower straight-four side valve engine,' explained Enoch to the world around him, 'not nearly up to the task. The later thirteen-point-nine would've been a better choice, but still, neither would be nearly good enough for the genius, Henry Royce, I'll warrant.'

'H'm, be that as it may, Enoch, but we've got two one-point-nothing horsepower tongas waiting to return us to the church. Shall we not keep them waiting?'

Enoch's nose was distinctly put out by not being invited to the palace for tea with the bishop, and he grumbled all the way through the final rehearsal about how it was unseemly for a man in his position to be excluded from the affairs of state. Cat reminded him more than once that those affairs belonged to a state which was not his to command, in which he had only a peripheral role as the official British busybody, but he didn't seem to want to hear that point of view, still less accept it. He was grumpy, even edgy, as they returned to the bungalows to rest and, in Cat's case, eat before the concert. Perhaps he was nervous about the performance, which wasn't at all what Cat would have predicted.

Enoch had been allowed to join the party later, as it assembled in the durbar hall, prior to setting off for the church. Cat remained close to Vij, cheekily running his fingernail across her back, where there was a gap between saree and blouse, when no-one was looking. He overheard the PA discussing cars with the bishop, who appeared to be interested only because his Morris had failed to reach the palace under its own power, since the engine died just as they had drawn level with the church, ominously. Very many willing hands had come forward to push the car into the palace yard, so little time was lost, but the episode reduced very greatly the dignity of the bishop's arrival, he felt strongly. It was clear that there was no-one else on hand who could diagnose and repair the problem, so Enoch's enthusiasm for motor vehicles had raised the bishop's hopes. But they were quickly dashed when it became clear that that enthusiasm went only to far as to include a detailed theoretical knowledge of technical specifications, and that wielding a spanner was not something he was able to do.

Cat was in his concert kit, white tie and tails, thoroughly enjoying the fact that his shirt, waistcoat and collar had remained unstarched since they were last washed, and so were soft and crumpled. He had thought initially that this would never do at the Albert Hall, but he was very comfortable here and felt that his playing might benefit from the ease of movement, so he contemplated the demise in general of formal evening wear for performance, and became sure it was a jolly good idea. Enoch was in his white tails again, cutting a dash it was true, but Cat did think that the tails made him look even shorter than he was.

The procession from the palace to the church was going to be early, in daylight, so there would be time for the concert and, back at the palace, a banquet to follow. There was the additional advantage that the people would be able to see the spectacle, lining the road which, at night, was poorly lit with only sporadic hanging lanterns. The Rajah and the bishop would lead the progress, with Mrs. D'Souza and Vij behind, the doctor having been deputed as a temporary rani for the occasion. Barton and Wigly would follow, attempting to give the impression that they were *both* royal advisors, Faiq Qifar would walk beside DM's senior imam and, behind them would be Cat and Enoch. Bringing up the rear, resolutely, defiantly, was the Rajah's uncle, whose name Cat still didn't know, but whose thunderous ill-temper was plain throughout the proceedings. At each corner of this coterie marched, in their own fashion, one of the elderly guards, holding their decrepit Martini-Henries to the present, their liveries freshly returned from the dhobi.

There was a surprisingly good turn out along the route, considering the aim of the walk-past was to honour an unknown bishop who, the next day, would consecrate a building which contained nothing of interest for any one of the locals. The imams had been requested to muster their flocks, and appeared to have been obligingly successful, raising the promise of good inter-faith relations, should anyone of a different faith ever come here again. The children appeared and disappeared like rabbits sniffing the air outside their burrows, as their heads darted in and out of gaps between the standing adults. Cat tried to spot Salma, whom he'd not seen since Enoch's singing had driven her out of the church, but he couldn't spot her amongst the others, and was concerned for her. He would have been very pleased if she came to the concert, which was open to each and everyone at no cost, but didn't think for a minute she would have the confidence to turn up.

Tucked discreetly away, barely visible behind a roof parapet, was a moving picture camera mounted on a tripod. Cat couldn't see the operator's face, as his head was held low behind the camera, but the movement of his arm as he cranked the machine was clearly visible. He peered up at the camera as he walked past, wondering where it had come from.

Unmissable, on the other hand, was Denis, whose prominence in the crowds was guaranteed by the combination of his nakedness and his position, at the front on a corner as promised, where he couldn't be missed. As the bishop approached, he stepped forward and bowed deeply in front of him. There was a gasp from all around, as if he'd laid a turd at the feet of a Mughal emperor, and Cat's heart leaped when one of the guards, with due regard to Denis's trident, hesitantly stepped forward and attempted to bar any closer contact.

'Good evening, bishop,' Denis peered round the guard to address the cleric.

'Good evening to you too, sir sanyasi.'

'I thought I'd introduce myself as I was at school with your father,' Denis declared with the all confidence of the Establishment.

'Good heavens, were you really? At Harrow?' the bishop pushed the guard to one side.

'Indeed I was. We were the two dusky scholarship boys.'

'Well, I never. And what was your name?'

'I used to be Selveratnam, Denis Selveratnam.'

'How extraordinary! My father spoke often about you. Well well well.'

'We were good friends, played together in the second eleven. I was at your Christening, you know.'

'I know, I know. Dear wife, this is one of my father's old school pals. Fancy that!'

Mrs. D'Souza didn't fancy that at all, and remained rooted beside Vij, from where she extended an undecipherable chirrup which was both greeting and farewell in one.

The bishop looked Denis up and down: 'When did you begin to relinquish this earthly life?'

'It was a response to nineteen nineteen. I couldn't carry on.'

'Ah, Amritsar,' nodded the bishop, sadly, 'yes, we must struggle to find our response to those dreadful events. Will you be coming to this very exciting concert, Denis?'

'I'm not sure I would be welcome in my present state, Jacob,' Denis indicated his nakedness.

'Nonsense! Our Saviour had a penis, don't forget.'

Vij, who had already turned round to face Cat in an attempt to hide her amusement, spluttered upon hearing this unexpected piece of intelligence, and had to to endeavour to turn it into a sneeze when the bishop's wife gave her a very obvious look. Cat tittered quietly to himself, proud at that moment to know Denis.

Denis tagged along with the party for the short remaining distance, reminiscing with the bishop as they walked together. The list of those known to be attending the concert was increased by one, as a result, the importance of which was shortly to be measured. An issue which had occupied both Cat and Enoch either side of the hours they'd spent preparing the programme was attendance, since it wasn't at all clear from where amongst the general public would come the incentive to attend a concert of foreign music in a building which many saw as haram, presided over by a Rajah from one religion other than their own, and a bishop from another. In the event, doubtless due to the cajoling of the imams, the church began to fill up quite respectably, and there was a good attendance. Not all of the pews were full – Cat estimated there were seats for two or three hundred people – but there weren't any gaping holes.

Almost all of those present were men, and all of them wore a taqiyah by way of acknowledging that the proceedings were something vaguely to do with religion. There was much gazing into the empty space of the church, which few had seen before, but there was a notable lack of pleasure on the raised faces, even amongst those to whom Faiq was giving an impromptu guided tour. For most in the audience the idea of a harmonium was familiar, if only the ubiquitous hand-pumped version found in temples and homes across the subcontinent, so there was interest in the church instrument on the basis of its size, but not otherwise, and just a handful of people walked round it in order to get a closer look. The hubbub of settling down in this strange environment didn't cease until Cat appeared from the vestry, carrying Parvati under his arm. This was a sight which, apparently, very few had seen before, and there was an audible gasp before the church fell silent. Cat smiled his welcome as he set Parvati down, lodging her end-pin in what had become his usual grout line.

'Good evening, everybody,' he announced, amazed at how greatly the acoustic had altered because of the crowd.

Enoch, by arrangement, repeated his words in Hindustani.

'We're terrifically pleased to see so many of you here this evening, and looking forward to playing for you.'

Enoch hesitated for a moment, unsure about the correct translation of 'terrifically' in this context.

'I am Cat Adam, Master of the Rajah's Music, and this is my first chance to play to you all. I'm jolly excited, I can tell you!

Performing with me is Enoch da Costa who is, as I'm sure you're all aware, the British Political Agent for Dhoosar Mathavassee.'

The silence which attended the introductions could have been taken in one of two ways. Either the audience was waiting attentively for the start of the programme, determinedly hushed like those attending a brass band concert at the Free Trade Hall, or they were grimly mute because they didn't want to be there at all. In either case, as Enoch launched into a complicated explanation of his composition, which included amongst his flow of Hindustanti the loan words *total serialism*, it became clear to Cat that there was a swelling bore of impatience which it would be best to dispel.

'So, if you are ready, maestro...' Cat interrupted Enoch.

There was a look, a moment's silence, before Enoch feigned a good-natured laugh, and took his place at the harmonium.

So many hours of rehearsal had happened over the weeks, for the simple want of any better pastime, that the duo were able to begin very precisely, without any visible signal passing between them. They hit the opening anacrusis as if they were a single performer, which delighted Cat, and he hoped that the audience had admired their synchronicity. But as he played, he looked up from time to time, and he noticed that minds were wandering. Open mouths and boggled eyes became the norm amongst the audience at large, whilst on the front row the bishop fiddled with his pectoral cross and the Rajah played footsie discreetly with Wigly, who had somehow managed to sit beside him. It wasn't clear what Denis, in his nakedness, was doing to amuse himself, but he certainly wasn't paying attention to the music. And it was plain that Mrs. D'Souza was once again fighting back her tears, whilst Vij's imploring stare told Cat all that he needed to know.

For all Enoch's extraordinary technical facility, he wasn't a skilled performer, in Cat's opinion, as his mind was too embedded in the music for him to be able to judge its effect on the audience; it was as if he played to please himself, and none other. As a consequence, he was startled when Cat began to pick up the pace of what remained of the sonata, failing to understand why he wasn't sticking to the tempi as rehearsed. He craned his neck above the harmonium to glare at Cat, which Cat had anticipated but which he ignored, using his greater experience to force the issue. The only way to please the audience with this prime example of total serialism, he was in no doubt, was to bring it to its close as soon as possible.

Sensing the greater energy, a rise in tension, the audience became more attentive, with the prospect some time soon of an event which they could understand – the end – hinted at. And there was a respectable round of applause when the closing dissonance became silence at last. Enoch was furious, Cat could see, as he dismounted to take a bow, but his rage was reduced by what he perceived as a respectable reception. Cat recognised that the applause was, in truth, a fulsome expression of relief that the sonata had ended, but he went through the right motions, taking a bow himself before stepping aside and acknowledging the superior genius of the composer with an expansive, and wholly dishonest, gesture.

'Stick to the tempi in the Mozart,' hissed Enoch as they switched places, 'I don't know what you thought you were playing at there!'

Cat nodded, as if innocent, wondering what the audience was going to make of the next item. He was confident that a pair of eighteenth-century soprano arias in the highest coloratura, as rendered be a man perceived by the people of the city as remote and off-hand, would arrest the audience's attention wholly, and not necessarily for the right reason. He remembered the effect of Enoch's falsetto on both Indira and Salma, and wondered if the presence of dignitaries would be enough to contain the audience. He couldn't help but contemplate the famous riot which followed the premiere of *Le Sacre du Printemps*, amongst a willing and musically-experienced Parisian audience, thinking that that could fade into historical insignificance if this male gathering decided they didn't like what they were hearing. Just as well the guards were here, he thought idly, looking round, puzzled when he couldn't see them anywhere.

As his second instrument, the keyboard had never become part of Cat's persona in the way the double bass had. He was an adequate player, but had to concentrate on what he was doing to the exclusion of all else, especially on the harmonium with all the foot-pumping as well. As a result, he reached the end of the second aria without much sense of how Enoch had sung, other than that the high F had been a terrible scream. He looked up at last to see the audience immobilised, in a state of shock, stuck to the pews not by appreciation for what they'd heard, but rather because they'd not been able to believe that they'd heard it at all. It was as if they'd witnessed an event as improbable as a hard frost on the streets of DM. Mouths were gaping wide, but not in the slack-jawed manner of the earlier boredom, instead they were each now held in a terrible rictus, with none more so than the bishop's. Unable for the time being to rotate his head on his neck, he stiffly turned his entire upper body in order to console his wife, for whom it had all become too much. Eventually a single clap from Vij signalled that applause was now required, if only to bring to an end this shocking experience, and it propagated around the nave like bubbles rising from rotting vegetation below the water's surface, until Enoch felt able to break out of his feigned reverie and take a bow, confident that the long silence was the result of a quite different type of recovery.

'Ah, the grief of bathos!' he muttered to Cat as they crossed once again.

Cat took up Parvati and pressed his cheek against her scroll. 'Ladies and gentlemen,' he addressed the audience, 'this instrument is over four hundred years old, and is a very special...'

As Enoch translated, a moment of doubt washed over Cat. Familiarity had led him to take it for granted that Parvati was just 'his' double bass, and he'd not given any real thought recently to exactly what she was, until just now when he'd stated her age. The madness of having brought such a precious instrument with him to the end of India suddenly seemed obvious.

'...you're about to hear it in one of the very few concertos written specifically for the double bass...' he continued, '...composed by Karl Ditters von Dittersdorf, who was a notable composer of the eighteenth century, a friend of Mozart and Haydn...'

How could this possibly be the place to keep Parvati? Would this be his first and final appearance as Master of the Rajah's Music?

'...one of the curiosities of his age, in Europe, was the rigidity of social ranking, and Karl Ditters, born a commoner, found himself promoted to a position in court which required him to be a nobleman, so he simply went to Vienna and had his status upgraded by the Emperor, becoming Karl Ditters von Dittersdorf in the process...'

He whispered an apology to Parvati, for the rough time he must have put her through.

'...but, as you'll hear, the music, and thus the man, remained genuine underneath it all.'

He plucked quietly each string in turn, to check Parvati's tuning, and to prime the bond which lay between them. He paused, looked into the audience to understand the scale of connection he needed to make with them, and was about to nod to Enoch when, from the corner of his eye, he saw a fleeting movement at the back of the church, as if a single leaf had twitched on an otherwise undisturbed tree. He hesitated, unsure what had happened, searched with his eyes – it was Salma! – she had crept in, and was hiding behind a pillar, but Cat could see her little feet sticking out. He laughed for joy, which pleased the audience as they felt it was for each and every one of them. So he laughed again, and this time they were correct.

The experience of playing the concerto to this smiling audience, of communicating beyond the restrictions of language, filled Cat with the will to find his best form. He felt that if anyone here didn't know all that was important to know about him and Parvati by the time they had finished, then he would have failed. And, as a result, his effort was tremendous, his performance magnificent. Parvati responded in turn, with wails, and giggles, and rumbles, and the sheer, melodious cheek of being an enormous instrument producing improbably high harmonics. If this was going to be the only chance DM would ever have to hear Cat and Parvati then, between them, they were going to make it count. Cat looked up from time to time, and saw bright eyes sparkling in the setting sunlight, as it turned the white of the interior to a warm red. There was movement everywhere, the small twitches people make when they have been taken over by music, whether a tapping toe or a nodding head, and at the back, still nearly hidden, Salma danced.

With a flourish, Cat and Parvati arrived at the final bar of the third movement, and brought the joyful piece to its end with Dittersdorf's repeated pizzicato octave Es. The effect was delightful, with spontaneous applause from every corner and, little by little, a standing ovation. Salma came out of hiding, and bounced as she clapped and waved at Cat. Enoch stepped out from behind the harmonium bearing on his face a look of unalloyed joy, knowing that he and Cat had gone beyond what was merely acceptable, that here, now, in Dhoosar Mathavassee, they had been brilliant. And Parvati had spoken in clear terms, making it plain that she was happy in India, that she was going to stick with Cat come what may.

The bishop, who held his grinning wife's hand whilst still clapping with his own, was persuaded to step forward to speak. 'Your highnesses, ladies and gentleman,' he began…

'SIT DOWN, MR. BISHOP!' commanded a booming voice.

There was immediate silence.

The Rajah's uncle stepped forward, and the bishop did as he had been bade. Cat couldn't make out what was happening, and looked to Enoch for some sort of guidance. None came.

The uncle spoke first in Hindustani, whereupon the general audience began obediently and silently to hurry out. As they left, a handful of armed men entered, each carrying a modern rifle, wearing khaki drill but no insignia. They positioned themselves at rehearsed points around the church, and stood with their arms ported, but at no point did they engage with the royal party as individuals, neither a look nor a sound. Cat's heart was racing, and he brought Parvati up into the horizontal in the hope that an escape route might become available. He looked towards Vij, who showed every sign of rage at being treated like this, but who was keeping quiet for now.

'It has become inevitable that changes are made in the governance of Dhoosar Mathavassee, and it is felt that the quickest and easiest way in which to achieve these changes is to remove you, Hurree, from your throne, and to install Prince Shankarrao in your place.'

There was a gasp from Wigly, otherwise this statement was received in absolute stillness.

'Let me allay your fears immediately. None of you will come to any harm, so long as you do as you're instructed. You are safe.'

Denis rose to his feet, a sudden movement which, if made by another, might have resulted in a reaction from the soldiers. But, having left his trident at the door and since it was unarguable that he had no other concealed weapons about his person, he was allowed to continue.

'I would ask you, your highness, two things. Firstly, why, if you mean us no harm, have we been placed under armed guard? Secondly, and here I refer to my former life in the law, are you aware that unconstitutional change such as you appear to be describing – a coup by any other name – is forbidden, and carries the promise of severe punishment, regardless of the rank of the offender?'

'Do sit down, you ridiculous old duffer!' instructed the uncle. 'You are under armed guard for your own protection, both to demonstrate the necessity of doing what you are bloody-well told, and to keep you safe from the attentions of any outside this building who might hold grudges against you. Is that clear?'

Denis, used to being called many things but not, apparently, a ridiculous old duffer, had nothing to say, and sat.

'As for the matter of what is and is not constitutional, what is and is not lawful, I have spent my life arguing with the likes of you who simply do not understand the nature of the princely states, and the power held absolutely therein. There is only one source of authority in Dhoosar Mathavassee, the rightly appointed heir to the ruddy throne, but that is not a matter of birthright under the laws of this state. My late brother appointed his elder son as his successor, it is true, but he wasn't fully appraised of your character at the time, Hurree, and I am confident that he would have chosen otherwise had you not been overseas at the onset of his final illness. I am removing you from your throne and titles, by force if necessary, on the grounds that it is both what your father would have wanted and what is best for this state.'

Silence.

'For the time being, I will take on the role and functions of divan for the new Rajah, exactly as I did for his father. He will be at liberty in due course to find his own man for the job, at which point I will voluntarily step down. Power for myself is not my aim.'

Silence.

'You will all be escorted now to the palace, where you will be fed and housed for the night. Doctor, you may return to your hospital. Denis, please go with her, I implore you. In the morning, you will gather your personal effects, which will be transported to the Royal Navy frigate which is at anchor off the quay. You will be taken by sea to Karachi, where further arrangements will have been made for you. I understand your automobile has broken down, bishop?'

'It has!' the bishop was remarkably assertive in his response.

'In which case, I'm sorry that you must leave it behind, as you too will be on the frigate tomorrow. It will be kept in a safe place whilst you arrange for its collection.'

The bishop didn't seem so assertive now that he knew he was going on a sea voyage. Mrs. D'Souza, on the other hand, looked positively delighted.

'But what about this church?' asked the bishop, with the bearing of a man already sea-sick, 'I'm here to consecrate it.'

'Oh bugger the bloody church!' harrumphed the uncle. 'Right, get to your feet, everyone, we'll make our way back to the palace.'

The soldiers, clearly well-drilled, created a tighter formation as the party rose. Hurree looked despondent, tears rolling down his cheeks, and had to be lifted from his seat by Wigly, using some force. They were herded towards the door like a handful of errant sheep, but with barely a sound being heard, and not a word spoken.

Slipping Parvati into her soft case, Cat followed obediently, only to see Vij disappear with Denis, heading for her clinic. She didn't look back, didn't try to exchange looks with Cat.

'I can't leave without saying goodbye to her,' he said glumly to Enoch, who walked calmly beside him.

'Just keep walking, Cat, for now. There will be no need for you to leave at all.'

'I don't understand. You heard what we were told in there. We're sailing away tomorrow.'

'Not necessarily. You can leave if you wish, but I'm not, and you don't have to. You are employed by the palace – well, loosely, I suppose – and that will still be true tomorrow.'

They walked on in silence, gazed at by onlookers from the shadows, as they passed along the dark road to the palace. Once they'd entered the palace compound, Enoch steered Cat off to the left, to make their way round to the bungalows along the vehicle track. The bishop's car had already been moved from where it had ended its journey, in front of the palace, and been pushed down the same track, so that it now stood between 2nd Bungalow and the water.

Cat's nerves had been so electrified by what had happened that he hadn't felt the burden of carrying Parvati under his arm until they were back in front of the bungalows, when he began to feel under direct threat no longer. Although this didn't amount to feeling safe, he relaxed a little and became aware immediately of the ache in his shoulder, so he carefully laid her down on his veranda. He went directly to her giant case, opened it and disappeared inside.

'Oh, for heaven's sake, Cat, you're not going to defecate now, are you? The hours you've spent sitting on the blasted box, trumping like a thirty-two foot diapason. It's nearly driven me mad! How can anyone… Oh!'

Cat emerged from behind the screen, clutching the stack of George V rupees Enoch had given him.

'I had no idea my private behaviour irritated you so much.' Cat muttered acidly, 'But who can tell what makes affection turn to irritation, in the way it does.'

'Yes, well, I've said it now.'

'In answer to your question, no, I was not going to have a shit...'

'How needlessly Germanic!'

'...oh, shut it, Enoch!' barked Cat, stuffing the notes into his jacket pocket, 'I was taking my money out of the biscuit tin, as I now intend to keep it on me. The only way they'll get it is if they kill me, and then I won't care.'

'Look, no-one's going to die, Cat, I can promise you.'

'And you would know that, wouldn't you, because this is all your work.'

'I resent that suggestion!'

'Enoch! Uncle Elephant said that there's Royal Navy frigate waiting. Not a frigate, or an Indian Navy frigate, but a Royal Navy frigate. And since he was so keen to stress that DM is its own place, the only way that a Royal Navy frigate is going to become involved in this is if you organised it.'

'H'm, yes, he wasn't supposed to say that the frigate was ours, actually!'

'Yes, well, *he's said it now*! All those trips to the telegraph station, all your fucking 'diptels', you've been planning this all along. You stated you were being a dove – I heard you, right here. You're a liar, da Costa, a filthy liar!'

'I was being wholly honest, my dear friend...'

'Don't you call me your dear anything!'

'Wholly honest. Might I remind you what noise doves make?'

'What the fuck are you talking about, Enoch?'

'They go *coup coup, coup coup*!' Enoch thought he had been hilarious.

'You utter cunt, Enoch. These are people's lives you're toying with here. How dare you joke about it.'

'You know the difference between you and me, Cat? Shall I tell you?'

'Well, you're bound to know the answer to even that, so, yes, why don't you.'

'You care about things, Cat. That's your problem.'

'My problem?'

'Yes, that's why you find playing music so difficult, because you care about it. I can just play it and be brilliant, but you have to be *musical*!'

'Difficult! Enoch, music is what I do!'

'Moreover, I have learned from experience that caring about people is a dreadful error, because they die.'

'Who died that you ever cared about, Enoch!'

'Prince Johnny died. I liked him, and he liked me. My brother died. They sent him home with half his face blown off. He couldn't bear it, so he asked me to help him kill himself.'

'You helped him?'

'He was brave, vain, a strapping fellow when he went off to war. By the time he came back, he was still brave and still vain, but he'd learned to think, and it was all too much for him – a great example of what Buchan said about thinking being injurious to health; 'few instances can be produced of studious persons who are strong and healthy'.'

'Oh, Christ, stop quoting other people at me!'

'I, on the other hand, have always been a thinker, always a cringing coward and never strapping, but it turns out I am vain, just like him, so whilst I couldn't possibly face being shot at, I could come here, where they sent me as a punishment for being half-caste, and I could fight my own battle in my own way, and prove them all to be idiots, and look, Cat, see, gaze upon me in my finest hour!'

'You're mad, Enoch, bloody mad!'

'But Cat, I have won, I have become Roe and Clive in one, I have changed the world. Look, I am the best, I am a winner!'

'Stark raving mad!'

There was a terrible scream, which took both Cat and Enoch by surprise. They looked up and saw Indira running frantically towards them.

'Sahib – oh Sahib – Wigly Sahib has gun – look for you!' she screamed again, running towards Enoch with her arms outstretched, scared senseless.

Enoch stood impassively, unable to rise to the task of offering her any comfort, motionless, until a shot rang out, followed by the sound of a bullet finding its mark behind them on the veranda. Cat turned to see that it had punched a hole in Parvati's case, clean through the opened lid, and he snatched Parvati up, clutching her close to him, an instinctual reflex which could have had no protective value against a bullet.

'Enoch! Enoch Da Costa!!' Wigly was lurching towards the bungalows, grasping in his hands one of the guards' old rifles, which he must have seized in the confusion of the moment whilst no-one looked. He was struggling to reload the single shot weapon, screaming hysterically as he approached, 'You absolute bastard, you'll pay for what you've done. You have destroyed our lives, everything, everything is gone – I'm going to kill you, you bastard!'

He stopped, pulled back the action lever on the rifle and took aim. Cat was overwhelmed by the drumming in his head, could hardly hear for the roar in his ears. He opened his mouth to plead with Wigly, but too late – a second shot rang out and Indira cried in pain, stumbled, collapsed onto the veranda at Enoch's feet, her head cracking into the timber like a dropped canon ball.

Cat lost control of himself and, still clutching Parvati, instinctively threw himself at Wigly before he could fire again. From the depths, he summoned one of his most hated memories, of cadet training at school, and screamed as he'd been taught when charging with a bayonet. The enemy froze as Cat drew closer, until he was upon him, when Cat's scream grew even more fevered and Parvati's sharpened endpin penetrated Wigly's sternum, effortlessly splitting the bone and piercing his heart. Wigly hung momentarily on the end of the spike as blood filled his mouth, his weight dragging Parvati down until he slid off and fell into a limp heap on the floor.

Cat stared in breathless disbelief at the corpse he and Parvati had created. He looked back to the bungalow, surprised at how far he'd managed to run, and saw that poor little Indira was dead, beyond question. Enoch, the craven cur, had run away, was nowhere to be seen.

There was no time for thought, no time for action, no time to stand and be counted. There was time only for flight, and Cat took off round the side of the palace, back towards the city, the one lucid thought in his blackened mind being that he had to reach Vij.

When he emerged into the square before the palace, he could see along the road a large mob gathered in front of the church, which was ablaze. Orange flames leapt high up the west end, and the crowd bayed jubilantly, rejoicing in every moment as popping sounds began to signal the beginnings of collapse for the unfinished tower. Cat didn't know what to do, sure that he couldn't pass safely within sight of them, and yet not knowing how to pass them otherwise. He placed Parvati beside him, on her endpin, and pressed her tightly up against a wall beside him, struggling desperately to catch his breath, to think coherently.

There was a gentle knocking sound, which Cat thought at first was Parvati speaking to him. Again it came, more insistently, and he craned his head forward as far as he dared, to see round her, and there, on the other side, was Salma, also pressed up against the wall. He wondered if she was mimicking him because she thought it was a game, but she pursed her lips and gestured shh, commanding his silence.

He nodded, when she whispered, 'Doktar ke paas – chalo...', and indicated with a sideways gesture of her head that he was to follow her. She slid along the wall, keeping flat against it, away from the mob, and disappeared into a narrow alleyway that Cat had never noticed. He followed, but not without difficulty since both he and Parvati had to negotiate the tiny opening sideways; her case scraped the wall, and Cat could feel the canvas abrade. Carrying Parvati, terrified, he struggled as best he could to keep up with his miniature guide, and she stopped every so often to allow him to catch up, but the paths were narrow and dark, and she would disappear within an instant down yet another hidden entry, only to have to return to show him the way when he missed her. Eventually, they emerged in a wider passage, which Cat recognised as being close to the hospital.

There were groups of men passing along adjacent streets, shouting, Cat could hear, all heading towards the burning church, but none which interfered with their progress until they arrived at the square in front of the hospital, which was a meeting point of passageways. An enormous huddle of covered women milled in front of the hospital, engaged in animated conversation about the events of the night, who spotted Cat just as it became clear that another group of men was about to pour into the square. He panicked completely, losing control, and tried to stop Salma going further, begging her to go back with him, but she cried out to the women and pulled him towards them. Spontaneously, they opened up their numbers, like a muster of giant crows, and wrapped themselves around Salma and Cat, moving as a body towards the alley at the side of the hospital whilst the mob passed by.

Once it became safe, the protective ring of women parted, to disgorge Cat and Salma, so they could make their way up the alley towards the rear of the hospital. But before he took a single step, there was a great boom in Cat's head, when, in an instant, everything became brilliantly lit by an orange glow and he was suddenly overwhelmed by a sense of calm and well-being. The terrifying pounding in his head had ceased, he was no longer short of breath, all his fear had gone. And so had his body. He stood, utterly awed, as he saw in the eerie glow his own self walk forward with Salma, hand in hand, who dragged him down the alleyway like a dog reluctant to walk. He saw himself carrying Parvati, struggling under the load, and how tensely he moved, as if every step was one more in the direction of the gallows, saw the back of his dress jacket covered in dust, the tails hanging limply.

He followed, aware that the inexplicable position in which he now found himself, had the other he been aware of it, would be a matter of considerable consternation, as the other he would have been unaware of the fact that this he felt so jolly good, both in mind and body. His steps were light, his thinking clear, his breathing – well, he wasn't breathing at all! Was he dead? If he was, it was of no consequence, because it felt so nice. And – oh! – he looked down at himself and discovered that the whole experience was pleasantly breezy because he had no clothes on, and that this felt entirely acceptable.

He saw that the other he and Salma found Denis and Vij waiting for them. The other he laid Parvati down, as Vij rushed to take him into her arms, where he stood, trembling, as she tried to soothe his anguish with her embrace.

'I have to stay,' she whispered to him, 'you know that don't you?'

'Yes, my darling, I do. And I have to go.' responded this he, the other he appearing to be incapable of speech for the present.

'But you must go. It's no longer safe for you here. It breaks my heart.'

'Mine too,' admitted this he, floating round the huddle in a complete circle

Vij clung tightly to the other he, as if trying to leave the imprint of her body on him, to make permanent the fleeting passage of their physical lives.'I'm so glad Salma was able to fetch you, my love.'

'She has been a little wonder,' Cat laughed, extending his arm to pat the little girl's head, whereupon it passed through her just as he would have expected of a ghost's arm. 'But the situation has become…'

There was another silent bang, when the orange glow disappeared into the darkness, and this Cat found his presence drawn irresistibly towards the other Cat. The two were combined, when he could feel the warm, soothing embrace of Vij's body at last. He breathed deeply, gasping for an extra puff of air, shuddering as he passed back into corporeality.

'...much more difficult...' he gasped again, '...than you think...'

He told Vij and Denis about the shooting, about Indira, that Enoch had just vanished, run away who-knew-where, and – Cat felt a shudder of grief spread down his back – that he and Parvati had killed Wigly, left him crumpled on the ground with a gobbet of blood oozing from his mouth.

'I didn't mean to kill him,' he wailed.

Salma held Cat's hand to comfort him.

'There can be no question of it being other than self-defence, Cat,' advised Denis, 'so you need not fear the law in this matter.'

'But you heard the uncle, Denis, here it's not your law or my law.'

'I should think, knowing how the new regime felt about the old, you'd stand a good chance of being in line for a decoration, frankly!'

'It's not funny, Denis-ji, and this isn't the point anyway. I have killed a man, and I don't know how I can live with myself. But I've done so many bad things, and this is just the worst.'

'You are not a bad person,' Vij stroked Cat's face.

'I will lead you to safety, out of the state.' Denis offered, 'We'll go tonight – it's not very far from here to the border.'

Cat became still, studied his friends, remembering this moment. He reached into his inside pocket, brought out his wad of notes and handed them to Vij: 'Will you use this money to help Salma, please, my love?'

'Of course I will, pyaare,' Vij smiled, tearfully, before explaining to Salma what Cat had asked.

Salma fell to the floor and touched Cat's shoes as an act of respect, but was distracted when Vij's cat decided to make an entrance. 'Salaam alaikum, billi,' she grinned.

'Billi angrezi me cat hain,' Vij patted her cat's head.

Salma gasped, not having known the meaning of Cat, and laughed cheekily at how inappropriate a name it was for her large friend.

'I must atone, Denis, and I will need your help. I will become sanyasi, like you, and seek purification of my soul. I will make it my penance to travel with Parvati as my companion and burden.'

'You must leave behind your double bass, Cat, surely?'

'No, Sir Denis, I must carry her. We know it is bad for her, but I'm certain she wants to share my burden.'

Cat began to remove his clothes, letting them fall to the ground one by one.

'What are you doing, Cat?' asked Denis.

'I know now what things are important, Denis-ji, and that my vanity isn't one of them. Like you, I will begin to abandon my earthly life.' As he undressed, he removed his spectacles, blinked owlishly around him and put them back on. 'Actually, these are made from cow's milk, so that makes them sacred, right?'

Denis smiled. 'You know this is not an easy life, Cat?'

'So what's new, Denis! My life in this body has never been easy. I know you will teach me.'

His concert kit fell on the dusty ground, unstarched and shapeless, a chaotic pile of rags, and he stood naked before his friends, vulnerable, ashamed, downcast, but sure that a brighter place lay ahead.

Cat kissed Vij one last time, wiped the tears from her face, bowed his head to Salma, picked up Parvati.

'Come, Cat-ji,' commanded Denis, 'we will leave this place together.'

'I am ready, Denis-ji,' Cat took his first step but paused, 'I, uhm, oh crikey – I wonder if in fact we might have just a small snack before we leave?'

29

I'm home now.

I couldn't stay in DM after the execution so, at some additional expense, had one of Sammy's people change my flight from Karachi to the next day, and arrange for Ali to fly me to the airport.

I stayed with my Nan for a while, since no-one was expecting me back so early in Altrincham; I was tired, in need of homely comfort in the bosom of all that remains of my family, so I called in at my flat only for long enough to deal with my packing before getting on a train. I knew she would be interested in hearing about my journey, and that she would make me her wonderful cottage pie.

Before I left, I wandered down to the archive for one last look, taking Lakshmi with me as my 'guard' to appease the Rajah. I'd been reasonably confident there were no more avenues for me to explore in my quest for Uncle Cat in DM, but wanted to be double check. We passed through the city entirely unmolested because, as I had suspected, the hanging that morning had passed for nothing. Say what you will about absolute monarchy, I can see that it makes certain aspects of government easier; it was clear that no general announcement of the execution had been deemed necessary.

Prejudicially, I hadn't anticipated that Lakshmi would be fascinated by the archive, but he immersed himself in it with scholarly attention whilst I browsed. He was drawn to the early materials, and I could hear him rummaging and making little humming noises to himself. Left to my own devices, I looked further into the post independence stuff, many of which were familiar because of my doctoral research. There was no sign of Uncle Cat, of course, but my eye was caught by an old VHS cassette, the only one in the archive, which was labelled by hand *WHICKER'S WORLD: DUSA MATHAVASI HO! (February 1984)*. I asked Lakshmi if he knew where I could play the tape, but he was too young to have any idea what it was (I only recognised it myself because I had had to teach a module on

Arendt in Altrincham, which inevitably involved Eichman and old archival materials). His response told me what I needed to know, so I returned it to its crusted shelf.

But I was so angry/dismayed/appalled with the authority which all these shelves upheld that I suddenly felt like stealing something, the second-worst sin a historian can commit. As a gesture it would have been a futile, but it wasn't a gesture at all, as I wasn't going to tell anyone – I was going to take this tape away as a souvenir, in the absence of a sun hat saying 'I've been to Dusa Mathavasi', a reminder of my trip. So I nonchalantly took it back off the shelf and kept it with me, hoping Lakshmi would either not notice or assume that such behaviour was normal amongst scholars.

He was a great comfort during what remained of my time in the palace, and I regret that we we couldn't develop anything which amounted to friendship because of my lack of Urdu. He walked me back to the palace by a different, longer route, and showed me places which were of interest to him in relation to local history. I valued taking in the atmosphere with him, my last look at this strange, teetering state, before it became wholly overrun with plate-glass and stainless steel.

That evening, I wasn't able to go to the roof and, even with Lakshmi for company, felt isolated from things which had seemed valuable. I had failed on the one hand to find Uncle Cat, and on the other lost the idealised, romantic vision of DM as a hidden paradise which, I saw at last, had fuelled my interest in the place from the moment I first heard about it.

I stood and looked out over the wooded area stretching out beneath my window, and marvelled at the history written in that landscape: I reflected on the capacity of British colonisers to behave so cavalierly with the lives of others, to adopt and then abandon princely states at their will; I hypothesised that the overweening control of the Qifars might have been the straw which broke the British camel's back; I wondered about Cat's life in one of those huts, and what went wrong so disastrously back then. I had to assume, with the archive for his period stripped, that nothing new would ever emerge now.

Then my eye was caught by a plume of smoke rising from the clearing, thick and black. Lakshmi knew immediately that it was from a funeral pyre, that they were cremating Yelda's body, a deliberate action contrary to Islamic burial customs, both as the final punishment and to prevent the development of a cult around the grave of a martyr. So it was that Yelda achieved the distinction of being treated like royalty, and I found myself completely unable to decide whether she would have been delighted in or appalled by the irony. In fact, she was already beginning to seem like someone I had met only in a dream, both real and unreal, and I could no longer see her face clearly in my imagination.

I was fully packed and breakfasted in good time the next morning, thanks again to Lakshmi, and waiting down at the front entrance when the car came to take me to the Qifar house. I hadn't expected anyone to see me off, indeed I had a strong sense that I had fallen out with the royal family as a result of being arrested, and then criticising Sammy, and that they were probably pleased to see me go. I doubted that Ali would have the first idea how my view of his family had developed during my time here, but then why would he? And why would he care anyway? Moreover, I wasn't about to express my views on the matter to the man who was shortly to carry me off in his helicopter. I felt like I was using him, which pleased me.

To my very great surprise, as Lakshmi loaded my luggage into the back of the car, a little voice behind me spoke my name, and I turned to find that Lulu had come to say goodbye. For a moment, a welling of doubt told me I shouldn't go, that I should stay here with her, that we could become lovers and exist in a state of passionate, conjoined bliss for all eternity. But I was finished with fantasies about this place, and so dismissed the thought for what it was – pure lust. She did give me her email address, however, and pecked me on the cheek, which made me take a very deep breath.

I sat up front in the helicopter, looking down on Ali's ridiculous menagerie scattering as we took off. We made one last circuit of the chersonese, and I was able to curse the remains of that blasted telegraph station for the damage it had done to me –

well, the damage it had allowed me to do to myself. At my request, we flew low over the reservoir and the clearing, so that I could see once more Uncle Cat's territory. The wretched scaffold was still there, of course, and I could see clearly the remains of the pyre. Ali casually informed me that Enoch da Costa's remains had been royally cremated along with Yelda's, making it clear he knew I had been at the hanging – and that I knew he had not.

Corpulent Mr. Bunta met me at the airport and, with ludicrous cheerfulness, said he hoped I'd enjoyed my visit to his homeland, before taking me to a very agreeable lounge, where I waited in some comfort for the misery of the fight home.

My Nan gave me a tremendous welcome, like a hero returned. I was so very happy to see her. I didn't admit it, of course, but there was a secondary reason why I wanted to visit; I knew she still had a VHS player.

She'd always been a fan of Alan Whicker, she said when I nonchalantly produced the tape, and we watched it together with rapt attention that first evening. I was able to point out to her some of the things I'd seen on my trip, and some of the gaps in the city as it was then, on the cusp of being developed. There was the boulevard before the central division had been built, with a very few, ancient cars running up and down it. There was the waste ground where the mosque would be built. There was the derelict old palace, the demolition of which being the singular event which had drawn Whicker to make the film. There was an interview with the current Rajah, together with Razi Qifar, both as young men.

The thing about Alan Whicker's output is that he went from the BBC to Yorkshire Television and, in 1984, back again. The fates really have conspired to keep DM a hidden place because the tape I had brought back with me was shot in 1984, by Yorkshire Television, presumably as the last film he made with them, just before he returned to the Corporation. For reasons which, I assume, were contractual, the film was never aired, and isn't listed in his filmography on IMDb, echoing the disappearance of DM itself.

Towards the end, there was an interview with an old lady called Salma Zafar, the most famous Dusa Mathavassian there has ever been, who had enjoyed an enormous career as a singer and Bollywood star.

From the lavish grandeur of her bling house, in a full set of pearls, she described in eccentric English how she had been a street child with no future, and that she owed everything to the great figure of Dr. Vijinalakshmi, who had adopted her and raised her alongside her own child, even before even she had married Mr. Bunta. She talked about an Englishman who had given money to the doctor for her benefit, who she thought might have been the father of her step-brother, and how she had first opened her mouth to sing because he was a musician. That he had been a very fat man and played an enormous double bass. That she couldn't remember his name, but thought it might have been Billi. That he had disappeared with a strange old sadhu on the night when Rajah Shankarrao took the throne. That he had been a lovely and kind man.

My Nan asked me why I was crying – a fair question, I suppose!

Me: I've found him, Nan! My great-great-uncle – your father-in-law's missing brother – he's here. That's him she's describing!

Nan: Well, fancy that!

Me: And I think we have a living relative there – well, in Karachi. OMG, Mr. Bunta, if only I'd known!

During the night, I received an email from Sammy, with the subject line *Tacitus*, in which he apologised for not seeing me off, explaining that he had been withdrawn because of the events of the previous couple of days. He said he had been thinking hard about the future of DM, and included a quote…

They have plundered the world, stripping naked the land in their hunger... they are driven by greed, if their enemy be rich; by ambition, if poor... They ravage, they slaughter, they seize by false pretences, and all of this they hail as the construction of empire. And when in their wake nothing remains but a desert, they call that peace.

He said it would be his life's work to modernise more than just the buildings, and that he hoped I would be able to return one day to see it.

My Nan thinks it would be a good idea.

So do I.

But where is that blasted double bass?

Further reading:

For an account of life in the pre-independence princely states of India:

Sarila, Narendra Singh. 2008. *Once a Prince of Sarila.* London: Tauris

For an account from one of the last of the Indian Civil Service 'heaven-born':

Mason, Philip. 1978. *A Shaft of Sunlight: Memories of a Varied Life*. London: André Deutsch

For an account of the great double bassist:

Palmer, Fiona M. 1997. *Domenico Dragonetti in England (1794-1846): The Career of a Double Bass Virtuoso*. Oxford: Clarendon Press

Roger Ashton-Griffiths
roger@ashtongriffiths.com

Printed in Great Britain
by Amazon

42276849R00142